Once a Cowboy

Once a Cowboy

A Raffertys of Last Stand Romance

Justine Davis

TULE
PUBLISHING

Chapter One

KAITLYN MILLER WAS glad she'd gotten here early. She liked to check out job locations beforehand, and the town of Last Stand, Texas, was proving well worth the time. She could see she'd be breaking out her camera equipment long before the actual assignment that had sent her here began. The job didn't start until Wednesday—probably because Jillian, her self-appointed boss, needed the time to sober up from a no doubt hellacious New Year's weekend— so she had a couple of days to soak up the atmosphere.

Jillian Jacobs would laugh at the very idea of a town this small having atmosphere at all; she'd lived years in New York City, and that was her idea of atmosphere. Kaitlyn agreed with what her father used to say about big cities, that you didn't really live longer there, it just seemed that way.

Kaitlyn had spent her childhood—the idyllic time before the storm—in a town even smaller than this. And she'd never gotten over missing it. She knew intellectually that it was the time of innocence and peace she was really missing, but her heart wasn't having any of that logic. She simply always felt the pressure ease when she got out of downtown

Austin and into the places that felt more like home to her, more like the Texas she knew and loved.

Last Stand was exactly the kind of place she thought of when she started feeling crushed in the city. The kind of place she'd love to live in again. And as soon as she got out of the financial hole she was in, she would. That the hole was not of her digging didn't make it any easier, however.

She parked the car she'd rented on Jillian's instructions—the woman didn't just want the big luxury sedan, she'd wanted it in a particular shade of green—on Main Street in front of a bakery called *Kolaches* where another, nearly new model of her own personal, tired compact SUV was just pulling out. The driver, a woman with pale blonde hair—a color as eye-catching as her own blah medium brown was overlookable—and a wide smile waved at her as she freed up the space.

And that, she thought as she got out of the car, was what she missed amid the hustle and bustle of the city. Among many other things.

However, taking this parking space might have been a mistake. She'd just caught a whiff of luscious, irresistible scent coming out of the bakery. It smelled sweet and felt warm and was a greater lure than she could resist. It was an indulgence she usually wouldn't allow herself, but one more deep breath of the aroma and her willpower crumbled.

One luscious cinnamon roll later she was walking down Main Street, looking at everything, her smile widening at the homey rightness of it with every step. She found herself grinning at the western wear store named Yippee Ki Yay, then looked across the street at the elegant Carriage House and the adjacent patio with tables and umbrellas. Then her gaze snagged on the statue in front of the library up ahead. Always curious about such things she headed that way.

She hadn't realized the name of the town stemmed from an actual battle. The date and a paragraph summary were on the plaque on the base of the statue. Kaitlyn wondered if there was a full history somewhere in the big, two-story stone library. She would bet yes; it was too interesting a story not to be told in depth.

The name on the statue's plaque, Asa Fuhrmann, re-minded her of the German heritage of this area. But the story beneath the name made her think of heroism every-where. Making a desperate run for ammo for the locals holed up in the only stone building around, the saloon, fighting despite the odds, definitely qualified. She found herself letting out a sad breath when she read that the wound he'd suffered in the process turned out to be fatal. She hoped he'd hung on long enough to know they'd won. Thanks to him.

And speaking of heroism, according to the second, small-er plaque next to a spot where a sizeable chunk had been gouged out of the statue's pedestal, more had occurred on this very spot. Last Stand's police chief apparently had the same kind of nerve the man immortalized here in bronze did. And she smiled at that.

We grow them tough in Texas.

She walked to the saloon, which was not yet open, and read the more detailed history of the battle there and stared in amazement at the bullet holes still visible in the stone walls of the building. She was definitely going to check out the library. She saw the coffee shop in the next block but decided her wallet couldn't handle both an expensive concoction and the cinnamon roll. No, convenience store coffee was going to be the best she could manage.

She headed back the way she had come, pausing again to look at the front wall of the saloon, wondering if that really was some kind of bullet lodged at the bottom of one of those holes in the stone. And wondering how she herself would hold up in such a situation. Considering how'd she'd done amid the chaos her life had become when her childhood had come to such an abrupt end, she guessed not so good. If it hadn't been for Nick…

She stopped in front of the western wear store with the smile-inducing name. And saw something she'd missed the first time. A placard in the window, indicating they had a few one-of-a-kind belts by local craftsman Rylan Rafferty back in stock.

Local craftsman. A rather mundane appellation for the kind of artistry she'd encountered in Austin a couple of months ago as she killed time waiting for her highness to arrive. She'd seen the saddle Rafferty had made for the former governor on display. When the assignment for this article came up, she'd recognized the subject and had accepted immediately, even if it meant working with Jillian again.

She glanced at her heavy watch and saw it was a little after nine. A chronograph, her engineer father had called the timepiece, and she wore it to honor him. It was a bit early to check into her room at a local B&B. She noted the store would open at ten. But the library was open now, so she turned around and headed back that way.

She was admiring the texture and solidity of the stone building, wondering when it had been built, when she reached the front door. Belatedly she realized someone was there, holding the door for her.

"Thank you," she said, stepping through quickly. Even at five foot eight she had to tilt her head back to meet the man's gaze. Deep blue eyes, shadowed by the brim of his dark gray cowboy hat, studied her rather intently for a stranger. But she had noticed the badge clipped to his belt, so assumed it was nothing more than his job. Just as it registered that he looked vaguely familiar, he nodded, tipped the brim of the hat to her in classic hat-etiquette fashion, and started to exit.

"See you tonight, Chief!"

The cheerful farewell from the woman just inside sounded rather teasing. She saw the man look back at the woman and roll his eyes. But he was smiling. Then what she'd said registered. He seemed young for that job, but he sure fit the bill for storybook handsome hero. And the hero part truly fit, if he was the man named on the second plaque out front.

"Chief?" she said to the woman inside as the door closed behind him.

The young woman had long, medium-brown hair close to her own shade, but with a rather startling bright red streak down one side that belied her staid attire of a businesslike white blouse and black skirt. She smiled, a warm, genuine smile. "Also my brother-in-law, so I get to rag on him. Welcome to the Last Stand library. I'm Joella Highwater. Looking for anything in particular?"

Highwater. The name on the plaque. Which answered her question; the man was the hero in question.

Kaitlyn gestured back out toward the statue. "The whole story behind that," she said. "I assume you have something?"

The woman's smile widened. "Oh, do we ever. In fact, you just passed part of it."

"Part of the story?"

"His family was part of the last stand."

She blinked. "Wow. And still here?"

"Lots of the descendants of the original fighters are. The Highwaters, the Herdmanns, the Raffertys, the—"

"Rafferty?"

The woman nodded. "Also one of the founding families, and they still live on their ranch a ways out of town."

It wasn't that common a name—it had to be the same family. And they were supposed to go to his studio, on a ranch nearby. "Is that…Rylan Rafferty's family?"

"Yes, it is," she answered. "You know him?"

"Only his work. I'm here to help do a story on him for *Texas Artworks*."

"I heard about that. I was surprised he agreed to it. He usually avoids the limelight."

Kaitlyn smiled at the oddity of that in this day and age of revolving fifteen minutes of fame. It was another reason she'd agreed to come do the shoot for the article, to meet an artist who didn't want publicity. "Rumor has it someone in Austin put in a call to suggest it to the magazine, and the magazine in turn dropped that name when they contacted him."

"Ah. A little famous person pressure. The former gov, maybe. Rylan likes the guy, and not just because he was a real boost to his career."

And she liked this woman, Kaitlyn decided. Friendly yet professional, and that crayon-red streak in her hair suggested she wasn't the stereotypical librarian. She led Kaitlyn to the library wall just inside the front doors, where there were three shelves labeled "Local Interest." Along with tourist guides and biographies of famous people from the town there were paper copies of what appeared to be the local paper, titled *The Defender*, which she supposed hearkened back to the battle the statue commemorated. The next two shelves were full of history books both old and new, first shelf Last Stand, second shelf Texas.

"If you want the most concise history of what happened at the last stand, this is your best bet," Joella said, pulling out a slim volume bound with a cover that was a facsimile of the famous Lone Star flag. "It covers only Last Stand and was co-written by one of our history teachers at the high school, whose family was also there. Her co-writer was Shane's—the current chief you just met—father, who was also our police chief before his death, and a very knowledgeable history buff as well."

Kaitlyn hesitated about offering commiseration on the death, but it didn't seem expected and might be out of place under the circumstances, so she didn't.

"Now, if you prefer your learning live," Joella went on, "and since you'll be out at the ranch anyway I assume?" Kaitlyn nodded. "Then you've got a built-in source for all the history you could want. In fact, if you want every little detail of what happened here, Maggie Rafferty, Ry's mom, is the one to ask. She knows our history inside and out."

"Good to know," Kaitlyn answered with a smile. "Thanks."

"I'll leave you to it, then."

The book was quite readable and infused with the great respect the authors had obviously felt for their town's history. Occurring between the Alamo and San Jacinto, chronologically if not geographically, it had happened when a wandering contingent of Santa Anna's troops had decided to widen their reach and take the little outpost, which at the time consisted of a blacksmith, a trading post, and the saloon. The saloon being the only structure offering any chance of survival—by then the locals knew about the slaughter of the defenders at the Alamo—those who could get there holed up in the stone building and made their stand. Thanks to the likes of Asa Fuhrmann, and those other names Joella had mentioned, including the Raffertys, those Texian fighters had held out long enough that the far bigger and better-armed troop decided the small outpost wasn't worth any more lives. And after winning, those fighters had decided to stay and make lives on the ground they'd fought for.

It was the kind of history that made her proud to be a Texan.

It was the kind of history that made her sometimes doubt if she was up to the standard.

Chapter Two

RYLAN RAFFERTY OPENED his eyes with a start, just as he was about to slide off his workbench stool and hit the floor. He jerked upright, one arm knocking his small sketch pad to the floor, the other hitting the toolbox on his workbench. The sharp, quick pain snapped him fully awake. He had no idea what time it was and wasn't sure he knew where his phone was to check. He'd done away with the clock that had been on the far wall long ago; his work didn't run on a schedule, and it was just another distraction.

As was his hair, which he now shoved back, stifling a yawn. It was time for a haircut. He tended to ignore it until it got to be annoying, getting in his way, and that tickle on his forehead was the first sign. Last night that errant strand had distracted him just as the solution to a design he'd been working on had flitted into his mind, and he'd lost it. He'd been up until the wee hours trying to recapture it. Unsuccessfully.

He picked up the sketch pad from the floor. It was bent a little at the corners, but that was more from carrying it around in his pocket than anything. Then he found his phone buried under a pile of discarded pages from the pad. Nine a.m. Late, for ranchers. He was lucky his family cut him slack. It was—he looked again—Monday, so he hadn't lost a day. That had happened a time or two and reorienting himself was an effort.

He was even aware it was a new year, which only three days into it was a minor miracle. Although it would be hard to forget that party at the Last Stand Saloon New Year's Eve. He'd imbibed more than usual in the process of toasting his two older brothers and their ladies, and then had collided with that woman outside the restrooms. She had turned…predatory, and only what little sobriety he'd held on to allowed him to extricate himself.

And he wondered what he'd have done if she hadn't had that wedding ring on her left hand. It had been a while, after all.

He shook off the admittedly cloudy memories. He walked over to his small kitchen setup, which consisted of a few feet of counter and cupboards, a small refrigerator, a microwave, toaster and coffeemaker. The coffeepot was down to the dregs and looked suspiciously thick when he swirled what was left. Wondered if there was any left at the big house. Decided, given his state, it was worth a try.

He blinked, then squinted as he stepped outside, pondered if it was worth it to go back for his sunglasses. It was Texas-sunny out, already too warm for a jacket. And a far cry from the rare bout of snow they'd had, fittingly, on Christmas Eve just ten days ago.

The day his brother Chance had truly come home.

That thought put a smile on his face and he decided he didn't need the shades.

Further proof of the miracle that had occurred was the fact that Chance and his redhead were at the house. He spotted Chance's palomino Dorado, and the ranch's docile guest horse, Latte, at the rail next to the front porch. His brother at the house, on a day that wasn't Sunday, the one day their mother's strict orders brought them all together. His smile widened.

That redhead, Ariel Larson, happened to be just inside the door when he opened it. Impulsively he pulled her into a fierce hug.

"Thank you," he whispered into her ear, so quietly he knew no one else would hear. "For my brother."

She seemed startled, but as he released her, she smiled. "I know," she whispered back, in those two words telling him she truly did know how worried they'd been about Chance.

Ry looked over to where that brother stood watching from the kitchen, a coffee mug in his hand—that boded well—and a slight smile on his face. Ry grinned at him. His brother actually smiling was worth a grin.

"Isn't he pretty?" His oldest brother Keller's fiancée, business dynamo Sydney Brock, had come up behind him. She was grinning as widely as he was, only at Ariel. "Why, he's almost as pretty as Cody."

Ry grimaced as Ariel studied him as if she'd never seen him before. Then, deadpan, she said, "Prettier, to me. I grew up in San Diego, where blond hunks are a dime a dozen."

"There is that," Sydney agreed, just as deadpan.

Ry let out a half-amused, half-exasperated sound, then headed for the coffeepot.

"I don't know whether to be flattered or insulted," Cody complained from the table where he was finishing up a plate of eggs and hash browns. Which actually looked and smelled pretty darn good. And there were some still in the skillets on the stove. He grabbed a plate.

"I," his mother said from her seat at one end of the table, to the right of her youngest son, "am just delighted to no longer be outnumbered by the men of this family."

"Hey," Keller said from his seat at, appropriately, the other end of the table, "it's still four to three."

"Which makes it about even, I'd say," Chance said, just as deadpan.

Ry turned to look at his brother, still disconcerted by the way he had come back to life since Ariel. Grateful, as he'd told her coming in, but still not used to it. He glanced at his mother, who was looking at Chance with her huge, loving heart glowing in her blue eyes.

He remembered Christmas Eve when, after Chance and Ariel had left to go back to his place, she had given them all their marching orders: they were not to disturb the pair in any way. They needed time alone. She didn't want anything to hinder Chance stepping back into the world, so no unannounced visits, no teasing, nothing. Spoken in a tone that brooked no disobeying, so firm even Cody had toed the line.

"Welcome back, bro," he said softly as, plate in hand, he walked past Chance and headed for the table. This alone was worth having come back home from his brief stint living somewhere else. The condo on Lake LBJ had been flashy, luxurious, and not his type at all. But then, the woman he'd lived with there had turned out to be all those things as well. And there had been no room for the way he worked, either in the condo or in Chelsea's life. Adjusting her own ways to another person simply was not in her rule book.

Ry was nearly through the eggs and potatoes when his mother, smiling at him—as she was at everyone these days— said, rather archly, "You plan on shaving before Wednesday?"

His brow furrowed as he swallowed the bite he'd already decided would be enough. "Wednesday?"

"Told you he'd forget," Keller said dryly, but one corner of his mouth was twitching.

"Forget wha—" He broke off suddenly. "Crap."

"Day after tomorrow, darlin'," his mother drawled, and now, infuriatingly, she was grinning. "Your week of celebrity bliss begins."

Damn. He'd known when he'd agreed to this feature interview thing for *Texas Artworks* that he was going to regret it. But it was hard to say no when a client who was also the former governor—and one of the maybe three politicians you could trust—was the one who sicced the magazine on you. That saddle he'd designed and made for the man was going to end up costing him almost as much in irritation as it had made him in money.

Or maybe not; the man had paid top dollar for it.

"I saw the article they did on Gabe Walker, the metal sculptor from over in Whiskey River last summer," Sydney said. "It was nicely done."

"He's a great artist," Ry said.

"Oh, yeah," Sydney said with a roll of her expressive golden eyes, "I keep forgetting you're not."

Ry shrugged. It was his standard response to those who insisted on calling him that if they were someone he cared about having a relationship with. If he didn't, he tended to snap about the third time they said it. His future sister-in-law was one he definitely cared about. He wanted that smile on Keller's face permanently. The man had more than earned it.

He rubbed at his chin; he'd gone beyond stubble a couple of days ago. And he needed that haircut. Maybe he'd splurge and go into town and have both done. Not like he was getting anything else done here. *Hey, just because the new project was a saddle for one of the biggest movie stars around, no reason to get moving on it or anything.*

And so a half an hour later he was heading up Laurel to

Main Street. He made the left turn and pulled into the strip mall where the barbershop was. Even through the window he could see by the two already occupied barber chairs that he was going to have to wait a bit on this Monday morning; apparently there had been a lot of not-shaving going on over the holiday weekend.

Still, he'd only been waiting about fifteen minutes when a chair opened up. As he was heading for it, Gary Klausen, an older man who worked at the hardware store in town, came in. Surprisingly, the quiet-seeming man looked as if he'd been on a New Year's bender. Jenkins, the barber who ran the place, called out to him that it would be a while.

Gary grimaced. "I'll have to come back later. I need to go open the store in twenty."

Ry got up out of the chair he'd just slid into. "Take Gary first. I can come back—I'm not on a schedule."

He thought Gary's thanks were a bit profuse for a simple offer to trade, but he smiled and headed toward the small convenience store at the other end of the mall, figuring he'd pick up his second cup of coffee for the day. Just before he got there, he spotted the last person he wanted to see at any given time, but especially today. Mr. Diaz, who ran the feed store and was the nexus of the Last Stand grapevine. The last time he'd collided with the guy, a tale that he'd been on a date with Sage Highwater—who in fact had only been talking to him about the custom saddle her family had had him do for her while he was still at Lake LBJ—had been making the rounds an hour later. Considering Sage's fiancé was a medal-winning former Marine sniper, that could have been life-endangering.

The man hadn't noticed Ry yet, but he would. Unless he got out of sight. He dodged through the nearest door, which happened to be a doctor's office. There were a couple of women in chairs in the waiting room, and another behind the counter, and all three looked up curiously. Ry smiled awkwardly and leaned around to look out the glass door just in time to see Mr. Diaz holding the door of the convenience store open for a young woman to leave before he went in. When the man vanished inside, he let out a relieved breath, feeling as if he'd dodged a bullet. He looked back at the curious occupants of the office, gave another awkward smile, mouthed "Sorry," and gave the door a shove to escape.

He almost flattened the woman who'd come out of the convenience store.

Ry swore at himself as she dodged backward, moving the cup she held, probably full of hot coffee, away from her body as she did. It sloshed but didn't spill.

For which you should be thankful, idiot. It could have burned her.

"I'm sorry," he said quickly. "I didn't realize you were there." She looked at the clear glass door, and he realized how stupid that sounded. "I mean, I was trying to..." He couldn't think of any way to explain that didn't sound even stupider.

Her gaze shifted from the door to the brass plate beside it. And then she looked back at him and smiled. And Ry blinked. He'd thought her rather ordinary, albeit with a nice shape and a graceful way of moving. And obviously quick reflexes. She'd danced out of the way as if she wore ballet shoes instead of worn, serviceable boots. And he'd noticed the large, heavy watch she wore, making her wrist look delicate. It resembled the one Chance wore, the one he called a chronograph, and seemed a rather distinctive choice for a woman.

But that smile was…amazing. It just seemed so genuine. Not the polite, meaningless expression people put on— Chelsea had been especially good at it—or the smirky kind of smile when people were being polite but thinking the opposite—Chelsea had been good at that, too, and at the end it had been too often aimed at him—but a genuine, from a good heart kind of smile. And it lit up those huge brown eyes, eyes with rather striking gold flecks here and there, eyes that looked as if they saw…everything. Even the tiny freckles in a spray across her nose added to the feeling of sincerity.

"It's all right," she assured him, and he was startled all over again. That voice was…wow. Low and rich and husky, the kind of voice that sent a tingle down your spine. And woke up areas even further south. "I'm sure you must be very distracted right now. Good luck to you both. Or rather, all three of you."

He stared at her as she walked on, on one level noticing she had the sweetest backside he'd seen in a while, on another wondering blankly what she'd been talking about, him being distracted and…needing luck? And what three?

His brow furrowed, he turned back, wondering how long Mr. Diaz would be inside the store. As he did, his gaze snagged on the brass plate the woman had looked at.

He groaned aloud, suddenly understanding.

It was the Last Stand obstetrician's office.

Chapter Three

"GET THAT FOR me, will you? There's a dear."

Kaitlyn smothered a sigh as she grabbed up the laptop bag. Of course the woman couldn't carry it herself. She had that heavy purse, after all. Full of every kind of makeup and lotion known to man. *One must maintain one's image.* If Jillian Jacobs had a mantra, that would be it.

She supposed an outsider would think she was just jealous. Jillian was obviously beautiful, whereas she was just as obviously not. Oh, she wasn't ugly, but she was no beauty like Jillian. Or her own even more beautiful mother. No, she was just…plain. Ordinary brown hair, ordinary brown eyes, ordinary height, ordinary shape. The only thing the slightest bit unique about her wasn't a plus in her view. Tiny freckles across her nose that made her always look like a kid weren't something she was happy about, but she didn't have the time or the patience to do what was required to hide them. They just were, and she lived with that fact.

She would have thought Jillian might tone it down a bit, since this was her first assignment at a new publication, and one with as much respect as *Texas Artworks*. But it apparently wasn't in her nature to ever do that. *You have to look and act like what you want to be.* That had been the other part of her mantra. Kaitlyn had silently wondered what that accomplished, if it was only the look and an act, but of course she'd said nothing. The woman had suggested her for this job, after all. No doubt because she didn't say the things she thought, but just quietly went along. Because she couldn't afford not to.

As they headed for the doors she wondered, not for the first time, why Jillian had even taken this job, given it wasn't normally her kind of publication. Wondered if it was simply, as Jillian claimed, expanding her horizons and her résumé, or if there was an ulterior motive. Rafferty had, after all, done work for a few politicians here and there.

Then again, she wondered why a class publication like *Texas Artworks* would hire someone like Jillian. However, she had read that the staff writer of the article she'd so enjoyed on metal artist Gabe Walker, Jackie Hayden, had been promoted to chief content editor, so perhaps they were just trying people out to take her place.

They encountered the owner of the inn on their way out. She'd met Frank Buckley yesterday and had been impressed with the former Texas Ranger on several fronts. And her opinion of him silently went up another notch when he merely nodded politely to Jillian, but gave her a wink and a nod. As if he knew exactly who and what the flashier woman was. As perhaps he did; she supposed you didn't survive being a Ranger for two decades, as the inn's brochure had said, without being able to assess people.

She remembered the words that had gone through her mind when she'd been in front of Asa Fuhrmann's statue. *We grow them tough in Texas.* It definitely applied here, too.

Another image shot into her mind, the man who had nearly knocked her down with a door Monday.

We also grow them beautiful.

Oh, yes, that definitely applied. She could admit that, because obviously he was safely attached. Why else would he be coming out of an obstetrician's office? Assuming it was the usual reason for a man to be there, she wondered if the child would be as beautiful as its father. If it would inherit that wild sort of edge she'd sensed in him, not just in the unshaven jaw and the sleek, dark hair with several thick locks that fell forward over his forehead to his eyebrows, but in the very way he moved, like some big cat—a panther or something. What must it be like, to have a man like that love you?

Lucky woman.

She smothered another sigh, told herself he was probably the sort who fell for women like Jillian, and together they would produce children as beautiful as they were. But somehow she couldn't quite believe that man she'd seen—for all of a single minute—would tolerate the likes of Jillian. Not when he could clearly pick and choose. Then again maybe he, like so many, only saw the surface and didn't care about the chilly heart and maybe/maybe not soul beneath.

But there was no maybe about one thing. Men like that didn't look twice at women like her.

Jillian paused at the desk in the lobby on their way out, no doubt to make some petty complaint or imperious demand. Even as the thought formed, Kaitlyn told herself to snap out of this mood, or she was going to blow this, and her chance for future gigs with *Texas Artworks*.

So she waited patiently as Jillian talked to Mrs. Buckley, then again when she turned away to take a phone call.

"So you're off to the Rafferty place?" Mrs. Buckley asked. Kaitlyn nodded. "Now that's a nice bunch of boys. Thanks to their mom and dad, rest his brave soul."

She managed to stifle her wince. So the Raffertys had also lost a father. Something in common, but unwelcome. "How many are there?" she asked.

"Four, although five now, because they've pretty much adopted the boy Keller—the oldest brother—had been fostering. Who is also the cousin of his fiancée, so it'll be official soon." The woman smiled at Kaitlyn's no doubt puzzled expression. "Then there's Chance. His fosters have fur."

Kaitlyn blinked. "Fur?"

The smile widened. "He takes on former military working dogs who…have PTSD, I guess is the best way to put it. He's got a knack, and has saved several they were afraid they'd have to put down."

An image popped into her head, of a monument she'd

gone to see, at the Joint Base in San Antonio. "Guardians of America's Freedom" the pedestal had said, beneath the statues of a military man and the four types of dogs used most frequently as military working dogs.

"That's…wonderful," she said, meaning it.

She was still thinking about that monument as they got into the luxury sedan Jillian had insisted on, that she'd picked her up in at the Austin airport last night. As she drove, she paid only as much attention to Jillian's nonstop dialogue as it merited, which meant just enough to pick out orders or instructions. True, the woman wasn't really her boss, but she thought she was and treated her accordingly. And Kaitlyn was in no position to complain just now. Making the payments she'd committed to and her own rent had been beyond tight this month, even after downsizing to the studio apartment that barely held her and her equipment. But she'd lived in worse, the building was clean, everything worked, and her landlord was a genial guy, so she didn't complain.

She did notice that Jillian assumed she knew where they were going, and that it was her job to get them there. Kaitlyn didn't mind that either; it was a nice car. Besides, she'd much rather be behind the wheel than trust Jillian to get them there.

"—do people live like this? It's so empty! Look at this, not a building in sight, nothing but hills and grass and rocks and trees."

Kaitlyn tuned back in to the ongoing parade of complaints as the woman's words and tone insulted the very thing she loved about being here. If she'd thought Jillian actually wanted an answer, she would have given her one, but she knew better. Jillian had no interest in anything she thought. Or anyone else who couldn't do anything for her. Oh, she grudgingly accepted Kaitlyn's photographs as adequate, even good, but there was nothing Kaitlyn could do to further her career plans and so she was to be merely tolerated. Or used, as a tool to produce photographs just as her laptop produced words.

The woman might not be the best writer around, but what she did have was a knack for getting people to say things they might not normally, either by using that beauty of hers, or simply by being relentless. It wasn't a tactic Kaitlyn liked, but then she'd never been one to push people so into saying things they didn't really mean, just out of frustration. And she had her doubts that the approach that worked with some, like the low-level politicians and the would-be business barons, would work as well with the kind of people *Texas Artworks* was interested in.

But look where Jillian is and where you are.

It wasn't the first time the thought had occurred to her, but as always she discarded it. If that was what she had to do to get there, she'd pass. She preferred to show the truth about people, and she thought she'd managed to do that in her pictures. Not the posed ones, not the ones where they knew they were on camera, but the ones she caught when they were unaware, when they were focused on something else, when they were simply being. That's what she loved.

Reminding herself she should be grateful, that she never would have gotten even a toe in the door at *Texas Artworks* if Jillian hadn't requested her, she murmured something noncommittal that she knew would be taken as assent, because who would ever disagree with Jillian Jacobs?

"This is it," she said as she slowed.

Jillian looked at the gate and the empty land beyond. "But there's nothing here."

Kaitlyn gave her a sideways look. "Do you have any idea how big an acre is?"

"I deal in city blocks, not acres," she answered sourly.

"Fine. Central Park in New York is eight hundred and forty acres. The Rafferty ranch is nearly four times that."

That got through to her, because her eyes widened. Then her brow furrowed. "How do you know that?"

"Little thing called research." She hadn't done all that much—she'd been distracted with her explorations of the town and its history. But she had been curious when she'd seen an official publication on that library shelf that gave the data on most of the local ranches.

Unexpectedly Jillian smiled. "That's why I want you with me, hon. You do all that kind of thing." She could be, when she exerted herself, charming. But Kaitlyn would never fall for it, because she knew what was underneath the charm, and it had scales.

She turned off the road onto the apron at the gated entrance. Pulled up as close as she could get, stopped, and put the car in park.

"And you got us here right on time, too," Jillian said. *Wow. Two compliments in one day. Would wonders never cease?* "Now all we have to do is figure out how to get in."

"It's not locked."

Jillian gave her a startled look. "What?"

She opened her car door. "It's not locked," she repeated.

"They don't lock their gate?"

"Welcome to Texas," Kaitlyn said, stifling her amusement. She guessed Jillian was used to locks, dead bolts, and chains on doors of any kind.

She looked toward the wide gate that crossed the entry drive. Was hoping she had the strength to move it; it looked pretty heavy. Jillian also got out of the car, although Kaitlyn knew it was not to help. It would never occur to her.

Kaitlyn took a step toward the gate, then stopped dead as movement in the distance caught her eye.

It was something out of every western movie she'd ever seen, every dream she'd had as a child. A lone cowboy astride a horse, headed toward her at a high lope. The horse was gleaming black in the winter sun, his mane and tail flying as his smooth, ground-eating stride brought them closer at a rapid pace. The man, wearing what looked like jeans and a dark gray shirt—if it had pearl snaps she wouldn't be surprised, in fact would be disappointed if it didn't—sat the saddle with the ease of long experience. The black felt cowboy hat he wore completed the dreamy picture, although the sunglasses threw off her image of the Old West.

"Oh, my," Jillian murmured, proving even she was not immune. There was something primal about the image. "You don't suppose that's…him?"

"More likely one of the ranch hands, or maybe a brother. The brief they sent said the whole family lives here."

"Weird."

And the fact that you think that weird is sad.

Although Kaitlyn had to admit, she wouldn't have wanted to live with her own family. But then, she didn't have a real family, and hadn't since she was nine. Sometimes she thought she'd never had one, but there were some good memories…at least she thought they were memories. But other times she thought she might have just made them up in her head, pretending she'd been like other kids.

The horse slowed a few yards short of the gate. Even before he'd completely halted the rider swung down with an easy grace that reminded her of something, someone. He patted the horse's sleek neck and dropped the reins to the ground. The big black immediately went from spirited mount to well trained and on standby.

The man pulled off the cowboy hat and hung it over the saddle horn with one hand while he rammed fingers through his formerly hat-restrained hair with the other. He pulled off the sunglasses and hooked them into a chest pocket on the shirt that indeed had pearl snaps. Then he started toward them.

Kaitlyn sighed yet again, but for an entirely different reason this time. The man moved as well as the horse. Powerful, lithe, supple... The analogy of a big cat popped into her mind again, and in the next instant it hit her. He was clean-shaven now, and his hair wasn't quite as wild, but it was him. The man from in town. The man who had nearly knocked her down.

In more ways than one.

Chapter Four

"NOBODY'S PREGNANT."

Ry groaned inwardly. He hadn't meant to say that, it was just the first thing that popped into his head when he recognized her as the woman he'd nearly clobbered with that office door.

The obstetrician's office door.

She just stared at him, probably wondering if he was crazy. Maybe she didn't even remember him. People generally did, for whatever reason, but this woman had a lot going on behind those big eyes with the intriguing gold flecks. He'd known that from the first instant he'd seen them.

He moved to pull open the gate. Since he'd never been able to recover that project solution that had flitted in and out of his mind, he'd been up working on his ranch chores since dawn. Until Cody's newest toy, essentially a video doorbell for the gate, had shown a car pulling in and Cody had texted him a warning. He was already aboard Flyer, so had merely turned the horse toward the gate and let him loose. Delighted, the big black had taken off as if his name were a literal description.

"I'm really sorry about the other day," he said as he came back to her from the gate. Was she the writer? That could make this more interesting than he'd thought.

"No problem. Should I be glad or sad no one's pregnant?"

That voice. It really had been that low, that husky, that rich. And it had the same effect now as it had had on Monday.

Belatedly, her words registered. Interesting, that she took the precaution to find out if this nonexistent pregnancy was a good or a bad thing before she said anything else about their chance encounter.

"I was only in there…avoiding someone." *No one to get pregnant anyway.* He gave himself an inward shake. "Long story," he muttered, thinking now was not the time to explain about the social makeup of Last Stand, and the place Samuel Diaz held in it. Then, looking into those deep, dark eyes, he asked, "You're Ms. Jacobs?"

"Of course she's not," came a second voice from his left. "*I* am."

He frowned slightly at the tone before he looked. Looked, and saw a gorgeous, shapely, platinum blonde with eyes of a lime green shade that he was certain wasn't normally found in nature—and he was from a family that threw some pretty amazing green eyes, as in both Keller and Cody—and puffy lips he put in the same category.

The woman was walking toward him, her hair bouncing

in long, perfect waves as she moved. She was wearing a green, silky kind of shirt that he was sure was chosen to match the eyes, and a darker green pair of slacks above a pair of matching shoes. High heels that couldn't be less suited to ranch life had she tried. Shoes like Chelsea had worn. He stifled a grimace.

She moved confidently, until just as she reached him one of those heels wobbled on the gravel. Instinctively he moved to grab her arm, keep her upright. And released her the instant she was steady again, wondering if the wobble had been for real or intentional. Funny, if it had been the other woman that question never would have occurred. That thought interested him. He would have to think about that, figure out why he was so certain so soon.

He'd looked up a couple of features Ms. Jacobs had done, just enough to make him wonder why she was the one doing this; she seemed to focus on bigger names than him. But he hadn't questioned it much beyond that, had even thought maybe he should be flattered.

"Thank you," the lime-eyed woman—definitely contact lenses, he could see the faint rim of them now—said, in what he was sure was supposed to be a sexy voice. Another interesting thought to be analyzed later was that it didn't have nearly the effect the other woman's had had on him. "And you are...?" she asked, a bit breathily.

He managed not to grimace, although he wanted to. "If you're Jillian Jacobs, I'm the guy you're here to interview."

The woman's smile was blinding. But Ry only caught a glimpse of it because a tiny sound, somewhere between a gasp and a groan, had drawn his attention back to the woman from the strip mall. The woman whose voice and smile he'd take over the flashy blonde's polished one any day.

But an instant after he'd shifted his gaze her expression cleared, before he could even put a description to it.

"Well," she said, her tone now impossibly dry, "that makes my job easy."

"Your job?" he asked.

"Oh, don't mind her," the blonde said breezily. "She's just the photographer. I'm the one who will make readers all over want to dump piles of money on you for your creations."

He barely stopped himself from rolling his eyes. *Hyperbole much?*

The reporter reminded him of someone else besides Chelsea, but he couldn't quite place who it was. Somebody he'd seen on television somewhere. Maybe giving a speech. Or maybe it was the emptiness behind the eyes that made him think that.

Or the dismissive tone in her voice when she'd said, "She's just the photographer."

This, he thought as he gestured them through the gate, closed it, then remounted Flyer, was going to be even worse than he'd feared.

KAITLYN HAD MEANT what she'd said. Rylan Rafferty was going to make her job very, very easy. Almost too easy. She supposed he could be that rare person who looked magnetic as hell in person, but it was lost in the transition to still images, but she highly doubted it.

She tried to imagine a shot she could take where he wouldn't look good, where he wouldn't exude that wild charisma. She couldn't.

But she could certainly imagine all sorts of shots she'd love to take. Him on that horse. Maybe grooming that horse. Or petting it. She was sure he did, from the way he'd patted the horse's neck as he'd dismounted.

Then a close-up with the emphasis on those stormy-gray eyes, that black hair falling over his forehead, and those thick, long eyelashes none of the tools in Jillian's bag could give her.

And him with the cowboy hat. Without the hat. Without the shirt—

She cut her own thoughts off sharply. That was a path she did not want to go down.

Still, she was glad she had the gravel road to use as an excuse to drive slowly enough to keep pace with the gleaming ebony horse's easy canter. And not knowing exactly where they were going as an excuse to keep watching the pair just slightly ahead of them. Black hat over black hair on a black horse against a sunny Texas sky. It was enough to warm this January day to summer.

The way they both moved had her wondering if perhaps on their website the magazine might go for some video, simply a clip of him riding, with the ease of someone who'd grown up doing it. Showing another side of the artist, a side that brought home that he was indeed a Texan. Her fingers fairly itched to have her camera in hand, filming this run across the land that was his family's. Already she could sense this was an elemental part of this man.

"Oh, I'm going to enjoy this," Jillian said, and Kaitlyn realized she was watching them too. Some primitive, stupid part of her yelped silently, *I saw him first!* She quashed it fiercely; that way lay pain.

She had no business even thinking about a man in that way, because her life wasn't her own, and wouldn't be again for a long while yet.

Besides, if Jillian had marked Rylan Rafferty as hers, that was it. She'd pursue him as relentlessly as she did her questioning, and that rarely ended in anything less than success. And heaven help the man if he fell for her and wanted more than just a fling.

She couldn't picture this man falling so easily, but she'd been wrong before. So very, very wrong.

Be nice to him, honey. We need this to go well. The words echoed in her head. Followed by Jillian's cogent assessment. *He likes the needy ones.*

The needy ones.

And no matter how much Kaitlyn told herself Jillian meant anyone not lucky enough to be her, she couldn't deny the truth at the core of the observation. Professor Louis Bates, subject of a profile Jillian was doing for a national publication, indeed liked the needy ones, for his own twisted reasons. And that's all Kaitlyn had ever been to him.

Her mind veered off the painful memory with the ease of long practice.

"Need another notch on the ol' bedpost?" She regretted the words as soon as they were out. She never did that, said what she was thinking, not with this woman. She waited for the inevitable slap-down.

"That," Jillian said, in the vocal equivalent of a leer as she watched Rylan Rafferty, "could take the entire bedpost down." Then she looked at Kaitlyn. "And I'm sure he'd never go for the needy type."

And there it was. She'd been put back in her place and now they could go on.

Kaitlyn drove, not sure which she hated more, this woman or the fact that she was in a position where she was forced to deal with her.

She paid just enough attention to the wheel to stay on the drive, the rest she kept on the horse and rider just ahead. A girl could look, couldn't she? Appreciate? It was just her bad luck to be what she was: a plain, ordinary woman most men, but especially men like Rylan Rafferty, looked right past.

Especially when there was a woman like Jillian in view.

Chapter Five

R Y HANDED FLYER off to one of the hands, who'd agreed beforehand with a grin, knowing how much he was dreading this. Now Ry was wishing he'd seen to the horse himself; he'd be calmer if he had something to do with his hands.

"I thought we'd do this where you do your work," Jillian said as he led them toward the house.

"Maybe later," he said. *Emphasis on the maybe.*

He was protective of his workspace out in the smaller of the two barns, and he didn't let strangers in easily. That space had been the second biggest reason, after his family, that he'd come home. When Mom had offered him the entire smaller barn now that the bigger one was finished, he'd jumped at it.

He'd known he'd probably have to allow access for this, but that didn't mean he was in a hurry to do it. Maybe he could limit it to just the photographer. He didn't think he'd mind her so much. If she was good, as he figured she must be if she was working for *Texas Artworks*, then she would probably respect the space. But photos of it would still end up in the article.

Great. Talk about lose-lose. Pictures of either his studio, or him, more likely both, in a magazine with a national reach. He reminded himself he owed the man who'd helped launch his work into profitability, and who had pushed for him to do this. "It'll raise your profile. You'll be famous, and so busy you can pick and choose your clients," he'd said. Ry had liked the pick and choose part. The famous part, no. *Right where I don't want to be.*

He tried to focus. He needed to at least pay attention here. Manners, he reminded himself. He could do manners. After having them drummed into him by both his parents, he darn well should be able to.

He felt the usual jab of pain at the parent who was missing from his life now, even after two decades. But the lessons his father had taught him before his death were perhaps the ones he'd learned best. And his mother, loving and tough at the same time, had made damned sure he, and his brothers, never forgot those lessons.

Speaking of his brothers, the youngest was clearly playing again.

"Whoa!"

It was that voice, the photographer's voice. He looked at her, saw her looking upward. She'd heard the sound and triangulated it barely an instant after he had. "My brother Cody," he explained. "He plays with drones."

"Cool," she said, and her smile this time was appreciative, and as genuine as the one he'd seen before.

"That's the message drone. Cody designed an app to go with it, so you can text in a message that can be downloaded on the other end."

The little device neatly sat down at the bottom of the porch steps. He went over and picked it up, then straightened to look at her again.

"Handy guy to have around," she said, and she was still smiling. And for some reason he found himself going on.

"Another brother lives out in the far corner of the ranch, and the cell reception out there is lousy, so we use it to reach him. He was probably letting Chance know you're here."

"Chance? Is he the one who works with MWDs?"

He blinked. "Yes," he said after a moment of surprise.

"The lady at the inn told me," she explained. "What a great thing he's doing."

"Yes, it is. Those dogs deserve his efforts."

There was a quick movement to his left, and suddenly the other woman was close at his side. Too close. Then the pretty blonde was grasping his arm. "You mean those…attack dogs?" Ms. Jacobs said, and something in her tone had Ry thinking she wasn't so much afraid of dogs as she was tired of not being the center of attention.

"They're hero dogs, not attack dogs," Kaitlyn said, an edge in her voice now.

The reporter ignored the comment and, not even looking at the other woman, said, "Why don't you go get all your stuff out of the car, dear?" This was accompanied by a flick of her hand, as if shooing off a pesky mosquito. A hand with fingernails that made Ry wonder how she managed to use a keyboard. If indeed she did; maybe she just dictated her articles.

And left it for some poor editor to clean up any goofs.

Oh, this was not starting well. She might be gorgeous, he was willing to admit that, but he could do without the attitude. It—and she—indeed reminded him of Chelsea, and he wasn't going to be fooled by that again.

But the photographer didn't protest, simply shrugged and turned as if to go back to the car as ordered.

"Hey," Ry said, "I don't know your name."

She looked back at him, seeming almost startled. As if she was surprised he wanted to know. "Kaitlyn. Kaitlyn Miller."

"Welcome to the Rafferty Ranch, Kaitlyn Miller."

It was more than he'd said to the reporter, and he knew from the slight widening of her eyes, those big brown eyes, that she'd registered that. "Thank you, Mr. Rafferty."

"Ry, please. Or at least Rylan, or it's going to be a long few days."

That got him another one of those smiles, and he found himself smiling back like a kid who'd given a right answer in class.

"All right. Ry."

And hearing his name, the shortened, family version, in

that voice pleased him far more than it should have.

"IT WOULD SEEM I misjudged."

Kaitlyn looked up at Jillian's softly spoken words, clearly meant for only her to hear. "What?"

"Apparently he does go for the needy type." Kaitlyn's jaw tightened and she went back to selecting the lenses and lighting she wanted in her carry bag as Jillian added, "Or perhaps it's those Southern manners I've heard about."

And only heard about, because you've certainly never practiced them.

One of these days she was going to bite her tongue hard enough to bleed.

"That must be it," Jillian pronounced. "He's just trying to make you feel included, because that's what they do around here."

She sounded relieved to have found an answer that satisfied her. And she was likely right—that's all it was, the extra attention he'd given Kaitlyn. Somehow he'd known she was the odd one out here and gone the extra mile to include her.

Somehow? All he has to do is look in a mirror, then at Jillian, then at you. Beautiful times two, and…not.

Kaitlyn slung the bag over her shoulder, once again deciding the doing without had been worth it; that multifunction lighting device, that she could set to mimic outdoor light, spotlighting, soft light, halo lighting and more, had been worth every penny and every missed lunch in weight saved alone.

They went up the porch steps to the door of the big ranch house, Mr. Rafferty—Ry—politely ushering Jillian in first, then waiting for her, also. She gave him a fleeting glance and a half-hearted smile; that realization of once more being on the outside had brought her down. She was going to have to marshal her mental tricks to snap out of it, roll out the self-lectures and—

She stopped just over the threshold, a tiny gasp escaping her. For a moment she couldn't go any further. She could only stand and stare.

The painting on the far wall of the large room was big, probably nearly three by five feet, but that wasn't what had stopped her in her tracks. It was the vividness of it, the brilliant colors, the scope, and the pure energy poured into it. The rough edges of rock escarpments, the softness of the hills seeming to roll endlessly to the horizon, and over it all the brilliant, unforgettable spread of the bluebonnets in full bloom, carpeting every spot where they'd taken hold in luscious color.

This had been done by someone who loved what they were portraying here, in all its Texas Hill Country glory.

Belatedly she realized she was blocking the door, and that Ry had necessarily come to a halt behind her.

"Sorry," she said quickly, and took another step inside so he could come in after her. "I was just thinking that the next time somebody asks me why I love Texas all I'd need to do is show them that painting."

Something changed in those gray eyes in that moment, and she thought she saw both pain and pride there.

"It is pretty," Jillian said, glancing at the painting.

Pretty was hardly the word for it. On impulse Kaitlyn asked, "Your work?"

"No."

The pain she'd seen in his eyes was there in his voice, too. Was it the artist who inspired it? She wanted to ask but couldn't bring herself to in the face of that pain. Then someone else came into the room—at a run—and the moment was lost.

The man in a hurry was tall, blond, with dark green eyes that were obviously genuine, and added a third to the total of beautiful people in the room. And Kaitlyn couldn't miss how Jillian was suddenly hyper-aware again.

"Looking for this?" Ry asked, holding up the drone.

"Yeah," the blond said. "I was just letting Chance know we have visitors. In case they're trying try off-leash."

Kaitlyn blinked. "Trying try?"

"T-R-I," Ry said. "It's the dog's name. Both for tripod because he lost a leg, and because he never stops trying."

"How clever," Jillian said, but her attention was still on the newcomer, whom Ry quickly confirmed was his brother Cody, as Kaitlyn had guessed from the drone.

"Lucas named him," Cody said. "Our oldest brother's

foster kid."

"That's very noble of your family," Jillian said. "Taking in foster children. And dogs."

Kaitlyn happened to be looking at Ry—as she already did too much—when Jillian spoke. And she didn't think she'd mistaken the flash of irritation that crossed his face. But he didn't respond, merely handed the drone over to his brother.

"So you're the reporter from *Texas Artworks*, huh?" Cody asked, looking at Jillian with obvious male appreciation. Which only made Ry's lack of the same more obvious to Kaitlyn.

She wasn't sure what it meant.

Or how it made her feel.

Chapter Six

RY TOLD HIMSELF he should be thankful Ms. Jacobs had zeroed in on Cody, if only because it got her attention off of him. But there was enough of a predatory gleam in those unnatural eyes to make him want to warn his little brother. But Cody was no kid, and if he wanted to risk the burn Ry was sure would come with a woman like this, it was on him.

Of course, he was sure of that burn because he'd been there himself. Already he knew instinctively Jillian Jacobs and Chelsea were the same type.

He noticed the photographer was also looking at the fair-haired duo. "That," he muttered, just loud enough for her to hear, "would be a little too much like looking in a mirror for me."

Her gaze shot to his face, as if he'd startled her. "That's probably why she's looking so hard," she said, and immediately looked as if she wished she hadn't said it. He had to bite back a laugh, but he couldn't stop his smile.

"Good to know," he said, eyebrows raised in an exaggerated way to show his lack of surprise. And then he got that smile again, that real, honest, open smile, with no artifice, no hint of it being something to hide behind. And as Ms. Jacobs laughed at something Cody said, in that way that rang hollow in his ears, he thought he'd take one of those smiles over a thousand of those flattering laughs.

Yeah, he'd better warn his little brother. Cody was indeed far from a kid at twenty-eight, but that didn't mean he'd run into the likes of this woman before. He spent too much time in skirmishes with Britt Roth—his childhood nemesis from the next ranch over—and with his tech toys. Of course, there had been his years at college, the only one of the Rafferty boys who'd actually finished that chore, and that time he'd come back from an exhibition in Dallas in an odd sort of mood, satisfied yet a bit wistful, but nobody, not even their mother, had been able to pry out of him what had happened. Which in itself was notable, given that if anything, Cody was too open. Which was why she'd been worried about him in the first place.

After a few more minutes Cody, clearly reluctantly, said he had to go. He had a meeting with the police chief about a new camera system for the station to replace the ancient one that had finally failed.

"He's not just having Sean do it?" Ry asked, referring to the chief's younger, detective brother, who was probably the only one in Last Stand who could give Cody a run for his tech money.

"Sean's out of town. With Elena, so he doesn't want to

bother him."

"Better hustle," Ry advised. "You don't want to keep Shane Highwater waiting."

"I know," Cody said with an eye roll. "That guy's scary as hell when he wants to be."

"So don't make him want to be by being late."

"I've heard that name before," the reporter said as she watched Cody go. "Shane Highwater, I mean."

"He hit the national news when he killed a suicide bomber a few years back. There was video that went viral. The guy was nearly to his target, a crowded arena. Who knows how many would have died and been injured."

"That's it. That's why he seemed familiar when I saw him in town Monday," Kaitlyn said suddenly. When she went on she sounded a little in awe. "I saw that video. The guy was holding a dead man's switch."

Ry nodded. Clearly she understood the significance of that. "Only reason Shane's not dead was that it malfunctioned."

"Wait," the reporter said, "you're saying he did that thinking he'd die, too?"

She sounded astonished at the very idea. Which told Ry even more about her than she realized, he was sure. "He's a Texan to the bone," he said.

"And we grow them tough," Kaitlyn whispered.

He looked at her. This was a woman who got it. "Where are you from?"

"I was born in Kingsland."

"Ah. The Slab. Great place. Took a trip there, when I was a kid." He remembered well the popular spot where the Llano River flowed over some rock slabs, creating pools, sandy beaches, water chutes to lie in, even some miniature rapids. It had also been one of the last trips with Dad; he'd been deployed again not long after. And hadn't come back alive.

"Points for not mentioning chainsaws," she answered dryly.

He laughed, glad of the distraction of her mention of the popular horror movie that had been filmed at a house there.

"Shall we get started?" Ms. Jacobs said, sounding irritated again and giving Kaitlyn an annoyed look. As if she couldn't stand not being the center of attention for more than a few minutes.

He'd been wishing ever since he'd said yes that he'd said no instead. Now that wish was even more fervent. If it was only the photographer, or if she'd been the writer, he might have ended up looking forward to this. But she wasn't, and since it was too late to back out, the best he could do was get it over with fast.

"Ms. Jacobs," he began.

She flashed him a lovely smile that he was sure was supposed to be engaging. "Please, call me Jillian." Then she glanced at Kaitlyn. "Why don't you head outside and do what you do, while we start the heavy lifting here."

It wasn't a question, it was an order. And it appeared Kaitlyn would obey without dissent. It was obvious who was in charge here. He understood that on things like this photos were only a part, that it was the story in words that mattered most to many. That he worked visually, with work you could see and touch, was probably coloring his reaction. But he couldn't help wondering if the woman who had reacted as she had to The Painting could really take ordinary photographs.

And he wondered what she'd think of his own painting by the same artist. But since it hung on the wall of the loft bedroom in his barn studio, he was never going to know.

Before that thought could derail him completely, he shifted his focus.

"Why don't you wait, and I'll show you around later."

He made certain his words weren't a question either. Start as you mean to go on, his father had always said, and he wasn't going to let this imperious woman completely run the show. Not here, on the ranch that had been his family's foundation for generations. Where he also didn't want strangers wandering around unescorted, even if they were here for a legitimate reason.

Irritation flashed in those lime eyes. But Kaitlyn said evenly, "He has a point, Jillian. Liability and all that."

"Oh. I suppose you're right." She said it grudgingly. Clearly the woman hadn't thought of that aspect, and it seemed as if she resented that Kaitlyn had. And honestly, neither had he; he'd only wanted a little more control over this situation he'd let himself be talked into.

He should have insisted they do this somewhere else, neutral ground. He was even more reluctant now to have his work space invaded. It was sacrosanct, and in the back of his mind he'd had the idea that the writer would stick her nose in for a quick glance, but the rest of the interview would take place here, or outside. But Jillian Jacobs didn't look like an outside kind of woman. No, she was more the elegant cocktail party type. With important people she could schmooze and contacts she could later turn to her benefit.

Well, that was harsh. Judge much? Still letting Chelsea affect your thinking?

Maybe he needed to lighten up. It was just his antipathy toward this whole thing that had him on edge. Maybe she was really a nice person at heart.

A nice person who said things like: "She's just the photographer."

Then again, maybe not.

KAITLYN HAD TO admit Jillian was good at this. She started with benign, expected questions, like where did he learn something like what he did—the basics from an old hand who did it over in Whiskey River, the next town over, the rest from trial, error, and a lot of discarded pieces—when did he decide to make it a career—he didn't, it just sort of happened that his work got discovered—and several other routine things that one would expect. And she found she was glad to still be here, able to listen and watch. She was intrigued in a way she rarely was. Intrigued by more than his incredible appearance and that cat-quick way of his, by more than how extraordinary he was going to be to photograph.

And fascinated by the way he had turned Jillian's dismissal of her around, using the same technique of a question that was an order in disguise, only with much more sense of command.

Jillian kept on with the ordinary questions a bit longer. Yes, his family had been here even before the battle that gave the town its name. Yes, four brothers, Cody she'd met, Chance they'd heard about, and Keller, the oldest, who ran the ranch along with their mother after their father had died.

Kaitlyn saw the flash of a long-carried grief in his eyes. A familiar look she recognized because she often saw it in her own reflection, on those days when she missed her own father to the point of a physical ache. She also thought she saw his gaze flick, just for an instant, to the gorgeous painting on the wall behind where Jillian was sitting. And a sudden certainty came to her, that explained the pain in his eyes and his voice when she'd asked about it.

His father. His father had painted it.

She studied the painting, which she'd been staring at a lot of the time anyway, with a fresh vision. The composition of the scene was perfect, with an outcropping of the stone that made up the Balcones escarpment beneath the Hill Country on the left edge, making the incredible expanse of the bluebonnet-covered hills seem even more like a luxury blue carpet, and the spot where earth met sky so close to the same color blue that the horizon was almost impossible to discern. A hawk of some kind circled above. She thought a redtail from the faintest touch of that color, exactly as it happened in real life when you only caught a glimpse of one of the raptors far above.

She shifted her gaze back to the man sitting in the chair opposite Jillian. Kaitlyn had taken the chair to one side, not wanting to be too close, knowing the woman would see it as an intrusion. She wanted her interviewee's attention solely on her.

She was still softballing, and he was answering easily enough. Kaitlyn sensed he was beginning to relax.

Don't.

If she could have sent a telepathic warning she would have. This was Jillian's way—luring her prey into a false sense of safety, then springing the trap with some loaded question to which there was no safe answer. Kaitlyn couldn't imagine what this man could have to hide, but everyone had secrets and she supposed he did, too.

"And how did it feel to be mentioned in the same breath as artists like metal sculptor Gabe Walker?"

Kaitlyn saw him take a deeper breath before answering and wondered why.

"I'm a craftsman, not an artist."

Kaitlyn blinked at that. The memory of the exquisite detail and the imagination that had gone into working every symbol of Texas, both official and not, into the leathers of a saddle shot through her mind. That was artistry, no matter what he thought or said. But at the same time, she remembered the sign in that shop in town. Was it by his choice it said craftsman?

He went on. "My work is more a matter of hand-eye coordination than any artistic vision, or whatever they call it. And I deliver what speaks to the people who commission it. So, I'm no artist."

Jillian's brow furrowed, a wrinkle-inducing expression she rarely allowed herself. Kaitlyn guessed she knew why; she couldn't imagine anyone at the level Rylan Rafferty had achieved being modest about it. But Kaitlyn wasn't sure it was modesty. There was too much feeling, too much intensity behind the words he'd said, and just as much of those same two things in those stormy eyes. Kaitlyn wondered if Jillian didn't notice this or didn't care.

"Of course you're an artist," Jillian scoffed, as if her opinion had the power to negate whatever powerful emotion caused him to believe that. Because he did believe it, Kaitlyn had no doubt. She also thought, judging by what flared in those eyes then, like lightning striking behind gray storm clouds, that with her casual dismissal of his words Jillian might have just train-wrecked this entire interview.

"Is that because you wouldn't be bothered with anything less than an artist?" he asked, and Kaitlyn didn't see how anyone could miss the edge in that deep, rough voice now.

"I don't—"

He cut Jillian off. "Why me? Don't you usually stick to the big shots, the people who get their names in the big-city, elite publications you usually write for? I'm small-time, compared to them."

Kaitlyn had to stifle a delighted smile. Clearly, he'd done his homework on her.

"You're not small-time," Jillian responded almost indignantly. To most it would have sounded like a defense of him, but Kaitlyn knew it was based in the woman's high opinion of herself. "A former governor and two senators own your work. Country music stars as well. And I understand you're going to be doing a project for one of the biggest movie stars in the world."

Kaitlyn remembered having seen that last in her research, about the latest Australian to take the world by storm. She guessed that Jillian was already figuring she could broaden her own fame by using that tidbit. But before she could dwell on it Ry was answering, still in that same tone.

"So that's what it takes to get your attention?"

"I believe it's what got *Texas Artworks's* attention," Jillian said stiffly.

This time Kaitlyn had to stifle what surely would have been a grin. He'd put her on the defensive, a position Jillian had little experience with. He'd turned it around on her, as if he didn't give a damn about what damage she could do to him. He'd more than done his homework, he was taking a stand with her.

Welcome to Texas, Jillian.

"And they've become a well-respected publication," Jillian added, still rather defensive.

"And so, worth your time?"

Kaitlyn remembered her silent warning to this man about relaxing his guard, and realized it hadn't been necessary.

"You're certainly worth my time," Jillian said, and Kaitlyn realized with a little jolt the woman had fallen back on her fail-safe: turning on the flirting.

"Well, now, darlin'," he said, the drawl so obviously put on Kaitlyn had to bite the inside of her lip to stop yet another grin, "then I guess the question is, are you worth mine?"

Chapter Seven

H E'D DONE IT now, Ry thought. The woman would write some scathing piece about his stubbornness, or arrogance, or misogyny—something. His mother would have had a fit at how rude he'd been. But damn it, he really didn't like her attitude. She had an air about her that just rubbed him like a saddle blanket shoved the wrong way. Those politicians and celebrities she usually interviewed might be used to it, but he wasn't. And he didn't ever want to be.

"Oh, I can make it worth it," she almost purred.

He managed a neutral tone this time. "I'll bet you could."

If I went for that kind of thing.

His own thought startled him. Why wouldn't he? Hadn't he just been pondering how long it had been for him? And here was a beautiful woman practically promising him to end that drought. Why wasn't he jumping at the idea?

"Oh, I could," she cooed. Then, abruptly more business-like, she said, "But let's get to know each other a little first. Tell me where you get your inspiration."

He felt a sense of relief that she seemed willing to move

on. And so he answered more generously than he might have, since he found the question annoying. "Every and anywhere. But as I said, I work for the people who commission the work. It's what they want that counts, what speaks to them that I try to deliver."

"How do you determine that?" It was the first time the photographer had spoken since they'd sat down. And she immediately looked at Jillian apologetically. "Sorry, Jillian. I didn't mean to interrupt."

Ry glanced at her, frowning. She felt she had to apologize for a simple question? And a question he didn't mind, something concrete and logical, not the esoteric kind about inspiration and vision. She flicked a look at him but quickly looked away, and he thought he saw her cheeks color slightly.

"You're forgiven," Jillian said to her, with a smile that at least seemed genuine. Then she turned back to him. "And given what you said, it is an interesting subject. How do you determine what, as you say, speaks to them?"

"Only one way," he said. "Spend time with them. Ask questions."

"So…you interview your clients?"

"In a way, I guess," he said, a little surprised at the accuracy of the question.

"Do you have a set list of questions for everyone, or do you tailor it to each individual?"

Okay, that was two decent, reasonable questions. He

should have known she didn't get to where she was by being stupid. "I start out with a list, although it's not written anywhere, it's just built on experience."

"What's the first question you ask?"

"What they're doing next weekend."

The woman gave him a puzzled look. He wasn't sure why, but he glanced at the photographer. And saw complete understanding in her expression, in those dark eyes. She got it, all right. How what a person did in their time off spoke of what mattered to them. What they put first in their life, after their work.

He found himself wondering what she put first when Jillian spoke again. "What if they tell you they're not doing anything?"

Another good one. Okay, maybe he'd misjudged. "Depends on how they say it. With boredom, or relish."

"And if it's boredom?"

"I focus on their work, whatever it is they do, since apparently they put their all into it."

"And if it's relish, what's your next question?"

"I ask them what they'd be doing if they could have any job in the world."

She seemed intrigued now. And her next questions were, he had to admit, intelligent. Probing without being invasive. Well, not too invasive. His mother had warned him he was going to find most of this invasive, him being who he was.

"We accept who and how you are because we know and

love you," she'd said. "But a reporter who makes her living prying into people is a different kettle of fish."

He remembered smiling at the phrase, knowing she'd picked it up from his father.

Well that's a fine kettle of fish you've gotten yourself into, Rylan.

I'll fix it, Dad. I promise.

A man's only worth the promises he keeps, son. Make sure you keep them.

And he had kept that one. He'd taken the vase he'd broken, one of his mother's favorite things, to the workbench his father had set up for him even at age ten, and spent three days after school putting it back together as best he could.

He tried to keep any promise he made, aided by the tactic of not making many. But he had made this one, to do this interview, and so he tried for cooperation while at the same time being very careful about what he said; some of his clients were, as she'd said, famous. He was sure they wouldn't appreciate him blabbing things that might have been said in confidence.

But the questions now didn't seem particularly high-pressure, and he was just thinking he might get through this when a dramatic, almost operatic ring drew Jillian's attention. She pulled out a phone in a jeweled case and looked at the screen.

"I'm so sorry," she said, "I do have to take this. Kaitlyn, why don't you get started while I do?"

"If Mr. Rafferty—Ry—is willing," the photographer

said.

She stood up, slinging the obviously heavy camera bag over her shoulder. The manners drilled into him long ago prompted him to consider asking if he could carry it, but when he stacked it up against how she might react to the inference that she couldn't do herself what she clearly usually did, he quashed it. He'd gotten off on the wrong foot with one half of this team, and he didn't want to tick off the other half.

They stepped outside. No photos inside the house without his mother's permission, he told her, and she was gone for the day. She gave him a look he could only describe as wondering, with a touch of wistfulness.

"What's it like, having a big family and all living together?"

"Well, we're not all under one roof. Keller and Sydney have their own quarters, and so does Cody—they're just attached to the main house. Chance has his place out in the west corner of the ranch, and he and his lady, Ariel, live there. Although we see him a lot more than we used to, thanks to her." He nodded toward the smaller of the two barns close to the house. "And I live in the loft over my studio, to keep from annoying everybody with my odd hours."

She smiled at that, and it seemed to remind her of something. "In there," she said, nodding back toward the house, "what were you thinking of?"

His brow furrowed. "When?"

"When she was asking about when you'd first learned you had talent. You were smiling, but all you said was you were about ten."

He raised a brow at her. "Double-teaming with the questions?"

She looked startled. "No! I mean, I wouldn't. Couldn't." Her expression changed, became worried. "I'm so sorry, I didn't mean anything. Can you please not tell her I upset you?"

He frowned. Stopped walking. She stopped beside him. But not too close, a careful couple of feet away. Just how hyper-sensitive was this woman?

"First, I'm not upset, I was kidding. Second, you're here as part of this too, so why can't you ask a question?"

"Jillian prefers I stick to what I'm good at and leave the heavy lifting to her."

That phrase again. Jillian had used it earlier. Inferring that the hard work was up to her. And belittling Kaitlyn's contribution to it. Was her work really so ordinary, her photos so mundane? He'd have to do a little research on that. Or have Cody do it, in a quarter the time. But now he felt badly about having touched what was obviously a nerve with her with his joke.

"So you're saying this is off the record?" he asked.

"Strictly a personal question, I swear."

She still sounded anxious. He didn't know what to do

about that, so he went back to her initial question. "When I was ten, I got a little rambunctious in the house and knocked my mother's favorite flower vase, one that had belonged to my grandmother, off the shelf and broke it. I was in so much trouble, because she'd warned me to settle down a couple of minutes before."

"Did she…hit you?"

Startled, he drew back a little. "Of course not. But when she called Dad in to mediate, I knew how angry she was."

She was staring at him, as if he were describing some strange foreign custom. "What happened?"

He started walking again and so did she, although she was still looking at him as if waiting breathlessly for his answer. "He told me I had to put it back together. Every shard. I'd never paid so much attention to detail before, to the shape of things, the way parts fit together. And that's when I learned…I liked that. Figuring that out."

"Then what?" she asked, smiling now, as if he were telling her the most interesting tale she'd ever heard.

"I started putting other things together. Seeing shapes in things, in a leaf or a branch, a stone, and putting them together."

Her eyes widened. "The twig man! On the shelf inside."

He stopped dead again, startled. The barely six inches tall figure was the first thing he'd ever made that looked like something. To his embarrassment his mother not only insisted on keeping it but also kept it on display. And she'd noticed the thing, among all the books and other mementos his mother kept out where she—and anyone else in the room—could see them.

"Yeah," he admitted. "First thing I ever showed her. Later, I met Dutch Benham, a master leather craftsman. He was getting on in years, so he taught me in exchange for some chores around his place. I loved it. It felt right."

He was, he belatedly realized, giving her a lot more than he'd given the writer. Would she keep her promise? Would it stay off the record? Not that he'd told her anything that he wanted kept secret. Except the bit about his father—he'd just as soon that didn't hit print. *Then you should have kept your mouth shut.*

"That's a wonderful story. And," she added hastily, "I'll never say a word. Although I think it would be a lovely thing to include."

"That, in essence, I owe my career to my father being a hard-ass about anything that hurt my mother? And vice versa, for that matter?"

"That's wonderful in itself," she said softly, this time without looking at him.

Something stirred in his gut at the way she said it. Again as if it were something totally foreign to her. He started walking again, not even sure where he was heading. The big barn, maybe. He could show her Bonnie's foal. People tended to enjoy that. And the baby horse already had his great-grandsire's charisma.

But his mind kept going back to the way she'd said those words, the touch of awe in her voice at the bits dropped here and there about his family. It made him wonder what her family must be like for such simple things to be amazing to her.

"I have a question for you," he said abruptly. She looked up at him then, as wary as a rabbit with a coyote in the neighborhood. "Why didn't she ask what I was smiling at?"

She gave him a shrug. "Probably because she assumed you were smiling at her. Men do."

He wasn't sure he liked being lumped in with that generic group, but he couldn't deny what she said was probably true. Jillian Jacobs was the kind of woman a man instinctively smiled at. Beautiful, sexy, and capable of turning on the charm. It was the capable of turning it off part that made him wary.

But was that what had put him so on edge he'd nearly blown up this meeting practically before it had even started? Or something else? She did remind him a bit of Chelsea, but he thought he was past blaming people just for looking like his ex.

But was he past the type? Or was he still that stupid guy who fell for the gorgeous looks, the practiced allure?

Damn. Maybe that was what this was all about. It was impossible to ignore how beautiful she was. And that she was—most would agree—just his type. Maybe he'd gone on the attack to keep distance between them. Maybe he'd gotten good enough at avoiding the Chelsea type that it had become automatic. That was good.

The thought that maybe he was still attracted to the type, not so much.

Chapter Eight

KAITLYN WAS UPSET with herself. Not an unfamiliar position for her.

Her thoughts took off running as they stepped inside the spacious barn, the bigger of the two here close to the house. On another level she was aware of the feel of the place, the scent of the hay, the sound of movement in the stalls. She noticed that a couple of equine heads had popped out through the open upper portions of the stall doors as they came in. But the greater part of her mind was processing those racing thoughts.

Ry had answered her when she'd dared to ask him questions now—as she'd said, strictly personal, things she had simply wanted to know—yet she knew she hadn't mistaken his frown when she'd dared ask one at the house. And there was only one thing different. The presence and absence of Jillian. So it was okay for her to ask something when she didn't distract him from Jillian.

This was not new to her. She knew her place. It was just that normally it was easy for her to stay there. But something about this man made her want to know more about him, how he did what he did, what he thought, what he felt, how his mind worked. In other words, she wanted to know everything.

And the fact that he hadn't let Jillian take complete control only added to her interest. Unfortunately it would, she knew, also pique Jillian's. The woman simply wouldn't tolerate anyone dimming—or resisting—her spotlight.

Not that Kaitlyn could. No, quiet, mousy little Kaitlyn Miller would stay in her place, the indispensable aide, the gopher, the quiet little mouse.

Enough with the rodent analogies. Even if it's not that kind of gopher.

"Fair warning," he said, snapping her out of her ruminations, "I hate having my picture taken."

She studied him for a moment, wondering why someone who looked like he did would mind. And just looking into his eyes snapped the leash she'd tried to put on her thoughts. And her mouth.

"Afraid your beauty will outshine the beauty of your work?"

He gaped at her. Actually gaped. His jaw dropped. He closed his eyes and gave a sharp shake of his head, then opened them again, as if to see if anything had changed. As if what she'd said was so impossible, he could only shake it off.

And suddenly she wasn't really sorry she'd said it.

"That," he finally said, and with a grimace, "was a very nice double-edged sword you dropped in there."

She couldn't stop her smile. He'd gotten it. If he said yes, he was conceited about his looks, if he said no, he was still tacitly admitting his own beauty existed. "Some things just are," she said simply. "And two of them were in that question."

He was still staring at her. Probably at her effrontery. Maybe he thought she was flirting, an idea so ludicrous she nearly let out a laugh at the very idea she would even try.

A rather pointed snort drew her attention, and she saw a black horse bobbing its head out from the stall labeled with a number three.

"That's the horse you were riding, isn't it?" she asked, glad of the diversion.

"Yes." She followed as he walked over and patted the horse. "This is Flyer. He's mine, which is why he's in stall three." He gestured with a thumb to the stall next to the black, labeled number one. "The gray there is mom's Seven. Short for Lucky Seven." He started walking down the barn aisle again, talking as they went. "The bay across from Flyer in four is Trey, Cody's horse."

"I'm noticing a theme," she said, looking at the horses as they passed them. "Although the Seven in one and Trey in four is a little confusing," she added with an amused smile. Then, as it occurred to her, she turned her head to look at him. "Your horse doesn't have a number name, so he's in three because...you're the third son?"

He grinned at her. It was devastating. It just shouldn't be

fair for a man to be so…so…much. "You got it. And here," he said as they reached the last stall, which was bigger than the others, "is Two. And his mom, Bonnie. Rafferty's Texas Bluebonnet, if you want the formal name."

She looked into the stall and something warm bloomed inside her. The two horses were clearly a mare and her foal, not simply because of their dramatic gold and black coloring but because of the way they stood so close together. That is, until the foal spotted them and came over to the doorway. He sniffed Ry, his upper lip mobile as he nudged his hand. Mom watched but seemed unconcerned.

"They're both lovely," she exclaimed as, at Ry's nod, she reached out to pat the little horse. "I love buckskins. Is he Two because he's the second buckskin?"

"No, because he looks exactly like his great-grandsire, Buckshot. So he's Buckshot Two."

She smiled at that. "This is starting to make sense. How old is he?"

"He was born last June, so he's coming up on seven months. He's being gradually weaned now, in fact this'll probably be his last night stalled with her."

"Is that sad, or exciting?"

"Probably both, but you'd have to ask them," he said.

"I don't think I speak equine well enough. Sadly."

"Your family didn't have horses around, huh?"

"No." *There was no family, period. Not like yours.* "Do you think…could I take a shot of them? It's just so sweet."

"I…sure. If you can do it without a flash."

"No problem," she assured him.

And it was a relief to dive into her bag, choose the lens she wanted and adjust the settings on the DSLR she mainly used. This was her turf, the place she felt at home, and was confident about what she was doing. And only when she relaxed into the familiar procedure, did she start to breathe normally again. And only then did she realize she hadn't been, really, since the moment he'd flashed that grin at her.

"So how did it go?"

Ry knew he should have skedaddled back to his place before Mom had arrived, but he'd come over to raid the cookie jar when Ariel had announced—via Chance, amazingly enough, which was reason enough to celebrate—that it was full of her custom macadamia nut chocolate chip specials.

"Okay," he said neutrally. "This was sort of a…groundwork day. The real stuff starts tomorrow."

His oldest brother, Keller, walked in as Mom asked, "So they'll be back early?"

He grimaced. "By the reporter's standards."

"Did you let them into the inner sanctum yet?" Keller, a couple of cookies of his own in his hand, asked.

"No." He gave his mother a sideways glance. "I didn't

allow any photos in here, either."

His mother studied him for a moment. "I'm surprised. I would have thought you would have, if it would avoid the other."

"Sacrifice the family home to save my studio? Thanks, Mom," he said sourly.

"You are a bit…manic about your privacy over there," Keller said, his tone mild.

"Genius burns and all that," his mother said, so cheerfully he knew it was intentional.

"Me?" he said in almost pure mocking indignation. "Chance lives as far away as he can and still be on the ranch, and you're picking on me?"

"That's because we don't have to worry about Chance anymore."

There was no mistaking the utter relief in her voice and expression, and Ry felt a blast of both love and admiration for this gutsy woman who had held them all together after the worst had happened. If there had been one unerring constant in their lives, no matter what chaos arrived, it was their mother's love.

He threw his arms around the woman who barely came up to his shoulder. "Love you, Mom," he said softly.

And when he looked up again, he saw his big brother smiling at him. He felt the urge to do the same thing to this man who had stepped into impossible-to-fill boots, but he knew Keller would just roll his eyes and tell him to do something constructive. Although maybe not, anymore. He'd lightened up so much since Sydney—and Lucas—had come into his life.

"Hey, good, you're here." Cody strode into the room, his two-in-one laptop in his hand. He carried that like most people carried a phone, because he said there were things he sometimes needed to do that required more power and a full keyboard. The keyboard that was now folded back out of the way so it was essentially functioning as a large tablet.

"Morning to you, too," Ry said.

Cody glanced around at the others. "I was up at six, so I already said good morning," he explained.

Ry smiled. He supposed he and his little brother were the most alike, because they both tended to get lost in their work as if it were another world, to the exclusion of all—and everyone—else.

"But I did do some deeper searching, like you wanted, on Ms. Jacobs." He made a wry face. "I only scanned what I found of her stuff, but you were right, she does mostly politicians and celebs."

"I wonder why they hired her for this?" Mom asked, looking concerned. "Surely not to…tear into you? *Texas Artworks* doesn't do that kind of thing."

"No idea." He gave her a wry half-smile. "Maybe it was because of who nudged them for the story. I'll ask her when they get here tomorrow."

"Speaking of they, I did a run on the photographer too.

Wow."

He raised a brow at the brother who was the only one to get the blond hair of the woman who'd birthed them all. But Cody had Dad's green eyes, while he'd gotten what Mom had said were her father's eyes. All of them were some combination of family traits.

"Wow?" he asked.

"She's good. Really, really good."

He held up the tablet. Ry stared at the image there, a breathtaking shot of the wall of a storm approaching what looked like the Gulf Coast. The contrast of the huge, swirling darkness punctuated by the brilliant flare of at least three lightning strikes, and the already restless sea, with the clear, blue sky it hadn't yet touched was beyond dramatic, it was awe-inspiring.

"And that's just the first one I found," Cody went on. "She's got stuff up on some stock photo sites that is amazing, and then there's a series she did for another magazine article."

Cody swiped a finger across the screen and another image appeared, this one a portrait of a man holding a little girl on his lap, with a book in one hand he was clearly reading to the toddler. The child's expression was rapt, entranced as she looked at what apparently were pictures in the book. But the man's expression as he looked down at the child was an echo of the one he'd just seen on his mother's face. The love fairly vibrated out from the image, and he wondered what it had taken to capture that moment.

"And this." Cody made the motion again, and this time it was a portrait of a little boy, probably a decade older than the toddler, holding a book himself while propped up by the trunk of the large tree he was under. Beside him, head resting in his lap, was a big, golden dog, looking up at the boy with worshipful eyes, as the boy looked at the dog with a similar expression of purest love.

"And this," Cody said again, and this time the image was an elderly couple sitting on a beach that looked somewhat like the one that storm had been headed for, leaning on each other. The man was looking at the woman beside him rather than the sea. And in his lined face was that same look—that love that was unshakable, eternal.

"My goodness," Mom said. Ry was glad she'd spoken, because he could not. "Were those published?"

"Yeah," Cody said, with a glance at Ry. "Along with an article about men in general that wasn't too flattering."

He blinked. "What?"

"You know, how we're arrogant, cruel misogynists, yada yada."

"Well, isn't that just interesting," Mom said. "For an article like that, she produces photographs that show exactly the opposite."

"Tell me Ms. Jacobs didn't write that one," Ry said dryly.

"Nah, her name's not on it."

Keller had been watching silently, but now said, "Why do you suppose she did those photos? Because she agreed with the sentiment of the article?"

Ry shook his head. If there was one vibe he hadn't picked up from Kaitlyn, it was man-hater. "I don't think so."

"Maybe," Mom said softly, "she did them because she didn't agree. And came up with photographs that are vivid proof it's a lie. Because no one with a beating heart and a shred of honesty can deny what those pictures show. The kind of love they show."

Ry thought about the woman he'd met. Thought about the way she'd reacted to the horses, especially Bonnie and little Two together. How she'd been so worried that she'd angered him by asking a simple question. That look in her eyes when he'd told her about his father's response to him breaking that vase. Her comments about his family, and the look in her eyes when she'd said them. And just from the way she acted, the fear of simply speaking her mind, all the apologies, he had a pretty good idea of what her life had been like.

"I think," he said slowly, "maybe she needed to remind herself that kind of love is possible."

Chapter Nine

"RYLAN RAFFERTY, HUH?"

Kaitlyn looked at the man she'd encountered on her walk along the creek the inn was named for. It was a quiet morning, calm so far since Jillian wouldn't bestir herself for another hour at least, and she'd quite enjoyed the clean-washed scent of everything after last night's rain. The creek was running fast, and when she spotted the sign indicating an overlook she'd followed it immediately. And had encountered Frank Buckley, the proprietor and owner of the Hickory Creek Inn returning from a check along the creek to make sure everything was in order after the rain.

"Yes," she said in answer to his question. "An article for *Texas Artworks*."

The man smiled. "That boy's really hit the big time now, for them to take notice."

She smiled back. "Apparently he was brought to their attention by someone with some clout."

Mr. Buckley looked thoughtful. And Kaitlyn remembered what she'd read on the web page for the inn when she'd booked the rooms, that he'd been a Texas Ranger for more than two decades, had retired after a crippling—for that job anyway—injury, and had turned his life to following his wife's dream of turning the family place into a B&B. She'd admired that and admired him for making that decision even though he'd been offered a desk job that actually would have been a promotion.

"Somebody with some pull, who used to hang out in Austin?"

She smiled at that. And tried not to think about how this man reminded her of her father. "Yes, Mr. Buckley. Somebody like that."

"Frank, please. Well, a Rafferty isn't one to say no to someone they think they owe something to."

"I believe that, after meeting him."

He studied her a moment, then said, "Come back up to the house. I'd like to show you something."

That surprised her, so she went willingly. She grabbed a mug of the best coffee she'd ever tasted from the table set up in the lobby before she took the seat he indicated. Then he went into a room behind the counter that served as the registration desk. A minute or two later he was back, putting a metal box on the table before her.

"He made this for my retirement ceremony, from the Rangers."

He pressed a thumb—not the one on his right hand, which had clearly been badly injured at some point, and she guessed was the reason for the retirement—on a small locking panel. It released, he lifted the lid, and she saw that inside the safe was a holstered weapon. His duty weapon, she guessed, but it was the holster that drew her attention.

It was intricately carved, the centerpiece of the widest part being a detailed replica of the Ranger badge. Around it were other symbols, including an eagle in flight, and a small image of this very building and the creek beside it. And all of it against a backdrop of the Lone Star flag, cleverly designed to look as if it were flying strong in the wind. And again she thought of Rylan Rafferty calling himself a craftsman. He was indeed.

But he was also, no matter his denial, an artist.

"It's amazing," she said, her voice barely above a whisper. "Such an astounding amount of meaning and symbolism, so beautifully rendered, in such a small space."

"Exactly," he said, in a satisfied tone, as if he'd made a guess that had turned out to be right. "That wild child of the Raffertys truly found his calling." She registered the appellation as the man went on. "Karina had commissioned it, but when she picked it up, he wouldn't let her pay for it."

She looked up at him then. "That's quite a way to say 'thank you for your service.'"

"Yes."

"Having met him now, I'm sure he felt it an honor to be asked."

The smile he gave her then was both genuine and warm. "Got his number already, I see."

She smiled back. "Would you allow me to take a photo of it? For the article? I don't have the final say on whether it would be used—"

She stopped when he waved a hand in understanding. "Chain of command, I get it. But of course you can. It's a beautiful example of his work, and you've clearly got the eye to see that."

"And it's quite a tribute to you."

"I'm proud that a Rafferty felt I'd earned it."

After she had finished up her shots of the beautiful holster and Frank had gone to put the weapon away, she repacked her gear. She was still pondering the obvious standing the Raffertys had in this community when she heard footsteps on the stairs, accompanied by a muttered complaint that there was no elevator in this place.

Kaitlyn, since she'd booked the rooms, knew there were ground-floor rooms available, including two that were specifically outfitted for those with disabilities or in wheelchairs, but the grandest suite, which of course Jillian required, was on the second floor. Kaitlyn's own room was also on that floor—she had to be close, in case Jillian called for her—but was a smaller room that Kaitlyn found no less pleasant. Especially when compared to her tiny apartment at home.

She moved quickly then, preparing a cup of coffee the way Jillian liked it. The woman accepted it without comment or thank you, merely as an expectation fulfilled.

"You're up early," Kaitlyn ventured.

"Who can sleep here? It's so damned quiet. I didn't even hear a single siren all night long."

Kaitlyn managed to swallow her sip of coffee without choking, but it was a near thing. When she could speak normally, she asked, "Is there something you'd like to do before we go back to the ranch?"

"I need to rethink my approach," she said. "I'll drop you off at that…quaint place, and you can get your pictures."

Jillian said it as if Kaitlyn were a kid with her first camera, or a selfie addict with a phone camera. She didn't react. She'd grown used to it, and if there was one aspect of her life she was confident of, it was her skill with a lens.

"Drop me off?" was all she asked.

Jillian nodded. "Then I'll go into town, such as it is. If this family is as well-known around here as they appear to be, surely there'll be someone around willing to gossip."

So now you're a gossip columnist? It was all Kaitlyn could do not to say the words out loud. But she knew she'd already strayed too close to the edge with the woman. She couldn't afford to lose this gig; the payment for the rehab center was due next week.

Last time, last time, last time, she chanted inwardly. She'd committed to paying for her mother's rehab one last time, more so she could walk away free than with any kind of hope it would take, since she'd long ago given up believing in miracles.

Then, eyeing Kaitlyn speculatively, Jillian added, "You seemed to connect with him."

Apparently he does go for the needy type.

The words echoed in her head. "If you're thinking about trying for a needy vibe, you know you don't pull that off very well," she said, her tone much dryer in her mind than it came out of her mouth. So much for keeping her sarcasm to herself.

Luckily for her, Jillian took it as a joke. "Of course I don't. Besides, you do it naturally. People let their guard down around you." Kaitlyn was a little surprised at the perceptiveness of that observation. She needed to keep reminding herself that Jillian didn't get to where she was by being stupid or unobservant. "So, perhaps you can wheedle something out of him. Some secret maybe, that I can use."

"What makes you think there is something like that?"

"Please. Everyone has something to hide."

Kaitlyn wasn't so sure about that. Then again, Frank Buckley's words came back to her. *That wild child of the Raffertys...* Just what kind of wild had he been? The kind who indeed had something to hide? Or simply the kind who had gone through the type of pain she knew too well, and had lost his way for a while?

Wild child.

The words also reminded her of her own thought, the first time she'd seen him, that he moved like a panther or some other big, wild cat.

"—you set him up for me, then I'll move in for the kill shot."

Kaitlyn snapped out of her thoughts. "Kill shot? What exactly are you after?"

Jillian waved a hand. "Just lure him in, get him talking. Like you did yesterday. Find me a pressure point."

Kaitlyn smothered a rueful chuckle. Lure him in? As if she were the kind of woman who could lure a man like that. Lure required allure, and that was Jillian's bailiwick, not hers. Although she had to admit she'd thoroughly enjoyed the time she'd spent with him yesterday. There were advantages to not being the kind of woman men immediately want to impress. Exceptions like the smarmy professor aside, she usually got to see the real person, who they genuinely were, instead of the façade put on for a woman they were attracted to.

And if it turned out she really, truly liked that real person she saw, and ended up wishing for more, well, that was her problem.

And of course, now that she knew Jillian *wanted* her to talk to him, her wayward brain would make doing so that much harder.

When they arrived at the ranch this time, the gate was open, and she felt a stab of regret. She would have enjoyed watching him ride up again on Flyer. And ride back. She'd always loved horses, and had wanted to learn to ride, had even started lessons back before. That's how she always thought of it, back before. Back before the end of her life as she'd known it.

With the ease of long practice—after all, more years had passed since that night everything had changed than she'd had before it—she redirected her thoughts. Thought about what she'd found in her additional research last night, going through the archives of *The Defender*'s website, old issues that had been scanned and added, going back to the days when the paper had first begun. Someone had had the foresight to save a copy of each edition, even then. She wondered what that person would think to see how those more-than-a-century-and-a-half-old issues were being read now, on a device that would seem as impossible as a trip to the moon must have.

She found the journey through history as engrossing as the book version, if only because it was fascinating to see the things that brought that life alive, the advertisements in the later editions, the announcements of births, deaths, and weddings, mentions of names she'd already encountered, including Rafferty.

Which eventually brought her to the more recent piece that had clarified much for her. An obituary for Kyle Rafferty, native son, killed in heroic action overseas at the too young age of forty-one. Beloved husband of Margaret, and father to Keller, Chance, Rylan and Cody.

The father who had created that painting that it hurt Ry to even look at. Probably just as it hurt her to look at the watch she wore. Yet she did it. Probably for the same reason that painting hung there, in plain, everyday view. Because some things—and some people—should never, ever be forgotten.

Chapter Ten

"WELCOME TO THE Rafferty Ranch," his mother said politely.

Ry noticed the blonde's fingers never stopped tapping on the polished stone of the counter she stood next to. And the frequent glances at the phone she held. Impatient? That was the vibe, anyway.

"Thank you," Jillian said, but it sounded rote. She gave the woman welcoming her into her home the merest of nods before returning her gaze to the phone. Ry's temper, usually safely caged, flicked its tail. Quinta, Mom's ever-present Aussie, gave the blonde a quick sniff and turned her back on her. Ry registered that as well.

Kaitlyn's smile, on the other hand—that dynamite smile—looked absolutely genuine. And when Quinta walked over to her, she immediately bent to greet the dog, whose tail wagged in approval. When she straightened to look at his mother, that smile was even wider. "It's a wonderful place, Mrs. Rafferty."

"Not the best time of year for beauty," Mom said. "You want that, you need to be here in April. Bluebonnet season."

"I love the hills in all their seasons," Kaitlyn said. "But if I wanted to see the full beauty and glory, I only have to look there."

She gestured at The Painting. Ry saw his mother's gaze narrow assessingly. Heaven help Kaitlyn Miller if Maggie Rafferty decided there was any falsity, any phony flattery in what she'd said. He didn't think there had been, but he freely admitted his mother was an excellent—better than he, certainly—judge of people. Especially their sincerity.

"I found out in my research before we came today," Kaitlyn said, her voice soft, her tone almost apologetic. "How he died, I mean."

Ry saw his mother go still. He stiffened himself, waiting for the inevitable platitude. It didn't come.

"His service, this place, that genius," Kaitlyn said as she nodded at the painting, "What a combination. How fascinating he must have been." Ry forgot to breathe for a moment. In just a few words, this woman had summed up the complexity of the man his father had been.

Mom drew herself up to her full five foot two. Ry knew from her expression that what Kaitlyn had said had struck a chord with her as it had with him. Emotion echoed in her voice when she spoke. "He was. All of that. The only thing he loved as much as his family and painting was this ranch, and as part of that, this country."

"We're lucky to have people like him," Kaitlyn said quietly. "For however sadly short a time."

After a moment his mother gave a short, decisive nod of her head. "Welcome to the Rafferty Ranch," she repeated, only there was genuine warmth in her voice this time. And he knew Kaitlyn Miller had, at least in his mother's eyes, passed muster. Perhaps more importantly, he saw by her expression and smile that Kaitlyn realized it.

"Thank you," she said softly, and the warmth in her voice was undeniable. And that was apparently enough to trigger Jillian.

"Kaitlyn will be taking her pictures today," she said in a tone imperious enough—and dismissive enough—that Ry saw his mother's eyebrows raise a bit. Jillian seemed to notice, for her tone was much more deferential when she went on. "I'll be in town, to get the atmosphere. I always try to do that on a story, get the feel for the place my subject calls home."

Ry didn't know which Jillian to believe, the imperious one, or the courteous one. He remembered the first moment he'd felt that jab of anger toward her. It had taken him a moment to realize he'd been ticked because of how she'd treated Kaitlyn. No one deserved that kind of disrespect. Well, no one just doing their job, anyway. But given he was going to be stuck talking to the woman for a while, he probably needed to adjust his attitude.

But he wasn't sure a day spent with Kaitlyn taking photos wasn't going to be even worse, in a very different way.

As Jillian drove off in the expensive rental car, Ry pondered the situation. It was funny, he would have expected the writer to be the more perceptive one, and yet it was Kaitlyn who had somehow known what to say—or perhaps what not to say—as she spoke of his father. Who had shown respect bordering on awe to both his skill as an artist and his sacrifice.

It hit him suddenly, belatedly…how had she known? He searched his memory, not that he really needed to—he was certain he hadn't told her Dad had painted that painting. He turned his head to look at her, study her as she chatted with his now-smiling mother. Obviously they had quite hit it off. They'd strayed into Last Stand history, a topic his mother could talk about for hours. Kaitlyn listened with every evidence of genuine interest and proved both that she was paying close attention and that, as a Texan herself, she knew enough of their history to ask things that put a spark of joy in his mother's eyes.

Ry watched and listened, enjoying it as he always did when his mother dove into her passion. Especially with a willing audience, which Kaitlyn clearly was. She'd just launched on the eighteen-minute battle of San Jacinto when her phone chimed an alarm and Mom announced she had to go, sounding almost reluctant.

"Meeting of the Daughters of Last Stand, about the upcoming Bluebonnet Festival," she said.

"It's the beginning of January," Ry felt compelled to point out.

"And it's the biggest event in Last Stand, short of the rodeo and Christmas. Never too early to start."

He gave her a smile and a wry shake of his head before bending to give her a hug. "Love you, Mom."

"Back at you, my precious son."

Ry felt himself flush a little; he wished she'd keep the extra syrup to the times when no one else was around. But she never had, and all of the Rafferty boys had learned she likely never would.

"Your mother is…everything she had to be, isn't she."

He looked toward Kaitlyn at the words that weren't really a question. He'd never seen an expression quite like the one she wore now. She looked wistful. Almost sad. "Yes. She is. Was. Always." Then, before he could talk himself out of it, he blurted, "How did you know my father did that painting?"

For a moment she looked even sadder. "By the pain in your eyes when you look at it," she said softly. He blinked, she shrugged. "I recognized the look. I've seen in it my mirror often enough."

He understood then. "Your father?" She nodded. "So you know the pain."

"Yes and no." He drew back slightly, puzzled. This time her shrug was accompanied by a sigh. "Your father died doing a noble thing. My father died because my mother's a drunk. A beautiful, alluring drunk."

The wistful expression as she watched his mother go

suddenly made sense. "Ouch," he said, because he could think of nothing else.

"Yes," she said.

"What happened?"

"On one of her binges she managed to set our house on fire."

His breath caught in horror. "Kaitlyn," he began, then stopped, having no idea what to say. It was a moment before she went on.

"She staggered outside in a drunken haze. Never even thought of me. Beau—my dog—woke me and we got out my back window. My—" Her voice broke. She swallowed. Oddly, she turned to look at the painting again, then went on. "My father thought I was still inside. He went back in to try and save me. He didn't get out."

It took everything he had to keep his voice anywhere near level. "She…survived?"

"Yes. The drunk survived, and the sweet, wonderful man who loved me died."

He didn't miss the implication that it was her father, not her mother, who loved her. "How old were you?"

"I'd just turned nine." Years younger than he had been. Just thinking it brought back memories of the pain, the disbelief, the raging anger. "Life's unfairness sucks. But then you knew that."

The last words were choppy, as if she'd fought saying them. He understood. And he did know.

"Sorry," she muttered. "I don't usually pour that out to virtual strangers."

To him, that felt like a compliment. "Sometimes that's easier," he answered.

"Yeah." She drew in a deep, audible breath. Then, steadily, she said, "Shall we get started? I get the feeling you'd like this whole thing over as soon as possible."

"Nothing personal," he said quickly.

She gave him another of those killer smiles. "I understand."

She glanced back at the painting, and he said rather quickly, "No photographs of that. That's…"

"Private. I understand that, too. What I was going to ask was if that location is here, on your ranch?"

"Yes. One of Dad's favorite spots. And for all of us, now." And before he'd thought he was saying, "You want to see it? It doesn't look like that now, of course but—"

"I'd love to."

"Do you ride? You can't really drive there."

"No," she said, and there was a touch of that sadness again. "I always wanted to, was going to take lessons, but then…"

Her voice trailed off. There was no doubting why. He could see it in her eyes again. No doubt that had been about the time her mother had destroyed their lives.

"If you want to try, we've got a lapdog of a horse, perfect for a beginner."

He saw a different sort of wistfulness, more of a longing, come into those huge brown eyes. "I'm supposed to be working," she said.

"So bring your gear. Take a shot or two."

She looked at him steadily for a moment. He wondered if she somehow knew he was stalling to keep from letting her, or worse the reporter, into his sacred space. Although again it flitted through his mind that if it was just her, he wouldn't mind so much. Maybe it was her eye for an image. Or her obvious perception. Or maybe it was something about the way Jillian had treated her, still nagging at him. He, like his mother, and his brothers for that matter, all had a tendency to root for the underdog. And he'd say that was exactly who Kaitlyn was in this relationship.

Or maybe it was just his reaction to what had happened to her as a child, how her father had died. The story was certainly horrifying enough.

Or maybe it was something entirely different.

Chapter Eleven

THEY WALKED TOWARD the second barn, which she noticed looked newer than the smaller one he'd indicated was also his living space. This one was also about twice the size.

"A recent addition?" she asked.

"Five years ago," he answered. Then, looking almost sheepish, he added, "It was part of Mom's plan to get me to come home."

"You were gone?"

He grimaced, and she didn't know if it was because he wished he hadn't said what he'd said, or that he didn't want to answer her question. "Sorry," she said hastily, for fear she'd offended him.

He gave her a curious look. "Why are you apologizing?"

"It's none of my business why you were gone. But Jillian will probably ask. How you ended up here on the family ranch, I mean."

"But we're off the record still, right?" When she nodded, he went on, his tone wry to the edge of bitter. "I was gone because I was an idiot who thought I'd found what my parents had together."

So he'd left for a woman.

Why are you surprised? Look at him. You know he's got to have them fawning all over him endlessly.

But he'd answered her, which surprised her. She'd really thought she'd stepped over the boundary. She tried for a neutral tone. "Didn't work out, huh?"

"Let's just say my year at Lake LBJ is something I remember with about as much joy as getting my wisdom teeth pulled."

"Ouch."

He shrugged. "Water under the bridge. I'm back here now, the setup is working well for all of us, and Mom's happy."

"Your mom," she said, with an emphasis she truly meant, "is a peach."

"That she is."

"The lady at the library said she was practically a living Texas history book."

"She is." He gave her a sideways look as they got to the small, human-sized entryway set in the main barn door. "You should ask her to see the letter to her children our five times great-grandmother wrote during the last stand, when she was certain she would die there."

"Wow." Her awe was genuine.

"I'd show you my copy—Cody scanned the original so we all have one—but Mom would really get a kick out of showing it off."

"I will ask her. I would love to see that real bit of history."

"You know a bit yourself."

"My dad read a lot about it, and sometimes he'd read it aloud to me." That too familiar combination of sadness and warmth filled her. "Even after I was old enough to read it myself. I loved listening to him."

"I get that," he said, his voice so gentle it was soothing. "I used to love to watch my dad paint. I had to be really quiet and not disturb him, but I didn't care."

"Exactly like that."

As he reached toward the smaller door she smiled at him, her eyes tearing up a little at the quiet understanding in both his words and his voice. He put a hand on the handle of the door, but then stopped.

"My turn for a none-of-my-business question."

Rather guardedly, she said, "Okay."

"When you told me about the fire…why did you look at the painting first?"

That was the last thing she'd expected him to ask. But perhaps she should have known, given he'd shown just how much his father and that painting meant to him. And she couldn't give him anything less than an honest answer.

"I needed to remind myself that there's beauty in the world, that it's not all pain. That there are people like my father, and like your father in it, and relationships like he obviously had with your mother, and with you."

He stared at her for a long, silent moment, and she wondered if she'd trespassed somehow, if she'd assumed too much, if he—

"That is one of the best things you could ever say about it. He would have loved hearing it. I wish he could have."

His voice went very tight on those last words. There was so much emotion in his tone that it spurred her to ask something she'd wondered since the first moment she'd watched him look at that painting.

"Do you think, if…he hadn't died, you would be who you are today?"

He drew back slightly, his hand still on the door handle. "What?"

"I just meant…if you hadn't had that tragedy in your life, would you be where you are? Obviously you could just sail by on your looks, but you haven't done that. You've found your calling and built a career on it. I just wondered if you think things would be different, if you would…"

Her voice trailed off weakly as he stared at her. Had she really done it this time, crossed the line?

"I can't give you an answer to that."

She had done it. Another apology rose to her lips, even as she wondered what it was about this man that made her forget where the boundaries were. "I didn't mean to—"

He waved it off. "I've just never thought about it like that." She let out a relieved breath. And then, with a lifted brow, he eyed her a little too pointedly for her comfort. "Sailed by on my looks?"

With one of the greater efforts of her life she met his gaze. She might not be a polished, elegant woman like Jillian, or a resilient, lively, and more attractive—at least to Kaitlyn—woman like his mother, but she was not a coward.

"Please. I'm assuming you have a mirror in that loft of yours?"

His mouth curled slightly. "Only to keep from cutting my throat while shaving. Which, I'll have you know, I did in your honor this week."

"Don't do it on my account. I'll bet you look even better with three-day stubble."

Where on earth had that come from? Where had any of this come from? She sounded like she was flirting! On a job, yet. She didn't do that, not with anyone, but especially not with sexy, gorgeous men way beyond her reach.

And this man, who was undeniably both those things and a genius talent to boot, was looking at her so oddly she could barely think.

"Just ignore me," she said hastily. "I'm much more tolerable with a camera in my hands."

You're not pretty enough to flirt, Kaitlyn. Just keep your mouth shut, and we'll do better.

Those words, delivered in that helpful, instructive tone she'd come to hate, had been the first time Louis's words had stung enough for her to doubt his intentions. She'd thought, with all his degrees and education, that he was able to see past the plain exterior to the heart and soul beneath. Fool that she was, she hadn't realized what he'd wanted was a weak, moldable woman he could shape into what he wanted. An adoring, grateful sycophant. He'd assumed she would be willing to accept that place in his life in return for his acceptance of her lack of beauty and charm.

Turned out she wasn't. And her determination to keep the vow she'd made then, to never kid herself like that again, was second only to her vow that this would be the last chance she would ever give her mother.

RY PONDERED THE mystery that was Kaitlyn Miller as he watched her get acquainted with Latte, the mellow paint they'd bought from the Walkers precisely because he was the calmest, most steady horse Keller had ever found, and it was always good to have one of those around for guests and newbies.

"He's beautiful," she crooned as she stroked the horse's neck. Latte, always willing to accept a new admirer, nudged her with his nose.

"That's his signal that you can touch his head," Ry advised her. "You've passed inspection."

She gave him a startled look, but immediately went back to the horse. Mystery wasn't the word for it. It wasn't that she'd complimented him—he'd had to learn early that people, especially women, seemed taken with his looks, while his mother had seen to it that he knew how surface that was—but what kind of woman felt the need to apologize for complimenting someone? She was a puzzle, and in the same way he'd been fascinated by figuring out how the pieces of the vase he'd broken went together, he was fascinated by what had shaped this woman into the puzzle she was.

And by the simple fact that her compliments meant something to him. It mattered that it was this woman saying words he'd heard before. And that had startled him. As had the fact that he'd felt a warmth stirring inside him that he hadn't felt in a long time.

You probably scared her, staring at her like that. Maybe she thought she'd trespassed or something, because she's here for a job.

He remembered Jillian's treatment of her and could see where she might be wary. Clearly the writer thought Kaitlyn should stay in her place. And that rankled him. Especially after he'd seen the images Cody had found. Maybe it was that he was a visual artist himself, but while he appreciated good writing, images such as hers were what sparked instant appreciation in him.

If you hadn't had that tragedy in your life, would you be where you are?

He truly hadn't ever thought about it that way, maybe because he tried not to think about it at all. He knew that life had blown up, been ripped apart as if by a Texas tornado. Keller had come home and helped Mom pick up the pieces, Chance had taken off to follow Dad's path into the military, and little Cody had retreated into his computers and gadgets. Him? Chance always said he'd gone to silent running after Dad's death, stepping back, not talking much to anyone about anything. And part of that was not spending a lot of time analyzing the impact that death had had on him and his life.

And here this woman he'd met just yesterday—well Monday, if you counted almost knocking her flat with a door in town—had spun it around in a way he found impossible not to think about. Would he have found his way to this? Would he have even thought about it if he hadn't been desperate to fill the void?

The old, all too familiar ache began to build. The end of one life had nearly brought about the destruction of five more, and only the sheer determination of his mother along with Keller's willingness to sacrifice his own dreams to hold them together had saved the entire Rafferty family. He wondered, not for the first time, if his father had had any idea how important he'd been to them, how rudderless and lost they'd felt without him, even though he'd often been deployed for long stretches. Perhaps it was a measure of what an amazing man he'd been that he'd still been their pillar, the nexus of their lives, despite the absences. That his death had nearly ripped the heart out of all of them, that—

Latte nickered, snapping him out of his heartrending

thoughts. And he found Kaitlyn staring at him, looking almost worried, and he wondered what kind of expression those thoughts had put on his face.

She started to speak, then hesitated. Finally, softly, she said, "He would have been proud of you, you know." He blinked, and she added quickly, "I know I didn't know him, but…I know the man who did that painting couldn't not be proud of a son who produces equal but different beauty."

He stared at her. How had she known, where his mind had gone?

And how had she so simply eased the old ache and given him the gift of a certainty he'd never really had? He'd thought Dad would be proud, but he'd never been sure. But now, thanks to this woman and her gentle words, her intuition, he had the thought that if he were here, Dad really might be proud of him.

And he couldn't find any words to explain how that made him feel.

Chapter Twelve

KAITLYN LOOKED AT the expanse before her with the same kind of longing that came over her every time she left the city. That she was here, on the back of a sweetheart of a horse who had never put a foot wrong—although she'd pretty much decided the camera would not come out while she focused on this first ever ride—and whose pace was so steady and even that she, a first-time rider, had never felt a moment of concern, only made the longing fiercer.

"I'm a little afraid of this," she'd admitted before they'd set out.

"Don't be," Ry had assured her. "He's as gentle as a newborn pup."

I didn't mean the horse.

She'd been a little surprised she hadn't blurted it out. Admitted that it wasn't the horse she was afraid of so much, it was being alone with him. Her mind—and mouth— seemed to lose all restraints under that particular condition. But she somehow managed to keep that one to herself. And was thankful for it; she much preferred being overlooked to being laughed at. Or about.

She'd known this place the moment he'd reined the gorgeous Flyer to a halt. Even without the carpet of bluebonnets, it was recognizable. They dismounted and he led her north as she scanned the breadth of the landscape before her.

When they reached the flat spot a few feet away, he stopped.

"This is it, isn't it?" she asked. "The scene in the painting."

"Yes. Not quite as dramatic without the blooms."

She glanced at him. Whatever had hit him so hard back in the barn, he seemed past it now. She understood; sometimes memories of her father welled up and overwhelmed her and it took her a while to find an even keel again. At least he hadn't seemed upset with her, even though she'd let her mouth run in ways she usually never did.

"I think it's more that it's dramatic in a different way. Not in color, but in shape and expanse, in the roll of the hills, the sharp edges of the stone outcroppings, and in the distant horizon."

He stared at her. He looked a bit…stunned. Had she done it again, somehow overstepped? Maybe this had been a bad idea, this ride alone with him. Staying here alone with him. Being anywhere alone with him.

She wasn't used to this. Her social life was beyond sparse anyway, but this had been a particularly long stretch, after the disaster that had been Professor Bates. The disaster that had shaken what little confidence she had. That had to be the only reason she was so…so…not herself. Why she couldn't seem to shut up around him, when usually a man who looked like this had the opposite effect on her, and she was unable to get out a coherent sentence.

"I'm sorry—"

"Stop it!"

A chill enveloped her as he snapped it out in obvious irritation. She really had done it now. She'd have to explain why he'd pulled out of the project, and Jillian would be furious. Not to mention she'd blown her own chance at any future gigs with *Texas Artworks*.

"I didn't mean to yell," he said almost immediately. "But just stop apologizing."

"I'd much rather stop saying things I need to apologize for," she said contritely.

He turned to face her then. His steely-gray eyes seemed darker than usual, even in the full sunlight. "You haven't said anything that would need an apology. So stop."

She frowned. "But just now, the way you stared at me, you looked…I thought—"

"I reacted because what you said echoes my own thoughts about it. Almost word for word."

"Oh." She felt her cheeks flush. She hated that she could never stop that; when you embarrassed yourself as often as she did, it would be nice not to have the whole world know. "Really?"

"Really. So that's one down."

She blinked. "One what?"

"Apology. I think we've got four or five left to go." She stared at him. As if ticking off a list he said, "Let's see, you apologized for stopping in your tracks to admire my father's painting. Shouldn't need an explanation about why that wasn't necessary. Then you apologized twice for asking questions. Good, solid questions, not silly, esoteric things about inspiration and vision. Didn't need those, either. And you sure didn't need to apologize for sharing the kind of pain we both know too well, of losing a father we loved."

She was still staring at him. She couldn't help herself. It wasn't so much what he was saying, that she hadn't needed to offer any of those apologies, it was that he'd listened. And not just listened, but really heard what she'd said. And remembered. She wasn't used to that, not on a job where Jillian was involved. The woman tended to suck up all the oxygen in the room, especially when it came to men. But Rylan Rafferty was obviously not an ordinary man, in more ways than one. Many more ways than one.

And he hadn't mentioned her most recent apology, for asking about him being gone from the ranch. Did that mean she had overstepped, and that apology had been needed? Or did it not count because he'd already asked her after she'd said it, why she'd apologized?

Her head was starting to whirl a bit with trying to figure this—and him—out. She opened her mouth to speak, realized she was going to start with "Sorry" again, and stopped herself.

"You were going to do it again, weren't you?"

It took everything she had to say with any amount of cool, "Mind-reading now?"

"I just figured that's why you stopped."

"Maybe I was going to say something else."

"Which you'd then apologize for? Is this how it usually goes for you?"

"No," she said wryly. "Usually I manage to keep my mouth shut when working with Jillian." The moment the words were out she regretted them, but under the circumstances she managed not to apologize.

"Why do you?"

"Work with her? Because she asks for me. This could be a career-maker for me. I need the line on the résumé. And the money," she ended bluntly.

He gestured back at her gear. "Equipment's not cheap, huh?"

"It's my mother's rehab that's not—" She cut herself off, horrified. She sank down to sit on the edge of a stone outcropping. Whatever it was about this man that blasted away her guardrails, it had to stop.

He was staring at her again. "After she killed your father, you're paying for your mother's rehab?"

"Again," she muttered.

"You apologizing again, or do you mean…this isn't the

first time you've paid for it?"

"It's certainly the last. I told her I'd do it this time because I'd promised I would if she really tried. And I won't be one of those who makes promises and breaks them without a second thought." *Like my mother.* "I vowed I'd stop when I turned thirty." She said it with fierce determination. This was a vow she would keep, even if it meant finally turning her back on the woman who'd borne her. And if that made her heartless, as her mother so often said, so be it.

Ry turned to look out over the landscape, as if he needed to process what she'd said. She'd never had a man, other than her father, pay such close attention to everything she said. It was a strange feeling. A little bit heady. But it also made her uneasy.

After a minute or two he said, very quietly, "Shane Highwater's mother drank herself to death at thirty. Shane was ten. The youngest kid, Sage, she was only two. I was always angry on their behalf, thought it was the worst thing that a mother could do. Now I'm not so sure. Maybe putting your kids through years of hell is worse."

"Be thankful for the mother you have," she said, meaning it. She'd only spent a short time with Maggie Rafferty, but she already knew she liked her. She was the kind of mother Kaitlyn would have wished hers into being, if it were possible.

He turned back to her then. "Oh, I am. Every day. We all are." The love that glowed in his eyes was unmistakable.

These weren't casual words thrown out because they were expected; he meant this from the gut. "I don't know where we all would have ended up if she hadn't held us together after Dad was killed. Certainly not here, together. And as tight as we are."

"She never remarried?"

"No. I think she had her hands full with us. And…she adored my father. Yours?"

Kaitlyn gave a sour laugh. "Twice. And engaged three more, although those guys had the sense to break it off before the wedding."

"Yet you pay for her rehab."

"She's my mother," she explained. Then his true meaning hit, and she blinked. "You mean I don't have as much sense as those guys?"

He shrugged. "Just wondering, when does the blood obligation wear out? Your father was loyal and look what happened."

She winced, but it was nothing she hadn't thought herself. And he was looking at her as if he knew that. And she decided she appreciated his bluntness. "Like I said, this is the last time. No matter what. I made that clear, told her the third time had better be the charm, because I wasn't doing it again."

"That had to be hard, standing up to your mother. We're programmed to do the opposite, so it takes guts, and the certainty that you're right. Good for you."

He said it like he meant it, with approval. And it warmed her, probably far more than it should have.

They remounted, Ry giving her a leg up, a procedure that was more than a little unsettling. It really had been a long time, if a simple helping hand set her pulse racing. Of course, when that hand belonged to the sexiest guy she'd seen in a long time…

They rode for a while, Kaitlyn savoring the feel of the horse's movements, the fact that she was riding at all, and that it was here, in this country she loved. Only something that powerful could keep her camera out of her hands. As they started down another hill she gave him a curious look, decided what she wanted to know was innocuous enough.

"So, you all work the ranch?"

He nodded. "Between us and the hands we have come in, we get it done. Of course Mom's worth about three hands all by herself. The woman's indefatigable."

She quashed another pang of envy. Her own mother had worked hardest at making sure she had the easiest life possible, which meant little effort and lots of booze.

They went up another rise, and Ry pointed toward a cabin in the distance, with a couple of outbuildings and what seemed to be a lot of fencing. "That's Chance's place."

"Where he works with the dogs?"

Ry nodded. "One of them, Dodger, a German shepherd, turned out so well our neighbor's borrowing him to help round up some horses. He's been down to just the one for a while, because he was a hard case, but he'll be picking up a couple new ones soon."

"I so admire that," she said.

"He's quite a guy, that brother of mine," he said, in a tone that told her he felt the same way. "And Ariel's been…a godsend. She pulled him—and Tri, the worst case he ever took on—out of a dark place. We were all worried."

She liked how open he was about that, and about crediting the woman his brother had found.

But then, she liked a great many things about Rylan Rafferty.

Chapter Thirteen

THEY GOT BACK to the main house just as Lucas arrived home from school. Ry watched as his mother came out to greet the boy, and she gave them a wave when she saw them riding in. He realized with a jolt that the boy was now a little taller than she was.

"I swear," Ry muttered, "that kid's grown another inch since Christmas."

"That's Lucas?" Kaitlyn asked.

He nodded. "When he got here, he was a couple of inches shorter than Mom."

"How long ago was that?"

He had to think back, to remember the day Keller had found the starving boy stealing raw eggs to eat from the chicken coop behind the big barn. "A year ago back in November."

"And he's been here since?"

Ry nodded as they rode up to the house. Lucas watched them approach, and Ry noted the boy seemed wary of the newcomer. But he always had been. After the tragic loss of both his parents, ending up in the system and eventually running away from the group home he'd been in, he'd been mistrustful of everything and everyone.

He'd been particularly suspicious of Sydney at first and working their way through the shock of finding he wasn't completely without blood family had been complicated by the developing relationship between her and Keller, the man he'd come to look at as a father figure. Ariel had also made him cautious, but he soon accepted her for what she'd done for Chance and the dogs, in particular Tri. He wondered how the boy would react to Kaitlyn.

Ry felt a little jolt, a combination of surprise and confusion. This wasn't the same. Sydney and Ariel, they had been destined to become part of the Rafferty family. Kaitlyn was…just a visitor. On a job. No, not the same at all. A few days and she'd be gone, never to be seen here again. He didn't know why the comparison had even occurred to him. He must have just been focused on Lucas's reaction, and Sydney and Ariel were the others it had been most obvious with.

But Ry also noticed that now, after a bit more than fourteen months here, the boy reacted more watchfully than as if he were personally scared. As if he considered the ranch his home now, a place to be protected. And even though Keller, and then Sydney, had done most of the work to get the boy to this point, it brought a certain satisfaction to Ry that surprised him a little.

"Hey, Lucas. Suck to be back in school after the holidays?" he asked cheerfully as they pulled up at the house.

"No more'n usual," the kid said. "Lots of homework already, but some of it's on cool stuff, like the solar system and space and stuff."

Ry dismounted, glanced over at Kaitlyn and saw that she'd slid down off the tall Latte without too much trouble. She pulled the smaller gear pack she'd taken with them out of the saddlebag.

"Lucas, meet Kaitlyn Miller. Kaitlyn, Lucas Brock."

"Hi," the boy said neutrally.

"Hi," Kaitlyn said, in much the same tone. "Nice to meet you."

The boy looked unconvinced. He nodded toward Mom. "She told me you were here. You're a photographer for this magazine thing, right?"

"I am."

He looked at Latte, then back at her. "Newbie, huh?"

"Very," she admitted, patting the horse's neck. "I'm lucky you have such a sweetheart here for people like me, who love horses but have never been on one."

"He's a good horse to learn on," Lucas said. Then, looking back at her, he said, "If you love them, how come you never learned to ride?"

Ry saw the flash of pain in her eyes before she lowered them, and he remembered what she said about the lessons that never happened. "Because the same kind of thing derailed her life as yours, only she was even younger," he said gently.

Her head snapped up, his gaze shifted back to her, and he saw the surprise flash in her eyes. Which were, he noted now, nearly the same deep brown as Lucas's, but more striking with the golden flecks. Belatedly he wondered if she was upset that he'd answered for her, when she'd seemed unwilling to answer herself. But then she gave him a fleeting version of that smile, this one touched with the remembered pain. Maybe he was reading too much into a simple expression, but he thought there might be a touch of "thank you" in there, too.

"Your parents are dead, too?" Lucas asked, the ferocity that had always been in his voice when he'd spoken of them when he'd first arrived missing now. He'd progressed to where he could at least talk about them, and them being gone, without pulling back into the hole Keller had coaxed him out of.

"My father is," Kaitlyn said, her tone just as level as she met the boy's gaze. "Thanks to my mother, who set our house on fire because she was drunk."

Lucas's brows shot upward. Ry, startled himself that she'd said it so openly to this boy she'd just met, could see him processing. Mom, he noticed, still hadn't spoken, but was just letting the boy think it through, as she had so often for them. But then her gaze shifted to him, and he saw that too familiar expression that told him she'd seen something more here, and that that maternal mind-reading had happened again. What she'd found this time, he had no idea.

"Wow. That sucks," the kid finally said. "What happened to you?"

"Foster care for a while." Lucas grimaced. "Yeah. And they weren't as nice as the Raffertys. You landed in clover."

She said it with a smile. The boy glanced at Mom, then at Ry, then looked back to Kaitlyn. "Yeah, I did," he said, a little embarrassed-sounding. "What happened after that?"

"They gave me back to her."

"Wow," he said again. "Did you hate her?"

Something about his innocent tone took any edge out of the question. Ry stayed quiet. This seemed important somehow, that Lucas communicate with someone who'd been through something similar to his own tragedy. And he had the sudden thought that that was exactly why Kaitlyn had done it. She had bared her own pain for Lucas's sake. A boy she didn't even know.

"I did," Kaitlyn admitted honestly. "Sometimes, when she gets drunk again, I still do."

Lucas's brows shot up again, and he drew back a little. "She still gets drunk? After that?"

Kaitlyn mouth twisted slightly. "She does."

"Man, that really, really sucks," the boy said, and there was a world of empathy in his voice. Then, unexpectedly, he looked at Ry and said, "I'll take care of Latte and Flyer if you want. Untack 'em and brush 'em and all."

"That would be great, buddy. Thanks," Ry said. He

watched the boy take the reins and walk the two horses toward the big barn. Then he looked back at Kaitlyn. Somehow, in the memories of similar misery, these two had made a connection.

"That," his mother said, speaking for the first time, and to Kaitlyn, "was a very kind and generous thing to do. I know how hard sharing your pain can be."

Kaitlyn only shrugged, looking a little uncomfortable.

"Don't belittle it," Ry said. "You reached him. He wouldn't have offered to do that work with the horses if you hadn't."

"I…it just seemed best to be honest. Like they weren't with me, a lot of the time."

"It was best," his mother said briskly. "But you'd be amazed at how many people wouldn't have known it or done what you did. Now, come on in, and have some coffee while I start dinner. We eat early on school nights. I swear, the homework they pile on that boy…"

She turned and went inside, leaving them little choice but to follow. Ry held the door for her and they followed obediently. His mother looked back over her shoulder at him as she started toward the kitchen.

"You do know what day tomorrow is, right?"

"Yes, ma'am," he said dutifully. "I've got an alarm set."

She nodded and kept going. Kaitlyn looked at him curiously. He shrugged and said wryly, "Friday's my day to start the coffee."

It only took her a split second. "And if you're deep into something you sometimes forget?"

"Exactly."

He pulled his jacket off once they were inside and he'd closed the door. Kaitlyn began to do the same with hers, a classic denim, lined with a blue plaid flannel. It looked well worn, and even mended in a spot or two. And he found himself wondering just how much that rehab was costing her.

"That's a really nice belt Lucas is wearing," she said. "A Rafferty original, I'm guessing?"

He took her jacket and hung them both up on the rack inside the door. "Yeah."

"Not every kid his age has something worth that much to wear." He grimaced. Personally he thought what Yippee Ki Yay charged for the things almost obscene, but the fact that they sold them as fast as he finished them indicated otherwise. "The image on the front beside the horse is this house, isn't it?" she asked. He nodded. "And I noticed his name on the back. Brock."

"Yeah."

"And two smaller names on either side of the bigger last name."

Did the woman miss nothing? "His parents' names." She just looked at him, and something in her gaze made him add, "They were good people. They loved him, and he knew it."

"And he loved them." She said it with certainty.

"Yes. And still does."

"Birthday present?"

"Yes. Everybody else in the family has one, so it seemed right."

She was quiet for a moment, and he thought she blinked rather rapidly a couple of times. "I was right," she said softly. "He landed in clover."

He watched her walk over and ask his mother if she could help and wondered just how bad her own foster experience had been. And on some other, deeper level, he was aware he was having to work to focus on that rather than the way she moved, the long-legged grace and the sweet curve of her backside.

"Go back to that cave of Cody's, will you?" his mother called out. "Let him know dinner will be ready in an hour. As long as he's here he might as well eat, too."

"Even Cody isn't crazy enough to say no if you're doing the fixing," Ry said to his mother with a grin, and turned to do as she'd asked.

Kaitlyn was already chatting easily with his mother and he was headed back to Cody's lair when he heard the sound of a car approaching. A quick glance told him it was the expensive rental, with Jillian at the wheel. He kept going.

Cody was, as usual, intent on the array of three monitors before him. Ry noticed one of them was showing what had to be a drone feed, because it was moving. The north boundary, he thought, then quickly amended the thought. The north boundary and Britt Roth, who was rocketing along the trail that ran parallel to the fence, aboard a powerful sorrel that gleamed red in the winter sun. Remembering the last blow-up between the two, he considered asking his brother if he really wanted to risk her fury again if she saw or heard that drone but decided not to prod that particular rattlesnake nest.

"Mom says dinner in an hour. And she's cooking, so you'll want to be there."

"What?" Cody said, almost absently, his gaze still fixed on the galloping horse and the woman astride it, riding as if born to it. As she had been.

Amused, Ry asked, "Is that what did I say, or what is she cooking?"

It still took a moment for him to disengage; his little brother had a tremendous ability to focus. Probably came with the brain. But finally he looked up at him.

"Mom says dinner in an hour," he repeated.

"Oh. Thanks."

"The maybe-not-so-intrepid reporter is back," he added. "She seemed pretty interested. And she's almost as pretty as you."

His brother flipped him a rude gesture.

Ry contemplated leaving Jillian to his mother for a bit. Maggie Rafferty had quite the knack for cutting people down to size, and if she felt someone had a seriously too high opinion of themselves, she didn't hesitate to do it. That she did it in the kindest and yet most unarguable way—and that she held herself to the same standard—was what had earned her the respect of most of Last Stand. It was a strange feeling, being the child of a town legend. And probably why they got along so well with the Highwaters, who were in the same position.

Yes, leaving Jillian to his mother for a little while might be worth it. If nothing else, perhaps Kaitlyn might pick up some tips on how to handle the self-important woman herself.

And why that mattered to him was yet another thing he shoved out of his mind.

Chapter Fourteen

MAGGIE RAFFERTY WAS, Kaitlyn had decided, the most amazing woman she'd ever met. And she'd met a few, photographed a few, some with well-known, if not quite household, names. But she'd stack Maggie up against any of them. And then stand back and watch with enjoyment as the pixie-haired blonde blew up their pretensions.

"I know it must be so hard for you," Maggie was saying to Jillian now, so sympathetically Kaitlyn couldn't believe the woman didn't realize it was put on. "You stand out so here, and I know there are a few people in Last Stand just like you expected to find, people who disdain big-city women like you."

"It's true," Jillian exclaimed, seemingly oblivious.

Kaitlyn saw something flash in Maggie's eyes, something akin to bright blue steel. "I'll bet you can't wait to get back home."

"I'm always happy to get back to civilization," Jillian said, clearly blissfully ignorant of the insult.

"Why, bless your heart," Maggie said.

Indeed. Kaitlyn was Texas born, and she knew perfectly

well those were not the kind words they appeared to be to those who didn't know better. She didn't see how anyone could miss the slicing blade just beneath the surface of Maggie's too sweet expression.

Yet Jillian flashed her most charming smile, as if delighted to find someone here in this hick town who understood her pain. Then she looked at Kaitlyn. "So did you get some lovely shots of our handsome subject?"

Kaitlyn grimaced inwardly. She'd already told Jillian that Rylan Rafferty was one who would require a slow workup to the more personal aspects of this. He wasn't the type who would pose flamboyantly for her lens, looking forward to his image splattered on glossy pages and screens across the state and beyond.

"Not yet. Getting there," she muttered.

She wondered again why the woman had taken this project. She was clearly not happy being here, and it was not the kind of thing she usually did. She said it was to expand her résumé, to show she could do any type of article and make it a hit.

"I want to go viral in every area," she'd explained once, as if having the most hits on a page were some sort of hard-won championship.

Jillian now made a show of quashing her impatience. "I have to go to Austin. I'll be there through the weekend." Kaitlyn wondered who was in town, what person who could help Jillian on her career path had arrived in the capitol.

"You'll have to call a ride-share in the morning, assuming they even have those here."

"She could take the stagecoach," Maggie said sweetly.

Jillian's head snapped around to stare at the older woman, which was a good thing because Kaitlyn nearly burst out laughing. Maggie's glance flicked to her for a moment. Just long enough to wink. With Jillian's head safely turned, Kaitlyn grinned.

"No need, we'll loan her a horse," came a deep, masculine drawl from the entry to the hallway the blond brother had emerged from yesterday. Judging by the kick of her pulse when she spun around and saw Ry there, leaning against the entryway wall with one shoulder, his ankles crossed, arms folded across his chest—that broad, powerful chest—she was surprised she hadn't sensed he was there. Like some helpless prey when the big cat was on the hunt. She wondered how long he'd been there, how much he'd heard.

He wasn't looking at her, he was focused on Jillian. Of course. Yet…his expression, that narrowed gaze, was not the usual rapt admiration she generally saw from men when they looked at the sexy blonde. Instead it was as if he were jabbing at her exactly as his mother had been. Belatedly, his words played back in her head. Loan her a horse?

He *had* been jabbing at Jillian.

But then he shifted his gaze to Kaitlyn and her breath caught. And driven by something she didn't quite recognize in herself and reverting to the Texas drawl she tried to restrain when she was elsewhere, she said, "Well, now, I'd like that."

The slow, upward tilt of one side of his mouth was like the sun coming up. To her, at least. She didn't know when making this man smile or laugh had become so important to her. She did know it made her feel as if she'd accomplished something significant. And sent her pulse rocketing off all over again.

"We'll see she gets back to the inn," Maggie said briskly. "And back here in the morning, if you want to leave right now." Kaitlyn had the strangest feeling those last three words were more of a suggestion than anything. She doubted Jillian had picked that up, however. And apparently so did Maggie, because she added, "You head on to the city."

Kaitlyn heard "where you belong" echoing in the air as if Maggie had said it. She had to stifle a smile and look away from Jillian. Jillian seemed oblivious again, and merely said a cheery goodbye as she left.

"Good," Maggie said, then looked at Kaitlyn. "Now you can stay for dinner."

Kaitlyn blinked, startled, and in that moment Maggie turned and vanished into the kitchen.

"You can translate that into she won't take no for an answer," Ry said helpfully as he shoved off from the wall he'd been leaning against and walked over to her. "So you might as well save the energy and give in."

And so that evening Kaitlyn found herself sitting at the

Rafferty dinner table with everyone except Chance and Ariel, who were off to pick up two dogs for his rehab program for MWDs. And, Keller said with more than a touch of satisfaction, to show Tri off to those who'd thought the dog would never make it.

"I wish I'd had a brother like you, who would have...stepped up," she said to Keller impulsively. She didn't even know why, except that it was true, and there was something about this family that invited such things. And she couldn't really regret that she'd blurted out the words, not when Keller looked embarrassedly pleased and his mother and Sydney delighted.

They all made her feel welcome, and comfortable. Except Ry. Who still made her nervous despite the prevailing ease in the room.

After that she was mostly silent, watching the family dynamic with more than a little bit of wonder. The talk went around the table, the give and take, everyone's words given attention and acknowledgment. She knew families like this existed, intellectually, but she'd never seen it firsthand before, let alone been a part of it.

But the Rafferty clan seemed determined that she be just that, a part of it. Over the luscious roast and vegetables, Maggie asked, "How did you get started in photography, Kaitlyn?"

Startled to be included, Kaitlyn stammered a little at first. "I...it was...high school. The teacher who ran the photo club. Nick Vega."

"He spotted your talent, huh?" Cody said.

Kaitlyn grimaced. "I think it was more he was trying to keep me out of trouble. Give me something else to do, besides—"

She broke off, realizing with a little shock she'd almost told them about the trouble she'd already been in, hanging with the wrong crowd and messing with the edges of a really bad lifestyle.

"Good teachers, ones who truly care, are rare and irreplaceable," Maggie said.

"Yes," Kaitlyn said, calmer now. "And he's one of them. He loaned me one of his old cameras and showed me how to use it." *And told me not to end up like my mother. The first time I ever knew that…everybody knew.*

"And you found your passion," Sydney said with understanding in her voice.

Kaitlyn looked across the table at the woman with the beautiful golden eyes. She'd only spoken to her briefly before, in passing, but even she had heard of The World in a Gift, the global enterprise the woman had built from the ground up. "Yes, I did. Thanks to Nick. His wife and son died very young, so we've become…each other's family. I owe him everything."

"Cody showed me some of your work. It's brilliant," Sydney said.

"And she," Keller put in with a loving look at the woman

beside him, "would know."

"Yes, she would," Kaitlyn said, meaning it. "So that means a lot. Thank you."

"So," Sydney said, that golden gaze fastened on Kaitlyn almost disconcertingly, "tell me about those shots you took for the male-bashing article."

Kaitlyn blinked. "I…"

She didn't know what to say. She'd hated that job, because every minute she put into it felt like a betrayal of her father, and in fact every loving figure she'd had in her life, who all happened to have been male. But she hadn't known the writer's prejudice going in. And she'd needed the money badly at that point, and what she'd made on that job had given her three months of breathing room.

And she'd hated herself every one of those months.

"You meant those photographs to prove exactly the opposite of what that article said, didn't you," Maggie said softly, and it was not in the tone of a question but of certainty. Kaitlyn shifted her gaze. Maggie's expression matched the tone, and Kaitlyn knew that, for her at least, the message she'd intended in those pictures had come through loud and clear. And that was the only thing that eased her self-disgust at having participated in the hit piece.

"Yes," she said. "It was all I could do. I didn't know what the slant was going to be until after I'd agreed, and then…I couldn't afford to back out."

"Sometimes we all have to do things we'd rather not."

Maggie's voice was brisk now, as if signaling that it was time to move on. "Are you still in touch with your teacher?"

"Yes. He's...having some problems physically at the moment, but his mind is as sharp as ever, and I see him regularly at the assisted living place he's in." She smiled. "It's a good place. We threw a big birthday party for him there last month, when he turned seventy."

"Places like that are hard to find," Ry said.

It was the first time he'd spoken since the topic of her work had been broached. He was looking at her intently as he said it. A little too intently. But then, Kaitlyn wasn't sure any steady look from him wouldn't be too much, for her anyway. And that speculative glint in his eyes made her edgy.

Or it was simply that he made her edgy.

"It took a while," she agreed, "to find the perfect fit."

"That's what I thought," Ry said, nearly as softly as his mother had spoken a moment ago. But there was a different note in his voice.

It was the sound of someone who'd had a suspicion confirmed.

Chapter Fifteen

RY DIDN'T THINK he was wrong that Kaitlyn had jumped to help clean up after dinner not only to be helpful, but also because she needed to move, to do something. And as he gathered up as many dishes as he could carry without risking breakage that would have his mother giving him that "You should have known" look she had down so well, he walked beside Kaitlyn into the kitchen.

"You're paying for your teacher's help, too, aren't you?" he said, keeping his voice low enough the others wouldn't hear.

"No." She didn't look at him.

"Kaitlyn," he began as she started to place dishes in the dishwasher.

"Not all of it," she amended, still not meeting his look. "Just…the gap his insurance doesn't cover."

"Does he even know?"

Her head came up then, and her gaze was fierce. "No. And he won't."

He couldn't stop himself and reached out to stroke a finger across her cheek. "That's where it comes from. The love in those pictures you took, blowing the premise of that article to pieces. It comes straight from you."

She seemed to shiver under his touch. That simple reaction sent a blast of heat through him he hadn't felt in…he didn't know how long. If ever. He—

"Pecan pie for dessert."

Ry's head snapped around. His mother's voice held nothing but her normal cheer, but he didn't miss the speculation in her eyes as she looked at them. And a touch of regret, as if she were sorry she'd interrupted. So was he.

Maybe.

But it didn't really matter—the moment had passed. Kaitlyn quickly finished putting her dishes in the rack and escaped. There was no other word for the way she almost scampered out of the kitchen.

"Rylan?" his mother asked quietly.

"What?" It came out a little sourly.

"Anything I should know?"

Your timing sucked, Mom. Or maybe it was the best. But he only smiled. "You already know everything, don't you?"

"An illusion I work hard at." She was looking at him in that intent, sees more than she lets on way he'd grown up with. She glanced toward the table where Kaitlyn had retaken her seat, then looked back at him. "I think I quite like her."

"It's mutual," he said. "She…doesn't know anything about a mother like you." He hesitated, but decided Kaitlyn had already said the basics in front of her when she'd told Lucas. "Her mother got out of that house fire, leaving Kaitlyn behind without a thought. Her father died going back in after her, because he didn't know she'd gotten out a window."

His mother's eyes widened with every word. And he knew he wasn't wrong about the sudden sheen of moisture in those beloved blue eyes. "That poor child," she whispered. "It's a wonder she's even functional."

"More a testament to her strength."

He knew what his mother would think if he told her the rest, that Kaitlyn was paying for that same heedless mother's rehab yet again. And knew that her help for the man who had set her on the career path she obviously loved would seal the deal. But those truly weren't his stories to tell; he wouldn't betray her confidence. That off-the-record he'd asked for, in his mind at least, went both ways.

They spent another hour around the table over the pie. His mother was going out of her way to include Kaitlyn, and Ry knew she'd come down firmly on her side. Then Sydney drew Kaitlyn, who said she had never been further from North America than Mexico, into the conversation with tales of her world travels.

"How long will you be here?" Sydney asked. "I'd love to talk to you about updating some of the photos on our website."

Kaitlyn looked startled. "I...we're only supposed to be

here for a week."

"Not we," Sydney said, as if she'd already drawn her own conclusions about Jillian. "You. Can you stay after that, and talk to me about it?"

"I…of course," Kaitlyn said, looking a little stunned.

Rightfully so, Ry supposed. After all, The World in a Gift was a global operation, a big name. It would be a huge opportunity, and a very impressive line on her résumé. Not to mention that he knew Sydney paid her people well. And he felt a burst of affection for his soon-to-be sister-in-law. And before he could figure out why her helping out Kaitlyn made him feel that, he was derailed all over again.

"Then you must join us next week. Wednesday night," his mother pronounced suddenly.

Kaitlyn looked startled. "Join?"

"We and a few friends are having a private party at the Last Stand Saloon. The annual 'survived the holidays' gathering."

"I don't—"

"Oh, please come," Sydney put in. "This will be my first one, too, so if you come I won't feel like such an outsider."

Leave it to Sydney to make it seem like Kaitlyn would be doing her a favor. She had the knack with people, and Ry admired it, and her. And again envied his brother more than a little for having found such a perfect match.

"I don't drink," Kaitlyn said flatly.

"No problem," Mom said easily. "Slater—he runs the

place—makes the most wickedly delicious peach lemonade."

"And if you go," Cody said, "we can use that to pressure Chance into going. Between that and Ariel pushing him, we'll get him there."

Ry stayed quiet, both to see what Kaitlyn would do and because he wasn't sure he wouldn't say something stupid. Her brow furrowed slightly, as if she were trying to remember something, but she seemed to push it aside as she leaned back in her chair and scanned the others. He saw the corners of her mouth twitch before she said, "Y'all are really something."

"What we are," his mother said cheerfully, "is a united front. Right, Rylan?"

She was looking at him a little too pointedly, as if she were very aware he hadn't said a word. He wanted to shrug and say "Whatever," noncommittally, but he could guess what that would get him. Then he realized—felt, maybe—Kaitlyn was looking at him. Waiting. As if it was his answer that mattered, that would decide whether she went or not. And he wasn't sure how that made him feel.

That seemed to happen a lot with her.

"Sure," he finally said. "You should come. It's a good time." *And you haven't had many of those, have you...*

It wasn't a question, even in his mind, because he already knew the answer.

She lowered her gaze for a moment, then looked back at his mother. "Thank you. I'd like that."

Ry was still pondering what he'd let himself in for some time later, after they'd adjourned to the great room for another hour or so, when he realized Kaitlyn and Cody were deep into a conversation. It was apparently about photo software, using terms that left him thinking it couldn't be more foreign to him than if they'd been planning a space excursion. When he found himself feeling a twinge of resentment at the sight of her and Cody with their heads together, alarm bells went off in his mind.

What the hell? What are you—jealous of your little brother?

He fought down the idea, but it put an edge in his voice when he finally said, "Let me know when you're ready and I'll drive you back to the inn."

He felt awful the moment he saw her expression change from animated to polite. "Oh. Of course, it is getting late. I should go."

Kaitlyn stood up quickly. His mother's look at him could have sliced bread. But then, suddenly, her expression changed, as if something had occurred to her.

"I'm so glad you stayed," she said to Kaitlyn.

"Thank you so much for having me. The food was wonderful, and the company more so." She glanced at Ry. "I'll get my things."

"I'll go get my truck."

He was glad to escape his mother's watchful gaze. For that matter, all of them were watching him a little too closely for comfort.

They were a couple of hours past full dark, and the truck's headlights arrowed down the road as he headed toward Hickory Creek and the inn. It was also cold tonight, maybe headed for a freeze. He hoped they were prepped for that, but then he smiled to himself. Keller would never miss something like that. His brother was rock-solid, and the ranch was in his blood and bones.

No, he'd be the one who'd completely miss what needed to be done. Hoses would freeze and split, spigots develop leaks, stock go without water until he finally realized and broke through the ice on the water troughs, while he was lost in his head somewhere. Even Cody would do better, because one of his fascinations was the intricate weather monitoring system he'd set up. It was also one of his most frustrating projects, and once after a storm he'd been sure would skirt them had hit with a vengeance, he'd said glumly, "The thing I've learned about predicting the weather is that nobody can be always right predicting the weather."

Remembering that storm, the towering clouds, the thunder, lightning, and pouring rain, he wondered yet again if there was a way to capture that in leather. He'd thought about it before but had never come up with a way to really capture the power and energy of a Texas thunderstorm. More depth maybe, but that would require a thicker material than could be comfortably worn. So it would have to be a saddle, a part that wouldn't need a lot of flex. Or maybe a bag of some kind, a briefcase or maybe even a purse. Mom might like that. Or she was always looking for donations to sell for her various fundraising booths at the Christmas Market or the Bluebonnet Festival. He could—

A movement from the passenger seat snapped him out of his thoughts and off of autopilot. Kaitlyn was pulling her jacket closer around her, and he belatedly realized it was cold in the truck cab as well. He reached down and turned on the heater.

"Why didn't you say something?" he asked.

She shrugged. He'd never met a woman who did that nearly as much as she did. "I thought it was off for a reason, like it didn't work."

"No," he said dryly as he slowed going into a dip, "it was off because I was off, in never-never land as my mother says."

She was quiet for a moment before she said, "And what beautiful thing will be born of that?"

He shot her a glance. She was smiling, as if she knew how his mind had segued from practicalities to imagination. Curious about how her mind worked, he asked, "With your camera, do you ever spend a lot of time trying to figure out how to best represent something?"

"Often," she said. Then, with a wry smile, she added, "Sometimes I even succeed."

"You certainly succeeded on that article Cody found."

She sighed. "I had to. I just had to. It was so wrong, and I had to show it."

"Because of your father? And your teacher?"

There was a moment of silence in the shadowed interior of the truck before she said, barely above a whisper, "The only love and caring I ever had in my life came from them. That article was the lie."

On the edge of his vision as he drove he saw her take a swipe at her eyes. And it drove him to say, in all seriousness, "Then let me say, on behalf of all mankind, thank you." Then, in a lighter tone, he added, "Not that all mankind deserves it, mind you."

"Neither does all womankind," she said, her voice steady now. And he wondered if she was thinking of the writer, or her mother. Maybe both.

When they got to the inn and went inside, to his surprise Kane Highwater was sitting at the desk in the lobby. The man grinned when he saw Ry's reaction.

"Scary, ain't it? But it's Frank and Karina's anniversary tonight, and he had a big night out in San Antonio planned. I'm just trying not to mess up too badly."

He turned to introduce Kaitlyn to Kane but stopped when he realized she was gaping at the man. A spark of irritation flickered. Then he nearly laughed at himself. He'd been told often enough he was good-looking, but Kane was in another class altogether. Even Ry's mother had called Kane uncannily beautiful.

But he was also lock, stock and barrel in love with Lark Leclair, the woman who had managed to bring the Highwater family back together again.

"You," Kaitlyn said in a tone that matched her expression, "You're Kane. I saw you at that show in Luckenbach last fall. Your voice…you were amazing."

The man behind the counter looked suddenly shy. He still, Ry guessed, wasn't quite used to the reaction his music got. "Thanks," he said. "It went well that night." Then, as if uncomfortable, he shifted his gaze to Ry. "You're coming next week, right?"

He nodded. "I'm under orders."

"See you there, then," Kane said, grinning again as if he knew perfectly well whose orders. But then, he knew Maggie Rafferty. "Lark's going shopping with Sage for something to wear."

Ry nearly laughed at the idea of the delicate, uber-feminine Lark taking the rough-and-tumble cowgirl shopping, for clothes of all things. "That ought to be interesting."

"How…fancy is this thing?" Kaitlyn asked, sounding a tiny bit alarmed.

"It's a saloon," Ry said, grinning himself now. "Slater doesn't have a dress code, but he does require you *be* dressed." *Sadly.*

He tripped over his own heated thought and was glad when Kane spoke lightly. "The Raffertys and the Highwaters, together again."

"Just how many Highwaters are there?" Kaitlyn asked.

"We started with five, now soon to be ten of us," Kane said cheerfully. And steadily, with none of the hesitation he'd once had in claiming that family as his.

"He's come a long way," Ry murmured as they started across the lobby to the stairs.

"That performance was stunning."

"I'm sure. But I meant with his family. He was gone for well over a decade." He looked at her then. "But that's a long, sad story. And his story."

She tilted her head slightly. "So the pain I heard in his music was real. Personal."

"Probably." As he walked Kaitlyn to the door of her room—it was the polite thing to do, after all—he asked, "Were you working that night, in Luckenbach?"

She nodded. "Another singer hired me for some publicity shots." She gave a slow shake of her head. "She was okay, pretty good even. At least, it seemed that way until he—" she nodded back toward the desk "—came on and blew everybody else out of the water."

"He was born with that voice. To him it's just something he always had. I think he still doesn't quite believe how good he is."

She stopped at her door, then turned to look up at him. "Kind of like you?"

He blinked. "What?"

She shrugged. Again. "He's an artist. So are you. And you're no more used to that than he is. But that doesn't make it not true."

"I'm not—"

"An artist. So you've said. Despite all evidence to the contrary. Maybe you should think about why you cling to that perception so fiercely."

She turned to unlock the door, leaving him a little stunned. Only the reflex of his mother's long training enabled him to reach out and open the door for her. His movement seemed to startle her, and she spun back. They nearly collided. She was so close he caught the fresh, sweet scent he'd already come to associate with her. The scent that reminded him of the peach lemonade his mother had mentioned.

He didn't even realize he'd lowered his head until she raised hers and her hair brushed his chin. She was close, so close, and the next thing he should do, the next thing he needed to do was obvious. So obvious. And his every sense snapped alert, ready, urging him on. He wanted that mouth, that mouth with the soft lips and the tongue that uttered those clever retorts. Wanted it so badly it blasted every logical, reasoned thought out of his head. And he moved that last critical inch. But at the same instant she moved as well, and his lips merely brushed her cheek.

She jumped, clearly startled. And that was enough to make him pull back. He'd never made a woman jump like that before, and that was warning enough to retreat.

Yes, she'd definitely been surprised.

But then, so had he.

Chapter Sixteen

KAITLYN WAS SURPRISED—AND if she were honest, a little disappointed—when the Rafferty Ranch truck arrived in the morning to pick her up, but with Keller behind the wheel. She almost laughed out loud at herself. What woman on earth would be disappointed to see the tall, handsome, green-eyed cowboy show up for her?

Only one who's developed a fascination for a dark-haired, stormy-eyed artist who denies he's an artist. One who got the crazy idea into her head that he'd almost kissed her last night.

As if the likes of Rylan Rafferty would ever want to kiss the likes of her. A man who could have any woman he wanted, with just a look and a crook of his finger.

"Thanks for the ride," she said to Keller, for lack of anything better to say. "I could have done a ride-share, really."

"It's no problem. I had to run into town for something anyway, so it only made sense." He smiled at her, and it was the smile of a very contented man. "Sydney was going to come along, but she got a call from London she had to take."

Kaitlyn smiled. "She's amazing."

"That she is," he agreed with that same smile.

Kaitlyn lapsed into silence, wondering if Ry had been grateful for his brother's offer. He must have been, since he didn't insist on picking her up himself.

Of course he was. You probably trumpeted it out that you thought he was going to kiss you.

"I wanted to talk to you anyway," Keller said.

Uh-oh. "You did?"

He nodded as he started the truck down the long, curving drive from the inn to the Hickory Creek Spur that would take them to the road back to the ranch. Kaitlyn shifted in her seat, ignoring the protest of muscles that didn't appreciate the new activity of riding a horse. But Keller didn't say any more, for long enough that she became puzzled.

"About?" she finally prompted. Funny, she had no trouble doing it with him, but if it were Ry there at the wheel she'd probably be intimidated into silence.

He took in an audible breath. "My brother."

She knew which brother he had to mean. And had the sudden thought that Ry had sent him to tell her to…what? Back off? Quit getting so personal? She didn't think he was the kind of man who would send someone else to do that, but then she didn't know anything about brothers and their bonds, or for that matter the bonds of a family like this one. She didn't know a darn thing about families like the Raffertys. She practically trembled, was afraid to say anything as she waited for him to go on. Finally, he did.

"Ry's a different sort of guy. Watching more than participating. And he sees…beneath the surface, I guess you'd say. Sydney says it's because he's an artist, and they look at things differently."

"He is that," she said, cautiously. "No matter how much he denies it."

He glanced at her before making the turn out onto the Spur. Odd, she thought, how a handsome guy like this inspired appreciation in her, but no longing. No, she stupidly seemed to save that for even more impossible men. For her, anyway. In this case one man in particular. It was no wonder he'd apparently sent his brother in to warn her off.

"Yes. And we don't really know why he keeps denying it." She opened her mouth to tell him what she thought, but realized she had no reason for the idea, only a gut feeling, and shut it again. "All we know for sure is, after Dad was killed, and before he found this…outlet, he was headed for trouble. He quit talking to any of us. Went completely silent. He was cutting school, getting into fights, and headed down a bad path."

"So his art saved him," she said softly.

"Yes. I don't think he meant it to become what it did, it was just something he liked to do, and there wasn't much of that, back then. He liked the ranch work, but that was about it."

"So he really was a cowboy?"

"Still is, when he needs to be." He smiled. "Our dad used to say once a cowboy, always a cowboy."

She managed a smile back. "It's a sort of mindset, isn't it?"

"It's exactly that." He gave her a sideways look again. "The thing is, he's always been kind of separate from people. Even us, sometimes, but everybody else, definitely."

She realized he was telling her this to warn her off—and she tried not to think of how embarrassing it was that he, or more likely Sydney had realized it was necessary—but she also thought she might be able explain a little.

"I think…it's more being one step back. I do the same, because I tend to look at people and things and see how they would photograph. It puts a slight…not barrier, but distance between us. It's not that I want to be apart, it's just that's where my mind goes first."

There were other reasons, of course, but she wasn't about to get into that here, with this man. *Hey, don't worry, I know your gorgeous, amazing brother isn't going to fall for plain, boring little me, with all my troubles.*

"That makes sense," Keller said as he slowed the truck to make the turn onto the road out to the ranch. "And it would explain why he reacts to you so differently. Because you get it, you're on the same wavelength or something."

She blinked, and went very still. *He reacts to you so differently.* She clamped down on a suddenly racing mind that was plowing through all the possible meanings of those words.

"But whatever it is," Keller went on, "he's more…here, more present, around you than we've seen in years." He gave her a wry smile. "We'd have been more worried than we were about him, if we hadn't been so worried about Chance."

"Meaning Chance following in your father's footsteps?" she asked, seizing at the change of topic.

"Yes. And we were afraid his goal was to end up the same," Keller said with surprising frankness. "But we didn't know where Ry was headed. Or what to do to help him."

"And then he found his calling."

"Yes. But he's still that step back, as you put it."

"I think it must be the artist in him. To be as good as he is, you have to be…observant. Of all the details of the world around you. And that takes a moment, before you can tune back in, sort of."

He turned his head for a moment then, to look straight at her. "Except around you. Around you, he's right there from the get. He practically vibrates."

There was an undertone in his voice that put her on edge. Warning again? And that quickly she was back to wondering if that's what this was. But why would he warn her? He could only be worried about his brother. He certainly wouldn't care if she was silly enough to fall for the guy and get herself hurt. But he couldn't possibly think she'd somehow hurt Ry? How could she? True, perhaps they connected on an artistic level—no matter his denials that he was one—but that was all it was. All it could possibly be.

My God, how did I ever have such an ugly duckling child?

You'd better look for an unattractive man who can't do any better, girl.

As she remembered her mother's rueful, pained words, she thought of how she would laugh her head off at the very idea that a man who looked like Rylan Rafferty would be attracted to her.

And that moment last night? What was that?

Proximity, that's all. An accident. No more meaningful than bumping into a stranger on the street.

"I'm just saying he's different with you," Keller said, a note in his voice that said he'd been waiting for a response from her, and when it hadn't come because she had no words, he thought he needed to explain.

She steeled herself, tried for a neutral tone. "Meaning?"

"Just…that it's good to see him like that."

There was such love in his voice it shook her. It reminded her of the way her father had sounded, when he soothed her after her mother had gone off on one of her binges.

She stared at him as they drove the final few yards to the ranch turn. "I really meant it when I said I wished I'd had a brother like you."

He pulled the truck to a stop at the gate. Then he shifted in the driver's seat to look at her. "I know you did. Sydney said you sounded like she felt, when she first came here." He grimaced. "Between the two of you, I'm becoming a believer that people should have to pass a test to become parents."

"And some people are born with everything it takes to do

it right," she said quietly, holding his gaze.

A slow smile curved his mouth. These Rafferty men were truly quite something. "I'm glad you're staying," he said.

Before she could react to that he was out of the truck to pull open the gate. She watched as he maneuvered the heavy metal structure with powerful ease. Found herself comparing his steady, rock-solid strength with Ry's quick, panther-like grace. She had to quash the heat that rose in her at just the memory of that first day when he'd ridden up on that black horse that was his match in beauty and flash. She tried to use what they'd just been talking about, that step back, that artist's eye, thinking about how she would capture with her lens the differences between the two brothers. Mentally she added another safety layer—Cody, the contrast to Ry with his opposite blond flash. She wondered where Chance, whom she hadn't yet met, fit on the spectrum of beautiful Raffertys. She had no doubt he did, probably in his own unique way.

And suddenly she wanted more than anything to do an in-depth series on them all, this family. The brothers were so different. Yet at the core, in all the ways that truly mattered, they were the same.

A product of their father's legacy, their mother's unfailing love, and the power and history of these Texas hills.

Chapter Seventeen

RY HEARD THE sound of the truck and knew they were here. He'd been reluctant to let Keller pick Kaitlyn up, and had tried to think of a way out when he'd arrived to start the day's coffee as required, but he couldn't make a big deal about it without raising the suspicions of the whole damned family. Because it was only logical, since Keller had had to go pick up a shipment of horseshoes anyway. Of course he could have volunteered to do that, too, but their mother was already watching him a little too closely for comfort. As if she knew Kaitlyn got to him.

I wish I knew how. But I only know she does.

He reached to close out the browser on his laptop that sat on his workbench, but lingered one more moment over the image he'd just found. He'd spent at least an hour on the stock photo site, starting with searching by her name, then realizing with a little snap of wonder that if he searched by subject instead, subjects she'd mentioned, he could almost always pick her shots out of a page full of images, even in thumbnail size.

Including this one, a dramatic, early morning shot of the

Alamo, at that time of day empty of tourists, and taken at an angle that cut out the stark modernity of the city that had grown around it. He'd known the instant he spotted it at the bottom of the page that it was hers. She'd caught the perfect angle of the sun's rays, the beams of light sweeping the eye past the more modern touches around the old mission, putting the building itself in a spotlight.

It looked as it must have on that March morning just before the final battle of the thirteen-day siege began. The light even had that same quality, and if she'd taken it on March 6th, he wouldn't be surprised. She was a Texan to the bone, after all. And it was the kind of detail she'd think of.

He heard the sound of his door opening. He jolted to his feet and spun around. Nobody ever just walked into his space, unless it was some urgent situation on the ranch and they needed help. They knew better. And then he realized.

Keller. He was pushing the door open. "Brought your photographer, bro," he called out cheerfully.

Too damned cheerfully. He knew exactly what he was doing. Because he was doing it on purpose. He had a sudden, flashing vision, of Keller and Mom, plotting this together. He swore to himself. Just because Keller had found his perfect woman, and more unbelievably so had Chance, and Mom wanted that for all of them, didn't mean they had to collude—

"Come on," Keller said to someone—like Ry didn't know who—behind him. As if the person were hesitant.

Smart girl.

But then, he already knew that. Kaitlyn Miller was definitely smart. And quick. And clever.

And as tough as she'd had to be. Texas tough.

And then she was there, with her hair pulled back in a ponytail today, dressed in her worn jeans and a blue and white and black plaid shirt, half tucked in at the front, and with her backpack of gear slung over her shoulder. He knew how much it weighed, and today she looked almost too slight to carry it. His mother's words came back to him.

That girl needs a little weight on her. I get the feeling she doesn't eat right.

Right? From what he'd learned about where her money went, he'd guess the more accurate diagnosis was she didn't eat much, period.

She's paying her own way and for a couple of others. He hadn't really meant to say it. The words just sort of slipped out under his breath. But his mother had heard—he could tell by the way her brow furrowed.

Or maybe, he amended now as he watched her nervously look around the open space of the small barn, she was just one of those people who ran at a high pitch, and burned off every calorie.

Keller backed away without ever actually setting foot inside, closing the door as he went. And Ry just stood there, fuming a bit at his brother, until he realized Kaitlyn had yet to meet his gaze. And it wasn't simply that she was looking around his studio, although she'd taken a quick, wide glance when she had first come in. No, she was studying the floor as if the simple, gray barn wood was the most fascinating thing she'd ever seen.

"I'm sorry," she said, still without looking at him. "Your brother is…"

"Yeah, I know." Keller was impossible to say no to. But he'd earned that status the hard way, and no one in the family would ever question it. Since he'd been thirteen the man had been the father figure in his life, even at only four years older. And if Keller hadn't stepped up, Ry had a pretty good idea of how things might have gone for the Raffertys.

Kaitlyn just stood there, but he could almost feel the tension coming off of her in waves. And it occurred to him, unsettlingly, to wonder what she and Keller had talked about on the ride here from the inn. Was it more than simply being here, in the place he protected so fiercely, that had her so nervous? Had Keller said something to put her so on edge? Make her so uncertain?

"You just going to stand there?" His irritation at Keller made his voice a little sharp, and her head finally came up.

"I know you don't like people in here," she began, and then stopped. And he didn't like the sound of her voice. Didn't like it at all. It wasn't quite fear, but it was more than hesitancy, and it made the sharpness of his own voice jab at him. He suddenly felt like some winter-hibernating bear who'd been disturbed, snapping out at the one who'd dared intrude.

"I'm a little…protective," he said, now sounding more like a sheep than that bear. "Come in, Kaitlyn," he added, making sure his voice was much gentler now. Sometimes dealing with her was like dealing with a horse who'd been abused. Understandable, given her life to now. And that in turn irritated him all over again, and he had the passing thought that it would be best if he never ran into her mother. Not that he ever would, of course, but—

Her sudden, audible intake of breath broke through his rambling thoughts. And he realized she was staring at his laptop, still showing her photograph. He seized on it, hoping this would get them past this awkwardness.

"It's a brilliant photograph," he said.

"I…thank you." She sounded disconcerted, and kept staring at the image.

"When did you take it?"

"About eleven months ago."

"Morning of March 6th?"

Her gaze shot to his face then. "Yes," she said, her voice barely above a whisper.

"I knew it," he said, and proceeded to tell her everything he'd thought about that image when he'd found it. Her eyes widened as he spoke, and he knew he'd struck gold with her, that he'd been right about what she'd tried to accomplish that day at this place that was sacred to so many Texans.

"How did you even find it?" she finally asked.

He shrugged. "Cody told me you had pictures up at the

site. Once I got there, finding them was easy. Your work stands out, Kaitlyn. The thought behind them, the care, the attention to detail, the framing, all of it makes them distinctive."

He didn't think he imagined that she was standing straighter now, and she suddenly seemed more steady. Solid. As if in this she had no doubts. This, at least, she was certain of. "Thank you," she said, and her voice echoed that certainty. "For understanding all that. And appreciating it."

He smiled at the change in her. And suddenly it felt right, her being here, in the place only family had been grudgingly allowed until now.

"Come on in," he said, meaning it this time.

She slid the backpack off her shoulder, then looked back at him. "Leave it, or bring it?"

She said it as if she understood completely what this place meant to him, how private it was. At the same time, he knew the magazine would expect photos of the place where it happened. And he realized he'd already decided. Because he trusted that, if she gave her word, this woman would keep it.

"Will you agree to not take anything of work in progress?"

He liked that she didn't immediately say yes, the answer that would get her what she wanted. Instead she looked thoughtful, as if she were thinking about—and more importantly understanding—why this was what he asked of her.

Then, slowly, she nodded. "I get that. And there's

enough of your existing work out there to take photos of. But…they'll want some of you working. The process."

He grimaced, but then, so she wouldn't think it was her, said with a roll of his eyes, "Genius burns, my mother says."

She smiled, that genuine, killer smile. "Exactly that. Would that be acceptable, if I make sure the actual work itself isn't clear?"

And again he was certain she would keep her word. Which was strange in itself—he didn't usually trust someone this quickly. Especially when it came to protecting this, the inner sanctum as Cody called it. To which he usually responded with a joke about Cody's lair in turn. Crazy how she always got him thinking about the workings of his family. Maybe because she'd never had anything like it herself. He hadn't asked, but he was fairly certain her mother had always been dysfunctional, maybe even always an alcoholic. And maybe that got him thinking about how lucky he was, even with losing Dad so young. He'd had a safety net, Mom and Keller had seen to that. Kaitlyn had had only herself, after her mother's addiction had destroyed her father.

He had to snap himself back to the present, with an inward shake. How did she do that, get him rambling in his head all the time? "All right," he said.

"Then we're agreed," she said, with another of those smiles.

And he had the oddest feeling that, with this simple act, letting her into his sanctuary, his entire life had shifted.

Chapter Eighteen

S HE HAD ENOUGH.

Kaitlyn told herself that repeatedly, and yet she kept framing and angling and hitting the shutter. Because once she started taking actual shots of Ry himself, she couldn't seem to stop.

Not that she hadn't taken a raft of the studio itself, because she had. It fascinated her, and that always sent her trigger finger on a rampage. She'd begun with the workbench, focusing on the tools themselves, and then the tool case he told her was a present from his mother, bought from The World in a Gift long before Sydney had come into their lives. She'd even taken shots of the debris scattered to one side, the remnants of his last project. She thought of the famous sculptor who said he simply cut away everything that wasn't his subject, and figured this must be about the same.

Then she'd shifted to the easel that sat to one side, then hesitated. It held a large pad of paper, and the top page held a pencil sketch, a familiar icon against an unexpected backdrop. The Liberty Bell, complete with crack, amid a bed of roses.

She'd lowered her camera. She should have known a man who could produce what he did in carved leather had to be able to draw as well, but somehow this had startled her. She looked over to see him watching her. "Looks like work in progress to me," she said.

He'd smiled then, and she knew she'd done the right thing. "It is. What do you think it means?"

Looking back at the image, she studied it a moment before asking, "That depends. What color are the roses?"

To her shock, he'd given her the most amazing smile she'd ever seen, and he'd sounded almost triumphant when he'd said, "I should have known you'd get it."

"So…they're the yellow roses of Texas, cradling the Liberty Bell?"

The smile had become a grin. "Exactly." Then he'd reached over and flipped the pad to a fresh, blank page. "Have at it," he'd said.

She felt as if she'd earned some precious prize. She was glad to have to focus on the process, making sure to capture the wadded-up sheets that littered the floor around it.

"I probably should have tidied up a bit," he'd said, sounding almost embarrassed.

"No," she'd said instantly. "This is much better."

Then she'd asked him to go to work.

And now, she was wondering for the first time in her career if her digital storage was going to be big enough. Because no matter what he did, be it working on that sheet of leather at the workbench, doing another sketch at the easel, or simply crossing from one to the other with that lithe, fluid way of moving that made her switch over to video a couple of times, he was the most beautiful thing she'd ever seen. At this rate, she was going to have to download and empty her camera storage to her laptop every night. And probably clear some things out of her cloud backup, because she couldn't afford to up the size just now but the thought of deleting anything she had of Ry was…unacceptable.

And then of course there was the way she kept having to tell herself that what was upstairs was none of her business.

I live in the loft over my studio.

Lived and…slept. That shouldn't rattle her so. But it did. Like everything about him did.

At first when he started to work, she could tell he was having trouble focusing. She was certain it was her presence. She only hoped it wasn't her specifically, but simply having anyone in here when he was trying to work. So she stayed as silent as she could, moving with care, trying to be unobtrusive.

But now he was there, deep into whatever image he was working on, although she didn't think it was the Liberty Bell one. Maybe something that didn't matter, since she was here with her camera. Then again, she couldn't imagine him doing anything that didn't matter in some way, and she wondered what marvel the foot-square or so piece would become.

She knew how intently he was into it when, after a couple of hours that had flown by, at least for her, his cell phone sounded an alert, and he didn't even seem to hear it. It vibrated on the wood surface of the workbench and he didn't even glance at it until a few seconds later. As if coming out of a trance his head came up, and she suddenly remembered his mother's teasing about an alarm to remind him Friday was his day to put on the morning coffee.

For a moment he just stared at the phone, as if he were having to work to remember what it was and why it had been rude enough to interrupt him. But then something seemed to occur to him, and he reached for it. He tapped the screen twice. And then a smile slowly dawned on his face, and almost without her volition Kaitlyn's finger pressed the shutter release. She didn't care if he heard it, she wanted that image of his profile, those strands of dark hair falling over his forehead, that strong jaw, the perfectly sized and shaped nose. And his mouth curved into a smile. That mouth that should require a permit.

That mouth that had been so close, just last night.

And then he looked at her, and her breath jammed up in her throat. Because that smile head-on was heart-stopping.

"Chance and Ariel are back," he said.

And once more she was overwhelmed by the pure love this family shared. It was like nothing she'd ever known. Even when her father had been alive, her mother's flaws had tainted things. Her eyes started to sting, and she turned away before he could see the tears gathering.

She didn't even hear him, he moved so silently. But then he was there, so close she could feel the heat of him, warming her.

"Kaitlyn? What's wrong?"

"Nothing," she managed. Barely.

He reached out and gently grasped her shoulders, turning her to face him. "Try again," he suggested.

She should have known. This was no ordinary, semi-oblivious male. He was an observer, and once tuned in he didn't miss much. The very thing that gave him his talent also made him aware when something caught his attention. He might need a little more prodding than the average guy to do that tuning in, but once he did...

"I'm sorry," she said, the familiar apology coming out more easily. "It's just...your family is wonderful."

"They are." He stared down at her. "Why on earth would you think saying that is something you have to apologize for?"

That, she couldn't answer. Because she didn't know.

And then, with those piercing, stormy eyes he apparently looked into her soul, because he said softly, "I'm the one who's sorry, that a good family is...such a revelation to you."

Her breath caught, and in her already tight throat it caused a harsh hiccup of sound that was even more embarrassing. And then she couldn't breathe at all, because he pulled her into his arms and held her. Simply held her, surrounding her with warmth and power and strength, and she felt all her embarrassment drain away. Or maybe it was that with him so close, with his arms around her, there was no room for anything except the amazing sense of comfort, of safety, of rightness.

She didn't want this to ever end. But when it did, when he spoke again, it turned out she didn't mind. Because what he said was, "Come on. I'll text him to be sure it's okay, then let's head out to Chance's place, so you can meet him, and Ariel. And Tri, the miracle dog."

He wanted her to meet the brother she hadn't yet met, and the woman who had apparently broken through to him. And no matter how much she tried to tell herself it was just a casual thing, so Chance would know she was around—he did work with dogs trained in war, after all—she couldn't seem to stop herself from thinking, or at least foolishly hoping, it was more.

"Drive or ride?" he asked then. "Or are you too sore to ride?"

That prosaic question snapped her out of her silly thoughts. "I do have some spots reminding me riding is new, but it's worth it." She meant it. She had loved the new experience, and couldn't turn down the chance to ride the sweet-natured Latte again.

He grinned at her. "Ride it is, then."

As she was putting her gear back into the pack, she paused. "Should I take my camera?"

"Do you ever not?" Her gaze shot to his face, but he clearly wasn't complaining, not with that grin still there.

"Rarely," she admitted. "Would he mind some photos of the dogs and what he does? Maybe I can talk them into using a shot in the piece."

"Mind, yes." She felt her cheeks flush, but Ry just went on. "Allow it, also yes. Because he knows any bit of attention helps the cause."

"Yes. And it's an interesting aspect of things here, where you work." There, that nicely slotted things.

She narrowed her gear down to what would fit in the saddlebags he'd gotten for her last time. Then she followed him to the barn, reminding herself every step of the way that she was here on a job, and had no business thinking of him...in the way she was thinking of him as she watched him move in those nicely snug jeans. She should just be glad he was being so...cooperative. Generous. Helpful. Kind. Thoughtful.

Wild. Gorgeous. Sexy.

Yeah, those too. It was crazy, she never, ever reacted like this. Especially to a man like this.

She hated what he did to her.

She loved what he did to her.

She had to get a grip on herself, on her mind, her imagination. Had to stop these thoughts. What she needed was a stop sign in her head. Or maybe one that said "Off-limits." In neon lights. Flashing neon lights.

But she wasn't sure even that would work. Not against Rylan Rafferty.

Chapter Nineteen

"WE'LL TAKE THE scenic route," Ry said as they mounted up—Kaitlyn a little gingerly with new-rider tenderness, but not so much that he was worried—and headed out. "Chance will want to show the newcomers around, and let them settle a little before visitors." He glanced at her. "They'll be in their runs except for Tri, so don't worry."

"I wasn't," she said quickly as they headed out past the big corral. "Aware, but not worried."

He nodded. "Those dogs are used to just about anything. Chance says it's just that their threat perception is out of whack. And Ariel says that to a traumatized warrior, every-thing is a threat."

"They sound like...quite a pair." She smiled warmly as she said it, and he was a little amazed at her obviously genuine warmth for people she hadn't even met.

"They're perfect together," he said, meaning it down to his soul. "And I will never stop being thankful she came to get Tri and met Chance."

"That's how they met? She came to adopt the dog?"

He nodded. Hesitated, but decided since it wasn't a secret, family or otherwise, he could tell her the rest. But he waited until they'd made the turn onto the trail that led down toward the stream, a branch of Hickory Creek that was sometimes merely a yard-wide flow, sometimes after a storm an uncrossable torrent.

"Tri lost his leg on his last deployment, a bit over two years ago, trying to save his handler's life."

"Trying? So…"

"His handler, who was a friend of Chance's, was killed." He gave her a sideways glance. "His handler was also Ariel's husband."

"Whoa. That had to be a strange path to tread," Kaitlyn said, clearly understanding all the ramifications of that.

"It was. But they're coming out the other side now, both of them."

He'd never expected to be so glad his brother had found his soul mate. At the same time, it made him a little nervous, because their mother seemed to have shifted her focus to him. As if she were going in chronological order and he was next. He and Cody had even joked about it.

You're next, bro.

Never gonna happen.

I know. That's why I'm safe.

Funny, now he found himself wondering if Cody hadn't just been joking, and why he had been so damned sure. Was it that impossible to think he might find someone who could put up with his crazy life, living in a barn, the erratic work hours, and the slipping into a different world when he was deep into a project?

He grimaced. *I think you just answered your own question, Rafferty.*

He got kind of stuck on that thought as they rode on. Kaitlyn had her camera out and was shooting whenever something caught her eye. And she was focused on that, leaving him with his thoughts. Which was not necessarily the best place for him just now.

He was actually glad when he heard her cell phone ring, because it derailed him from wondering why he was thinking about this love thing so much, when he'd thought it well and truly put away for some nebulous time in the future. It was just watching his two older brothers fall—that was it. As for Kaitlyn, it was just that she was the first woman he'd spent a lot of time with lately.

And what about the admittedly gorgeous Ms. Jacobs? He silently answered his own question again. *She's way too aware of her own appeal. Unlike Kaitlyn, who seems to think she's completely unappealing.*

He reined Flyer in, and Kaitlyn looked at him as she did the same with Latte, pushing her camera to one side.

"We go much further, you'll lose the cell signal," he explained, and she nodded in understanding.

She pulled her phone out of her jacket pocket and tapped the screen. He saw her expression change when she looked at the display. She smiled, but it was different than the smile that sent those weird sensations through him. No less warm, but touched with…worry?

"Nick?" she said when she answered, telling him it was her mentor calling. An instant later the worry in her expression vanished.

And that explained it, Ry thought. She'd been worried something was wrong, but apparently he'd called himself, so even if there was a problem, it wasn't so serious he couldn't manage a phone call.

But after listening for a couple of minutes, the worry returned. "Tomorrow morning? All right," she said. "I'll be there." A pause. "No, it's fine, I'll be there." She tried to smile, as if he could see her even though it wasn't a video call. "I want to be there, so hush."

When she slipped the phone back into her pocket the attempted smile vanished.

"Is he all right?" Ry asked, a little surprised at the urgency he felt about a man he didn't even know.

She gave him a startled look, and he knew it must have been in his voice. "He says he will be. But then he would," she added with a wry quirk of her mouth.

"What is it?"

"He's been having some heart rhythm trouble, and has to have a pacemaker put in. Tomorrow morning at nine."

"Hey, that's not so bad," he said, trying to sound reassuring. "And it helps. Dutch—the guy I learned leatherworking from—had one, and he said he felt much better afterward. He used it to make jokes any time he didn't want to do something. Said he didn't feel like it, his battery must be dead. Even though they last ten years or more."

She stared at him for a moment, and he thought he'd stepped in it, that he'd made too light of it. The guy meant a lot to her, maybe she wasn't ready—

She laughed. And he breathed again. Crazy, how making her laugh seemed so…special.

Then she became serious. "I'm sorry you lost him."

That was like her. To jump from her own troubles to someone else's. "Me too," he said simply. "But that tough ol' bird made it to ninety-six. So your Nick has a lot of years to go yet."

"I hope so," she said. Her brow furrowed again. "He insisted them doing it on a Saturday is routine."

"I don't think medicine is a Monday to Friday, nine to five kind of thing."

She smiled at that, and he felt an echo of what he'd felt when she'd laughed. He found himself noticing the freckles across her nose again, tiny and scattered. They reminded him a bit of the spots across Mom's Aussie Quinta's nose. He wondered how Kaitlyn would feel about that comparison to a dog. He suspected she wouldn't mind it at all.

Unlike Ms. Jacobs, who had looked at the sweet, loving dog with distaste. But then, Quinta hadn't cared much for her, either. Kaitlyn, she'd liked. Right off, she'd liked her.

And the dog was an excellent judge of people, so he knew that was part of the reason Mom had been so quick to welcome Kaitlyn and sidestep the blonde.

She pulled her phone back out, looked at it, then put it away again.

"Where is he?"

"Up in Temple."

"Good hospital there," he said.

She nodded. "That's where it's being done." Her brow furrowed. "Is there someplace in town where I can rent a car?"

He thought about her situation, knew that renting a car was probably an expense she couldn't truly afford. But for her friend and mentor, she would add another load to what she was already carrying.

"I'll take you."

She looked beyond startled. He was a little surprised himself. He'd only said it on impulse. "Temple's almost three hours from here."

He shrugged, liking the idea now, if only because she looked so stunned that someone would offer. "Only two and a half if you avoid Austin. Always my choice," he added with a slightly crooked smile. "We'll have to leave by six to get you there in time to see him beforehand, which I assume you want to do."

"Of course I do, but no, you don't need to do that. I can—"

"I know you'd find a way to get there, but why not save that energy and put it into looking after Nick?"

He was kind of proud of that one. From what he knew of her—more than he usually would but not nearly as much as he wanted—he guessed that would be the key. And it was.

"That's incredibly generous of you. Thank you."

He belatedly realized that he could have just offered her one of the ranch vehicles. They could spare one for the weekend. Or his own, for that matter. But even as he thought it, he resisted the idea. He wanted to do this. For her. With her. And that had him rattled enough that he stayed silent as they rode on. After a while she seemed to have processed the situation with her mentor and tuned back in to her surroundings. At least, he assumed so because out came the camera again.

As they went, he made sure to take a gradual path that would cause her the least jostle—alone, he would have sent Flyer rocketing straight down, leaping whatever obstacles got in the way—down to where the stream flowed below. And once more she took out her phone, then put it back.

They paused before crossing the stream. "It's about average now," Ry said. "But after a big storm here or to the north we have to watch it. Easy for a calf, or even a full-grown cow, to get caught by a flash flood."

"That would be awful."

Further on they stopped in a couple of places when she asked, so she could get a shot she wanted. Once even climb-

ing—agilely, as if she did it often, which he didn't doubt—
atop a fairly tall outcropping of limestone to frame a shot
back down toward the stream just the way she wanted.

And she'd humbled him a little in the process, so focused
on her goal that she seemed to barely notice, when he offered
her a leg up to the stone ledge, that for a moment they were
pressed together almost intimately.

*So that's it, Rafferty, you just don't like that there's a wom-
an who doesn't fall all over herself trying to flirt with you?*

He laughed at himself. Remembered Keller relaying his
buddy the police chief's sage advice: it's best to laugh at
yourself before anyone else does.

He figured that applied to getting over yourself, too.

Chapter Twenty

KAITLYN MANAGED TO at least corral—funny how she'd started thinking in ranching analogies—her concern about Nick, since there was nothing she could do to help right now anyway. Even if she was there with him, he'd be telling her to quit hovering and stop fussing over him.

She was having a bit more trouble reining in her thoughts about a two-and-a-half-hour drive alone with Ry.

She had meant what she'd said about his generosity. There was no reason for him to offer not only a ride but himself as driver. But he had, and if she were honest, it was probably for the best, since she would be thinking about Nick. Maybe not too distracted to drive safely, but that was a maybe she now didn't have to worry about.

"The dogs should be settled by now," Ry said after a glance at his phone's screen for the time. She supposed wearing a watch would be pointless for him, since he spent so much time being unaware of time. "We can head over."

"Lead on," she said, remembering when they'd been out that first day—she was startled when she realized it had only been yesterday—and he'd pointed out the cabin and outbuildings in the distance. She knew there was no way she'd find them on her own, and in fact he started off at a right angle to the direction she would have guessed.

Face it, you're hopeless without landmarks.

When they topped the last rise before the small house, Kaitlyn saw the quartet standing by the fence of a small corral next to the first outbuilding. They looked like a family to her: the man, the woman, the dog, and the horse. The man was tall, although she guessed a bit shorter than Ry, and lean and wiry where Ry was muscular. He wore jeans and a lightweight jacket over a gray shirt, and a baseball-style cap out of camouflage material. The woman was tall, slender, with long hair a gorgeous shade of red. She was in jeans as well, and they looked worn by usage rather than style.

The dog at their feet, alertly watching them approach, had to be Tri, unless Ry's brother had more than one amputee in residence. But she guessed it was, from the way the dog had taken that guarding sort of position, directly in front of the woman. Guarding, but not threatening. He looked like the dog from the monument she'd seen, lean and racy as he got to his three feet and swiveled so he could see them straight on.

When the dog barked Ry reined in, and she stopped beside him. Chance looked around and spotted them, spoke to the dog, then waved them down. When the man moved, Kaitlyn got a better look at the horse standing inside the corral, apparently quite liking the way Ariel was stroking his neck.

"Shouldn't that be Cody's horse?" she mused aloud as they started down the hill, studying the bright golden color, with a mane and tail nearly as blonde as Jillian's hair, but obviously naturally so. Even as she thought it, she pictured what a striking image the opposites would be: black-haired Ry on the golden palomino, and Cody on the black Flyer. She thought she'd like the contrast more, but then, she was...different. Odd, as Jillian had told her the first time they'd worked together.

Or weird, like every guy you've ever gone out with has said.

But Ry laughed. "Pretty enough, isn't he?"

"Which one, Cody or the horse?" she asked, the corners of her mouth twitching.

He laughed again. She could get used to this, making him laugh. "Either way works. Chance jokes he rides Dorado so Cody doesn't have to."

"It would be nearly blinding." She couldn't seem to help smiling, because he was.

"Also not wise. Cody tends to wander sometimes, and for all his flash, Dorado is not just a pretty face. He's a fiery beast, Mom says."

"I'll bet your brother keeps him in line."

"He does. Guess he got used to giving orders."

She watched as the man in the camo hat leaned over to kiss the redhead. She glanced at Ry, and saw the smile on his face. A loving, pleased smile.

"Just seeing them makes you happy, doesn't it?" she

asked as they reached the flat and started toward the house.

"It does," he said. "He was carrying around a ton of guilt, for something he couldn't have helped. And only Ariel could help him put it down."

"Only Ariel?"

"His guilt was over the way her husband died. Chance had himself convinced he could have stopped it."

Kaitlyn looked back at the quartet by the fence. She thought about what she already knew, that Ariel's late husband had been Tri's handler. With that added on top of it… "Then what I'm looking at here is practically a miracle."

"Mom calls it a Christmas miracle, since that's when it happened," Ry said, and when she looked over at him again at those words, he was watching her so intently it was unsettling.

In the end she found it one of the most pleasant afternoons she'd had in a while. Ry introduced her to Chance and Ariel in an odd sort of way, by name first and with why she was here, officially, almost sounding like an afterthought. As if for a moment, Ry himself had forgotten. That gave her a very strange feeling she didn't have time to dwell on right now.

She was formally introduced to Tri by, interestingly, Ariel. The dog made a careful inspection, apparently decided she was no threat, and seemed to relax, sitting at Ariel's feet again.

"You passed," Chance said, making her smile.

"Amazing how far he's come," Ry said. "You wouldn't had dared let him out off-leash before Ariel came along."

"She straightened us both out," Chance said, with a look at the redhead that made Kaitlyn's eyes sting, knowing what she knew about what these two had gone through to get to here. She thought of Keller and Sydney, what they were like together. And clearly these two were just as meant to be, and perhaps even more of a wonder, since he was the one the entire Rafferty family had been the most worried about. And looking at the couple now, the idea strayed through her mind that if there was hope for him, there was hope for anyone.

"Come on in," Ariel said, gesturing toward the door. "We're still unpacking, but there's coffee on. As long as you like plain and simple, basic black with cream and sugar if you want."

Since that was all she'd been able to afford for a very long time, Kaitlyn simply smiled and said, "My brew of choice."

The cabin seemed more spacious inside than she'd expected, probably because the compact kitchen and living room were all one large space. But she barely noticed that before her gaze fastened on the painting on the far wall. She didn't have to ask; it was clear it was by the same hand as the one in the main house. It was, she'd swear, of the stream they'd just crossed, except at a higher flow. At sunrise, she thought, judging by the faint wisps of mist the artist had managed to portray with a most delicate touch. And the wide-open Texas sky over the rolling land of the Hill Country was the crown of it all, captured forever by a seeing, steady hand.

She gave a slow, wondering shake of her head. "He was truly brilliant," she said softly.

The moment the words were out, she realized Chance had gone very still. The ex-soldier looked at his brother.

"I didn't have to tell her," Ry said quietly. "She guessed."

"Well, well," Chance said, an odd sort of expression coming over his face as his gaze became more pointed. Not surprise, but…acknowledgment? Understanding? Or simply a secret shared between brothers that others weren't privy to? She wouldn't know about that, having never had any siblings, let alone brothers. But then Ariel exchanged a glance with both men, and it was a knowing one that threw her theory right out the window.

No, she wasn't sure what it was all about. But she was certain that the smile on Ariel's face was pleased. And that made her feel oddly pleased herself.

As they sat at the small kitchen counter with mugs of coffee, Kaitlyn listened to the story about their trip to pick up two new residents.

"They seem pretty bonded, so this will be interesting," Chance said. "And this guy," he added, nodding at the dog who had plopped happily in a bed against the far wall, "has become quite the ambassador. He really eased the other dogs into cooperating."

"Brothers in fur, huh?" Ry quipped.

Chance smiled. "They did seem to recognize him in that way."

"Where are the new kids?" Ry asked.

"In kennels, for the moment," Chance answered. "Once they settle from the trip, probably after we feed them, they'll be out in the runs."

"You'll have to come back and meet them," Ariel said. And oddly, she was looking at Kaitlyn, not Ry. But maybe she just assumed Ry would be back.

"I'd love to," she said, meaning it.

"You should have her take some photos," Ry said. "She's really good. The way she frames stuff, her lighting choices… You can pick her work out amid a bunch of others, because it draws your eye."

Kaitlyn's breath caught, she hoped not audibly. He'd told her this, but somehow him saying it to someone else felt different. Because it obviously wasn't something he was just saying to put her at ease?

Or was it just that he was saying it? And it meant more coming from him?

Because he was an artist himself, she told herself firmly. That was why it meant more. Because it wasn't just somebody who had no artistic eye, it was someone with a keenly developed one. That's all it was. It couldn't be more.

She couldn't allow it to be more.

Chapter Twenty-One

H E NEEDED TO distract her. She was clearly worried. She'd been looking at her phone as if she were expecting a horrible call at any moment, ever since he'd picked her up at the inn at six. It was a chilly, stormy morning, but she still wore only the same denim jacket. He wondered if she even had anything else, anything warmer. Or maybe she was just so distracted with worry she hadn't thought about it.

"It's really become a basic procedure," he said. "They won't even put him completely out, just a local."

He glanced at her as he spoke. He saw the worry in her eyes, but she managed a slight smile anyway. "I know. I looked it up at the inn last night." Her smile quirked upward at one corner in that wry way she had. "Free Wi-Fi," she said.

And suddenly the start-stop with her phone yesterday made sense. She'd wanted to do that research right then, but he guessed she probably had a pretty tight data cap.

He pondered his next words for a moment as he drove, wondering how to say it. He finally went for casual. "You've got that at the ranch, too. Cody's got it rigged so you have access anywhere within sight of the main house."

She blinked. "That's a big area."

"And he's a big nerd," he said with a grin. "He can set you up with a password for while you're here."

"He'd do that? What if I was some kind of hacker or something?"

He waited until they'd negotiated a curve in the road, then glanced at her with a raised a brow. "Are you?"

"No, but what if I was?"

"I'd wish you luck," he said with a smile. "It takes my little brother about fifteen minutes just to describe the security he's got on that system. Another ten about routers and repeaters and mesh and I don't know what all."

"He sounds like a handy guy to have around."

"He is. I'll have to play you the music he did for me."

Her brows rose. "He's a musician, too?"

"Not exactly. But he put together a version of Verdi's 'Requiem,' with something he calls a virtual orchestra, that I blast out when I'm stuck. It really gets things moving." And somehow he knew she'd appreciate it, despite the modern, electronic edge, although he sometimes wondered what Verdi would think of this reimagining.

"And the drones?"

His smile faded. "He doesn't really explain those. Because we all know what his goal is there."

She just waited. He glanced at her again, saw she was

looking at him. But she just waited. She wouldn't push. Funny, when it came to her work, she was confident, even bold, but here, now, she wouldn't even ask for an explanation of his rather cryptic statement. She wanted one—he could see that in her eyes—but she wouldn't push.

He turned his gaze back to the road, and it was a good half mile before he finally said, "Our father was KIA because a spy drone inadvertently gave away their position. The motor noise."

It only took her a moment. "So he's working on a silent one?"

"Yes."

"Is that even possible?"

"For military use, at distances beyond battery power? I don't know. I do know if it is, Cody will figure it out."

"And won't that be a wonderful tribute," she said softly. "But then, all of you are. To what an amazing man he was."

"He was," Ry said, and found to his surprise he could barely get the words out. Before she had arrived, it had been a while since his throat tightened up like this about his father, but when she said things like that, all the old emotions had come roiling back. Maybe because he knew she meant it in all the ways they did, for all the same reasons. What she'd said to Mom proved that.

His service, this place, that genius...what a combination. How fascinating he must have been.

Yes, she got it.

They were on the outskirts of Austin—he was intentionally avoiding Interstate 35 until they were north of the city because this was as close as he wanted to get even early on a Saturday morning—when, as she started tapping a finger nervously on the armrest, he said, "He'll be all right. It'll help him."

"He will. I just…" Her voice trailed off.

"I know what he means to you."

"I wouldn't be here if it wasn't for him," she said in a rush. "I was on a really bad path."

He hesitated, then said it. "I've walked that path."

He felt her quick glance, saw it out of the corner of his eye. "I know," she said.

He frowned. Then it hit him. "Keller," he said with a grimace.

"Afraid so," she admitted.

He lapsed into silence, wondering what had brought that discussion on. Had that been why Keller and Mom had been insistent that he pick her up yesterday? Had they decided she needed to be warned about him? That he was too weird for someone like her?

When that thought hit, he stared straight ahead, only the necessary focus on his driving. Because that thought was based on an assumption they had no way of knowing. He'd never indicated she…got to him. So there was no way they'd know that Kaitlyn Miller had him thinking things he hadn't thought in a long time. No, that wasn't true either. She had him thinking things he'd never thought. Things like together and forever, linked.

But they couldn't know that. He'd never told them.

Maybe you didn't have to.

He groaned inwardly. Mom. How often had they all joked about her capacity for mind-reading? How she seemed to know things they'd never, ever told her. As if when she'd carried them some sort of mental connection had been formed, and it hadn't ended when they'd been born. But no, she'd been able to do it with Dad, too.

Don't ever try and put one over on your mother, Rylan. I've tried. She'll know. She always knows.

Kaitlyn had lapsed into total silence, and he wondered if she regretted telling him that. And had to bite his lip to keep himself from asking how and why the subject had come up at all with Keller.

"Ever done a shoot in Austin?" he asked instead.

"Some. For a couple of music shoots. And the Congress Street bridge."

He grinned at that. "The bats. I saw your shot of them. Great stuff."

"They're amazing, the way they take off all at once like that. I'm glad people have left them alone."

"They're a tourist attraction." He wanted to keep her talking, and he was curious, so he asked, "What's been your favorite ever shoot?"

She hesitated a moment, and he had the feeling she was

staring at him, but was too busy watching the little silver car that had just cut in front of them to make sure.

"You'll think it's silly," she warned.

I doubt it. "What was it?"

"I did a shoot for one of the animal rescues in Temple last fall. Animals up for adoption. It was hard, because I wanted to take them all myself, but my favorite because they all got adopted by Christmas."

"I'm not surprised."

"I was. And so were they."

"They wouldn't be, if they'd seen those shots you did for the men-are-evil article."

She sighed audibly.

"Look," he said hastily, sorry he'd brought it up, "I get that you had no choice, once you were locked in. So you fought back the only way you could, and made the whole thing a farce."

She hesitated again, then said, "A couple of those photographs were published elsewhere, later, after I got the rights back. They went up on a blog countering the gist of the first article. It ended up with more reach than the original."

Clear of the rude little vehicle now, he glanced at her, one corner of his mouth lifting in a half-grin. "Nicely done."

"Least I could do."

Glad she was at least not mired in worry at the moment, he kept going. "What about the most exciting shoot?"

"Skydiving," she said without hesitation. He almost did

some rude driving himself as he gaped at her.

"You went skydiving?"

"Had to. That's what the people paying me were promoting, a skydiving school east of San Antonio."

"How was it?"

"Terrifying. Exhilarating. And a few other 'ings' I won't mention."

"Wow." He meant it. Jumping out of a perfectly good airplane had never been on his list of things to do in life. "How'd you come down—no pun intended—after that?"

"I went to Gonzales. It's only about fifteen miles south of there. A little time thinking of what they faced down and I was fine."

He glanced at her again. Let out a compressed breath and gave a wry shake of his head. "No wonder you and Mom hit it off."

"Did we?" It sounded as if it had escaped from her before she thought, because she hastily added, "I mean, I really liked her, and she's been so nice to me, and—"

"You did," he said, hating the life she'd led that made her so uncertain. How did somebody who felt that way about herself manage to also be so confident about her work, brave enough to go skydiving for a job, and be so determined to counter unfairness where she saw it in whatever way she could? She was a walking dichotomy, was Kaitlyn Miller. "In fact, you had it made from the moment Quinta decided she liked you."

"She's such a sweet dog," Kaitlyn exclaimed.

"And a very good judge of people. I think Mom would take her assessment over anyone's."

"Even yours?"

He grimaced. "Especially mine. I don't have the best track record with people."

"I know the feeling," she said, her tone heartfelt. "I've hit some big dips in that track."

He glanced at her. "Another thing we have in common, huh?" That seemed to unsettle her, because she looked away quickly. "Who was your worst?"

"A…professor Jillian went to interview. I completely misjudged him." Her voice had gone flat, and he wondered if her misjudgment had had personal consequences. "What was yours?" she asked, hurriedly, as if she was afraid he was going to ask her about it. "The Lake LBJ lady?"

So she remembered that. "Her name's Chelsea. The lake was where she wanted to be. Didn't realize I was as much décor as the chrome and glass of her condo."

"Whoa." She gave him a sideways look. "I mean, you're pretty and all, but décor you're not. Or a chrome and glass guy."

He rolled his eyes. *Pretty? Really?* "Half the time I was afraid I'd break something. The other half I felt like a house pet."

She let out an unladylike snort that made him grin. This was the Kaitlyn he'd wanted to see again.

"You'd make a pet like a wildcat would," she said dryly.

He gave her a sideways glance. "I think I'll take that as a compliment."

"How it was meant," she said.

By the time they joined up with Interstate 35 north of Austin, leaving them less than fifty miles to go, the atmosphere in the truck was…he couldn't think of the right word for it. Friendly? Pleasant? Relaxed? Convivial? They all applied, but none were exactly right.

Warm, maybe. He could go that far. Because there was a sort of warmth between them. The problem was the next word his mind wanted to fasten on was *affectionate*. And that was not a direction he wanted to go.

Did he?

He made himself look to the west, where far out of sight lay the lake he'd once lived next to. If that adventure hadn't proven his instincts about people—especially women— sucked, he didn't know what would.

Yet this woman had passed muster with his mother, brothers, Lucas, Quinta, and even the wary Tri. That had to prove…something, didn't it?

Just drive, Rafferty. That's your job here. Just drive.

When they got off the interstate and down onto West Central in Temple, he was glad he had to pay attention to the unfamiliar streets, so he could quash the useless thoughts whirling in his head.

Chapter Twenty-Two

"IT'S JUST NOT the same," the man sitting in the wheelchair insisted. "Film has a certain quality, a depth, a warmth."

"Yes, it does. But they each have their place, don't they?" Kaitlyn said.

She'd been delighted to see Nick looking much as he always did. Dr. Bailey, the electrophysiologist doing the procedure, or EP as he told them to call him, was just leaving the room as they arrived. He paused long enough to reassure her that all would be fine, that in reality it was a fairly basic procedure that was almost as routine as anything involving the heart could be.

"Dr. Muir informed me that Nick is her favorite patient, so I wouldn't dare mess up," he said with a wide smile.

It had made Kaitlyn smile as well, because she suspected the genial Dr. Muir said that about all her patients. Then again, she did seem to have a particular soft spot for Nick.

There was paperwork to do, and that took a while. Ry had assumed he'd be waiting outside the room, but once Nick had found out he'd given her a ride all the way here from Last Stand he'd insisted on meeting him. And that had been…interesting. Nick knew about the job, of course, and when she'd introduced Ry as the subject of the assignment, he'd turned an interested eye on him.

"Kaitlyn showed me pictures of your work. Very impressive."

"Thank you," Ry had said.

"Just don't call it art," Kaitlyn couldn't resist putting in. Ry shot her a sideways glance.

"Oh, I wouldn't," Nick said.

Ry had looked back at Nick. Judging by his smile, he was pleasantly surprised at that. "Thank you. It's a craft."

She could have warned him he was about to be dismantled, but she didn't. She just watched as Nick reduced Ry's insistence to rubble.

"There's a good eye, skill, and a deft hand there. And the stellar choice of elements to include. Plus working in essentially three dimensions yet also flat, a sort of bas-relief in leather. Not to mention the fact that you create items of actual use. So all that puts it far beyond mere art."

Dr. Muir arrived just in time to head off whatever reply Ry might have made. Kaitlyn had gotten to know her after Nick had given her medical power of attorney—as Kaitlyn had given him in turn—when he'd started having problems and Kaitlyn knew it was typical of the woman that she would show up even though she had nothing directly to do with the procedure about to be done. Nick was her patient and she took that very seriously.

It wasn't until after they'd wheeled Nick off for the prep and Ry had wandered out saying something about coffee, that she hit the post-op treatment information page of all the papers they'd handed her. Reading it, she far too belatedly realized that she hadn't gone far enough looking this up last night. Nick would have to stay in the hospital overnight while they monitored both the incision site and the settings of the new device. He'd had been making light of it all, probably so she wouldn't worry, and he hadn't bothered to mention that.

Her mind started to scramble. She would have to find a place to stay, somewhere close by, then a way to get Nick back home, then a way back to Last Stand by Monday, when Jillian was due to come back. She really hadn't thought this through—her main goal had been to get here to him and deal with the details when she arrived. But now—

"Here." She looked up to see Ry holding out a cup of coffee to her. "One sugar, one cream," he said, as if she'd asked.

"I…thank you." She took the cup, feeling a strange tightness in her throat at the simple fact that he'd noticed and remembered how she liked her coffee.

"Problem?"

"I…" She hesitated, feeling foolish. But there was no way around admitting it. "Nick made this whole thing sound so minor I didn't even think about it, so I didn't realize until now Nick will have to stay overnight."

Ry only shrugged. "Nurse outside mentioned that."

"You might as well head home. Thank you so much for—"

"You already thanked me a dozen times," Ry said, cutting her off but not rudely. "So we need to know what time he'll be released tomorrow."

"It says here it will be after noon."

"But you'll want to be back here earlier, I'm guessing?"

"I...yes." She grimaced. "If Nick still had his place I could stay there, but—"

"Don't worry about it. There's a place less than two miles away that had a couple of rooms available."

She stared at him almost blankly. "What?"

"I don't know how nice it is, but it's close." She was still staring, stuck on a *couple* of rooms. "We don't have to be there until five. They'll hold them until then."

We? "How do you know—"

"One of the nurses told me about the place, and I called while I was in line for the coffee. Oh, and he also said there's a store up the road about three miles on the right that should have anything we need for tonight."

She knew she was gaping at him now. "Rylan," she began; for some reason this seemed to require his full name. "You don't have to—"

She stopped as he put his hands on her shoulders and crouched down to look her in the eye. "Stop. This is your family we're dealing with. Your real family," he amended, with emphasis on the adjective.

She couldn't stop the moisture that welled up in her eyes. "He has no one else." *Neither do I. Or I didn't, until now.*

"And in essence he saved your life," Rylan said softly. "So here we are, and we'll handle it."

She didn't know what to say. Even when the tears overflowed and trickled down her cheeks, she couldn't look away from those deep gray eyes. And when he reached up to brush the droplets gently away with the backs of his fingers, the strangest combination of warmth and need billowed through her.

And she realized with a jolt that this was what it felt like when a Rafferty had your back.

"IT SAYS THAT it's okay to talk on your cell phone, but you have to use the ear on the other side," Kaitlyn was saying as Ry moved his pencil over the page open in his small sketchbook. He carried it with him regularly, never knowing when he might see the answer to a design problem somewhere. He wasn't sure what had started him on it here, just that watching Kaitlyn, so thankful that Nick had come through the procedure perfectly, had made him reach for it.

That, and that Nick had a fascinating face. A mix of the cultures that were his interesting heritage, which according to Kaitlyn was Cuban and French. His fingers had started itching the moment he'd seen the man.

"And," she went on, "they'll give you an ID card, in case you set off a metal detector somewhere."

"I wasn't planning on flying anywhere any time soon," Nick said, his tone dry as Kaitlyn sat beside the bed instructing him, while holding his hand. But his expression was unmistakable; she was indeed the family he didn't have, just as he was for her.

"Well, maybe you'll feel like it now. You shouldn't have any more dizziness or palpitations, and you can exercise again. Maybe even go for hikes again."

"With my favorite fellow hiker?"

Ry looked up and knew who the man meant by the way he was looking at Kaitlyn. With love, just like Mom looked at all of them. And now Lucas, Sydney and Ariel, too. This was why Kaitlyn was doing without, so that Nick didn't have to. And doing it with class, making sure he didn't know so he wouldn't feel the guilt Ry was certain, watching the older man now, he would feel.

"If you want," Kaitlyn said.

"No one better," Nick said, and his gruff tone didn't hide his emotions at all.

Ry was smiling as he went back to his sketchpad. He was so wrapped up in what he was doing he was caught a little off guard when Kaitlyn excused herself to go to the ladies' room, leaving him alone with Nick. Nick, who didn't waste any time.

"I owe you thanks for driving her all this way."

He shrugged, a little awkwardly. "No problem."

"Especially since you're the celebrity she's there to photograph."

He couldn't help it—a burst of laughter broke from him. "Celebrity? Hell, man, I'm just a rancher with a knack that people seem to like."

That made Nick smile, and Ry thought there might have been approval in the expression. "She said you were modest."

Ry blinked. "She did?" She'd talked to this man who was her surrogate father…about him?

"She also said you're staying until tomorrow."

"Until you get home safe," Ry said. "She won't be easy until then."

"And you arranged it all?"

He shrugged. "She was…distracted. Worried about you." He met the man's gaze, held it. "You mean the world to her, you know."

Nick studied him, his dark eyes alert and intent. Whatever relaxant they'd given him had clearly worn off. "Seems you've gotten to know her pretty well in a short time."

Ry wasn't at all sure what to say, and somehow another shrug to those words seemed wrong. Almost insulting, somehow. At the least a dodge. Which, if he was honest, is what it would be.

"She's…special."

"Yes, she is. And she's had a rough go of life."

"I know."

"You know what happened? Her father?"

"The fire? Yes." He shifted, a little uncomfortable at the intensity of the man's voice. Whatever they'd given him had most definitely worn off.

"And her mother?"

"If you want to call her that," Ry said sourly.

"And I don't much like that woman she's working with, either."

"We're in agreement on that," Ry said with a grimace. "From what she said, I think Ms. Jacobs and Kaitlyn's mother are cut from the same, self-centered cloth."

Nick nodded. "No scruples at all."

"I don't think she's a drunk though. She's too sharp."

Nick tilted his head slightly as he looked at him. "Kaitlyn told you all this?"

Puzzled, Ry said, "Yes. Why?"

"She never talks about it. Never. Rarely even to me, and I'm as close to a father as she's got, now."

"I know that, I—" Ry stopped abruptly.

A father. Kaitlyn's father. Essentially that was who had been grilling him for the last two minutes. Suddenly he felt as if he were back in high school, asking Andrea Whitfield's father if he could please take her to prom. Except this had been more of a third degree than that had been, because Mr. Whitfield had known his family. Nick didn't know him, or his family. He only knew he loved Kaitlyn like a daughter.

And he was the man who had handed Kaitlyn her salvation and her calling when he'd handed her a camera.

He leaned back in the chair beside the bed, a bare couple of feet away from the one Kaitlyn had been sitting in. He couldn't really put a name to the feeling that had come over him, only knew that a large part of it was thanks that she'd had this man in her life. And that made him smile.

"Next?" he said.

Nick frowned. "Next what?"

"Next question in the third degree," Ry said, keeping his smile in place. It wasn't difficult, because he was truly glad Kaitlyn had had this caring man in her life.

And why it mattered to him so much was something he'd have to think about later.

Chapter Twenty-Three

KAITLYN SAT ON the edge of the bed in the room Ry had gotten for her. She felt a little numb, as if her nerves had been on overload until Nick got through this, and now, exhausted, they were shutting down.

She looked around. It was a room that could be anyplace at all...except for the Lone Star on one wall, and the old photographs on the opposite wall of various railroad yards, the industry that had built Temple when in the 1880s several railroads made the town a division point. It had been mostly shacks, tents, and saloons then. She doubted any of them, if they even still stood, had the history of the Last Stand Saloon.

They say back in the beginning Temple was nicknamed Tanglefoot, because it was hard to walk down muddy streets if you were drunk.

Ry had said it in the lobby, gesturing toward an even larger photo of the old west version of the town in the lobby. She'd given him a doubtful look, thinking he was making it up just to distract her, but the clerk at the desk had backed him up. Then again, he was the one who'd told Ry the story in the first place, they both admitted with a laugh.

Well, part of it fits, because tangled is definitely how I feel right now.

She sighed, wishing she could avoid the rest of the evening and have it just be morning and time to go get Nick out of the hospital. But at the same time, she was—rather breathlessly—looking forward to the time in between. And spending it with Ry.

Of course, that might not be his plan. After all he'd done, maybe he'd just want some peace and time away from her.

She heard a sound, realized it was her stomach growling. Odd, she hadn't felt hungry. Maybe those nerves had shut down, too. But on the heels of that sound came a knock on her door. A two-tap; short, sharp and quick. She knew who it was without getting up to look, because who else would it be? Telling herself it was silly to think that she'd somehow known he would knock on a door exactly that way, she got to her feet. And because she'd been a woman alone for years now, she did take the cautious look through the peephole in the door.

Every weary nerve in her body snapped back to life.

"Tired but not dead, huh?" she muttered, then shook her head. She wasn't just talking to herself, she was talking to body parts. Just because when she'd looked, he'd both been far enough back to avoid the distortion of the fisheye effect of the glass, and been looking off to one side, at another guest passing by, and she'd gotten the full punch of his profile.

Her finger itched for the camera shutter, and she wondered if she would ever tire of taking photos of him. Judging by how many she'd taken yesterday, she doubted it. Put him in front of her and she was like someone with a full auto machine gun, the snapping of the shutter nearly constant. That's when she wasn't in video mode, trying to capture the way he moved.

She reached for the doorknob, consoling herself that at least he didn't know this was unusual for her. For all he knew, she always took gigabyte upon gigabyte of images.

He was turning back as she pulled the door open, touching a hand to his head as if he were tipping a hat to the older woman with the man walking past. Cowboy hat or not, Ry had the manners. Kaitlyn knew she didn't mistake the woman's appreciative look, which despite her age was likely as much for his looks as his courtesy. Which she completely understood.

"Hey," he said, that lethal smile flashing. "I'm starved. Are you up for going somewhere for dinner, or you want me to go get something?"

Kaitlyn just stared at him. The combination of that smile, her nerve endings deciding that this man required a response no matter how numb they were, and the utter oddity of someone besides Nick worried about whether she ate or not, was overwhelming. She knew she was standing there dumbstruck, but she simply could not think of any words.

His brow furrowed slightly when she didn't speak. "There's a little place right across the parking lot the guy at the desk says is good. Of course he would, since it's close, but hopefully it's edible. If you're too wiped—and I understand if you are—tell me what you want and I'll bring it back." He smiled again, a little more hesitant now. "I'll even call and read you the menu if you want."

"I…" She swallowed, tried again. "No, it's all right, I'll go." Wait, that sounded like she wanted to go alone, and she didn't. She definitely didn't. "Let me get my wallet."

"You won't need it, unless you want a drink."

She blinked. "What?"

"Alcohol. Wouldn't blame you after as wound up as you've been. But now you know Nick's going to be fine, so if you want a beer or some wine or something—"

"No."

He looked suddenly chagrinned. "Damn. I'm sorry, Kaitlyn. I forgot."

She knew he meant he'd forgotten she didn't drink, but she was stuck back on not needing her wallet. Was that his tactful way of letting her know he was paying? As he had for these rooms, and gas, and the most valuable commodity of all, his time?

How was she ever going to pay him back for all this?

"It's all right," she managed to get out. She knew she

needed to eat, and she also knew she wasn't up to having that payback discussion just now. "Let me grab my key."

"Make sure you grab your jacket, too. It's cold."

She only nodded; she'd already noticed he had his on.

And so a few minutes later, after a walk in the brisk air across the parking lot, she found herself sitting across the table from him in a booth in the small but friendly-seeming diner. It was busy enough that they got the last available seating, and she wondered how many of the people present were here for the same reason she was: a loved one in the big hospital a short distance away.

"Meat loaf's the best tonight," the weary-looking waitress said when she came over, menus in hand. "But you'd better say so now, we're getting low."

"Always willing to give it a shot," Ry said, then added with a smile, "You'd have to go some to beat my mom's, though."

Either his words or the way he said them perked the waitress up. Maybe she was a mom who appreciated another mom being appreciated. Kaitlyn knew that kind existed, totally unlike her own. Or maybe, being tired, the harried woman had just now noticed she was serving a guy who looked like he could have walked off a magazine cover as the flavor of this or any other year. "How about I bring you a little bite, so you can see for yourself?"

She did just that, a small bit of the meat concoction speared on a toothpick. Ry took it, and tasted it as thoroughly as if he were judging some contest at a county fair.

"Okay, that's good. Really good. Still only a tie, mind you, but better than any other competition Mom's had. What's the secret?"

"Best Texas beef. And the chiles."

"Duly noted," he said.

When the woman took their orders and headed for the kitchen, she was smiling. Kaitlyn had gone along with the meat loaf as much out of curiosity as anything. Curiosity about what it tasted like, not, she told herself firmly, because she wanted to know what he liked.

"Do you always charm the wait staff at restaurants?"

He shrugged. "Just try to appreciate them. I did my share when I was in school, and I know how much fun it's not." He wiggled a brow at her. "You thought I was charming?"

"Please," she said, raising a brow right back at him; she was feeling better now; the breadstick she'd grabbed when the basket appeared on the table had revived her a little. "You could charm the rattles off a snake."

One corner of his mouth quirked upward in that way that made her pulse kick. "Pardon me if I don't try that one."

"Don't like snakes?"

"Don't mind them all that much, but they always make me think of what Chance said about my ex-fiancée, after I found out she'd been cheating on me for a while."

She wasn't sure she wanted to hear it, especially when she

found herself feeling pleased by the sour tone of his voice when he talked about the woman foolish enough to lose him. But at the same time, she was too curious not to ask. "Which was?"

"He just gave me that thousand-yard stare of his, utterly expressionless, and said 'And here I thought when she was MIA she was just out shedding her skin.'"

She burst out laughing and was embarrassed when she realized she'd sent a couple of breadcrumbs flying. But he was smiling, so she couldn't feel too humiliated. Besides, it was his fault. Well, his and Chance's.

"I can picture that," she managed to say after swallowing. "What did Keller say?" She was endlessly fascinated by the workings of this family.

"He just said welcome home, but the subtext was definitely 'You never should have left.'"

"What about your mom?"

He smiled again. "She said she'd call her a bitch, but that would be an insult to Quinta."

She laughed again, feeling more relaxed than she had since she'd gotten the news about Nick. No, to be honest, since she'd taken on this project.

"I'd have to agree on that. She's such a sweet dog."

He nodded. "Even Tri likes her."

That got them off onto a discussion of Chance's *They Also Serve* project, and how many dogs that were nearly written off he had saved. She told him about going to see the monument to MWDs, and asked if he really thought his brother would let her do some photos.

"As long as you keep him out of them," he said.

"Too bad," she said. "All you Raffertys are darn photogenic from your mom on down. So are the new additions to the family, including young Mr. Brock."

He ignored the implicit compliment to him and focused on her last words. "Those three," he said, clearly meaning it, "are the best thing that's happened to us in a long time."

Over the savory meat loaf that arrived—it really was that good and she would eat every bite, because who knew when she'd have a meal like this again—Kaitlyn silently pondered the differences between being part of a family that had contracted down to two people who could barely stand each other versus one that was so full of love that it could easily expand to welcome others. So full of love that it could adapt to such varied people, from eldest Keller to youngest Cody, then take in Lucas and accept Sydney and Ariel and still have love to spare.

It was something she'd never known.

It was something she'd always wanted.

And something she'd never have.

Chapter Twenty-Four

WHEN SHE OPENED the door to her room, a blast of heat seemed to wash over them. Ry blinked, drawing back a little. He glanced at Kaitlyn, who lowered her gaze, half-shrugged, and said, "I was cold."

"What you were," he said firmly as he ushered her inside, "was hungry. And tired."

"Maybe."

"You've had a hell of a twenty-four hours, Kaitlyn. You're exhausted."

"Maybe."

Exasperated, he nudged her inside and shut the door behind them. And almost immediately he regretted it as the heat of the room enveloped him. He pulled off his jacket and tossed it on the chair beside the small table in the room. He saw her gaze follow the jacket, more intently than the simple act deserved. What the hell was she thinking?

"Are you always so stubborn?" She was staring at him now, wide-eyed. Almost shocked? Sometimes he just did not understand this woman. "What?"

"I..." Her voice trailed off.

He was a little tired himself, and he had to reach for some patience. He pointed. "Bed. Get in it."

She paled. Oddly, he noticed the tiny freckles across her nose stood out more. Then she looked down again, as if the rather wildly patterned carpet under their feet held the answers to everything.

"Kaitlyn?" He was worried now. She looked so…broken. Her shoulders had slumped and suddenly she looked fragile, and very, very vulnerable.

She didn't look at him. She just said, in a voice that matched how she looked just now, "I know how much I owe you, but I…"

Her voice faded away as she glanced at the bed he'd pointed at. The bed designed for two. And at last it hit him. What she was thinking.

"Son of a—" He bit back the oath. "Do you really think—never mind, obviously you do." His voice went hard, because what she'd assumed, that he'd want that kind of payment for just helping her out a little, stung him to the core. "Thanks for the compliment, thinking I'd take advantage of an exhausted woman dealing with the man she thinks of as a father in a hospital just down the road. For thinking I'd take advantage period."

He turned on his heel and headed for the door, then looked back at her. She hadn't moved.

"Good night, Ms. Miller," he said harshly. "Be ready at nine to go back to the hospital."

He didn't slam the door on his way out, but it was a near thing. It wasn't until he was at the door to his own room, reaching for the key in his jeans pocket, that he realized he'd left his jacket in the too-warm room. But he wasn't about to go back now; he'd get it in the morning.

Twenty minutes later, despite his own weariness, he was still pacing the floor of his own room. Because the tired was matched by the anger. What the hell? What had he ever done to make her think he would ever expect that kind of payment for a simple favor? Nothing, that's what he'd done. Of course Britt, Cody's nemesis, had once said he invited those thoughts just by existing and looking the way he did. She'd done it in her "just one of the guys" way so he'd laughed her off, but it came back to him now with a whole different edge.

Did Kaitlyn think he expected her to fall into bed with him just because he'd helped her out a little, or because of what he looked like? She'd implied the former, but she'd actually said something else.

Obviously, you could just sail by on your looks.

He swore under his breath, still pacing. He needed help with this. He wasn't used to having to dig this deep to figure someone out.

Obviously, you could just sail by on your looks.

He stopped dead. Had he been? It was hard not to know the effect what he looked like had on some people. In fact it annoyed him more often than pleased him, because he'd had nothing to do with it. And because his mother had pounded that fact home to him, and how much more important the inside was than the outside. For a moment he wished he could talk to her.

Great. Get in a tangle and first thing you want to do is talk to Mommy?

He could call Keller, but he was a working rancher, and it was late. He was also a newly engaged man, who had better things to do and was probably doing them if he was awake at this hour. And Chance was still off-limits under Mom's orders; besides, he was still just finding his own way out of the darkness he'd been in for too long. Cody, well, he was pretty much clueless when it came to anything that wasn't run through a computer.

No, a woman. That's who he needed to talk to. A woman who'd understand, and maybe be able to explain this to him. Which brought him back to Mom.

He glanced at the phone he'd put on the nightstand beside his own empty, two-person bed. He could text her. Then if she was asleep, he wouldn't disturb her, because he knew she had texts silenced at night, saying if it was that urgent they should just call.

But what the hell would he say? *"Hey, Mom, Kaitlyn thinks I want her to pay me back for helping her with sex. Why?"*

In the end, he picked up the phone and texted nearly that—without the mention of sex. She might be the smartest woman he'd ever known, but she was still his mother.

Her answer came back quickly enough that he knew he hadn't awakened her. And it was so simple, so blindingly obvious he felt stupid for not having figured it out himself. He sat on the edge of the bed, staring at the exchange on the screen.

Why would Kaitlyn think she has to pay me back somehow for doing this?

Perhaps because she's always had to pay, one way or another.

It was true. He knew it was, down deep, without having to think about it. Kaitlyn had paid for every step of her life, be it the addictions of her mother, the death of her father, or her generous spirit that led her to try and help both the one person in her life she still loved and the one who had wrought such destruction. She was still paying, and it was a steep price.

And it stung him beyond measure that she thought he was just another who would take from her. In a way he found particularly repugnant.

Obviously, you could just sail by on your looks.

Her words hammered in his brain once more. Even his father had seen it and had addressed it when he had officially become a teenager.

You've got that magic, son, that attracts people. When you get a little older it will attract women. A certain kind of man will use that as a weapon. Don't ever become that kind of man.

His father had never been more serious than with that instruction. It had also been the last piece of advice he'd ever given him; he'd been killed on the next deployment.

He'd tried to live by that advice, but he was starting to wonder how often things had happened easily for him because of it, without him realizing it. Something he'd never thought much about until Kaitlyn, and seeing how she'd had to fight her entire life.

His parents had built a foundation so strong, so steady, that it had survived his shattering loss. Kaitlyn had had nothing after her father's death except a heedless, self-centered mother who clearly had never been able to truly address her destructive illness. Who had left it to her daughter to deal with.

When it came right down to it, despite losing Dad so young, he'd been lucky. Because Mom was a rock and had held them all together, and then Keller had stepped into some very sizeable boots.

Kaitlyn had had nothing. Except, when she managed to survive to high school, Nick Vega.

They would take care of Nick—he would see to that. But that drive home to Last Stand was going to involve some discussion. He didn't like those kinds of talks any more than the next guy, but this was a special case.

Kaitlyn was a special case.

That resolution made, he finally made use of the tooth-brush the hotel provided, stripped and went to bed. And actually fell asleep quickly, thinking he had everything mapped out and handled. But the dreams that followed centered mostly on the idea Kaitlyn had planted, of them sharing that matching bed in her room. Only his subconscious corrected the error in her thinking, and in his dreams she came to him, eager, wanting, nothing of payback or owing in her mind.

And he awoke more than once in a heated jolt, his body aching in ways he hadn't felt in a very long time.

KAITLYN KNEW SHE needed sleep, yet she couldn't seem to get more than an hour at a time. Then wakefulness stole her mind again and set it to racing. But one thing was consistent. Her brain would not let go of the images she herself had planted, by thinking Ry wanted sex from her. As if he would. Even if it was all she had to offer.

But when he'd practically ripped off his jacket like that…

She should have known better. She'd fallen back into the old trap, set and sprung by Jillian, and had insulted a man who would never want or even think of such a thing in the process. If nothing else, Maggie Rafferty would never allow any of her sons to devolve into that mindset, no matter how beautiful they all were. And she'd done it, Kaitlyn was certain, without beating them down or denying they were as attractive as they all were. Ry in particular.

Unlike her own mother, who had never missed a chance to remind her that she had inherited her father's ordinary looks instead of her own glamorous beauty. It wasn't until she was sixteen that she'd confronted her about it.

"Then why did you marry him?"

"Because I was careless enough to get pregnant with you, and I didn't want to have to support you myself."

Her mother had said it easily, almost casually. She remembered the chill that had filled her, and enabled her to ask coldly, "Why didn't you just get an abortion?"

For the first time her mother had looked uncomfortable. "Your father and I reached…an agreement. I didn't abort, and he would take care of us both, no questions asked."

That was the first time she'd realized the full extent of her mother's mercenary instinct.

"Why are you being so honest about it?" she'd asked, surprised at the candid answer.

She had flicked a hand in that careless way she had. "Part of the agreement was to never tell you about it. But that doesn't apply anymore, since he broke his end and died, leaving me to deal with you."

That had been as close as she'd ever come in her life to assault. "He didn't just die, you murdered him!" She'd shouted it with all the rage she'd carried into her teenage years. "You're a drunken waste, and I hate you!"

"And you ruined my life! I'll be glad when I'm legally done with you."

The too vivid memory hit hard. Kaitlyn erupted out of the bed, back to a pacing of the floor that was beyond restless and halfway to frenzied. She knew how worked up she was when that hideous scene came back to her in all its painful clarity. Most of the time she was able to keep it buried. Deep.

She turned on her heel when she ran out of floor space near the door. In the spinning process she brushed the table and something slipped to the floor.

The jacket. She bent and picked it up, meaning to put it back on the chair where he'd left it, accidentally she was sure. Because he'd been so angry with her. Rightfully so, after the way she'd insulted him when all he'd done was take the thing off because it was so warm in here.

But suddenly she was clutching it in both hands, lifting the shearling to her face, breathing in the clean, sage-like scent she associated with him. Something fell, hitting the small table beside the chair. It sounded like a book, papery, but with an edge. When she looked she saw it was the small spiral-bound sketchpad she'd seen him with before. Before she thought, driven by a need she couldn't even name, she was reaching for it, flipping back the bright orange cover.

Her breath caught when she saw the image on the first page. A pencil drawing, done in the same sure way his other work was done, a minimum of lines portraying a maximum of detail. But that she would have expected. What she hadn't expected was that the drawing wasn't of some symbol or natural element for one of his projects. It was of people. Two people.

Nick. And her.

It was a moment when, as she sat beside his bed, she'd reached out to touch Nick's hand in the same instant he'd done the same, and they'd ended up clasped together. They had both smiled, pleased that they had shared the need for contact. It wasn't the warm, engulfing hug Nick usually gave her, but it was the best they could do until he was up and around again.

She stared, her breathing shallow as she saw what Ry had captured. Two people who treasured each other. Nick was her father in all but blood, the closest thing she had to one now, anyway. And she knew he looked upon her as the daughter he'd never had. Which was sad, because he would have made a wonderful parent to a big, sprawling brood. The kind of parent Maggie Rafferty was, producing amazing adults the world needed more of. And somehow, in a small pencil sketch, Ry had captured all that and more.

I'm no artist.

His insistence seemed foolish in the face of this obvious, concrete proof to the contrary. So why did he insist, why did he cling so hard to that "craftsman" title and reject this amazing talent?

She thought she knew. Because there was only one reason that made sense to her. She wondered if he even realized it himself.

She stared down at the sketch, wondering if he would give it to her if she asked. She would love to have it and would treasure it like few other possessions she had. At the very least Nick had to see it. She knew he would see what she saw in it, and it would mean as much to him.

But then she remembered how furious Ry was with her. He wouldn't give her the free bar of soap from the hotel bathroom. But maybe he would give it to Nick, and she could get a copy of it. That would do.

She toyed with the page. She could just tear it out of the sketchbook right now, without asking. He was already so mad at her, what was one more offense? But she knew she wouldn't. This was something personal for him, and as angry as he was, she didn't want to make it worse.

You've still got a job to finish.

Her effort at cool calculation failed completely. Which told her she'd made yet another in her long string of mistakes; she'd gone and fallen for not only the subject of a job, but an utterly unattainable man.

She started to pull her hand back, to let go of the page with the drawing. But she saw another penciled line on the page beneath it, and she couldn't stop herself from looking.

She gasped aloud. Because this drawing was her. And yet it was not her. The woman in the image had her features, was recognizable as her and yet…not. Because this woman was lovely. Something about the angle of her head, the smile curving her lips, the big, luminous eyes, resulted in something far more attractive than she would ever be in reality.

She didn't know what to think. He couldn't really see her this way. He probably was just using her as a basis, to draw what a genuinely beautiful woman would look like.

That slowed her racing heartbeat a little. It had been an…exercise, that's all. Take a basic, ordinary person and make them look wonderful. The same kind of thing she sometimes did with angles and lighting. That's all it was.

And now that she had that figured out, she could breathe normally again. Because the idea that Rylan Rafferty actually saw her this way was probably the most harebrained thought she'd ever had.

Chapter Twenty-Five

R Y STOPPED WHEN she put a hand on his arm just as they reached the hospital elevators. She hadn't said more than ten words this morning, and that was fine with him. Until they were alone together on the way back to Last Stand. Then that discussion was going to happen, when both of them were trapped in the cab of his truck.

How the hell had they piled up so much between them in such a short time? Their first encounter had been just a week ago tomorrow, and it was pushing it a bit to count that, since it had been that moment outside the doctor's office.

He shoved his uncharacteristically scrambled thoughts aside; there was a job to do right now. And obviously she had something to say, so he didn't reach for the button to summon the elevator yet.

He'd seen her shiver when they'd left the hotel and walked toward his truck. It had dropped below freezing last night and was still in the thirties, judging by the frost on the patch of grass outside the lobby. Her worn denim jacket was no match for that. He'd shrugged off his own shearling jacket and put it around her shoulders, startling an "Oh! No, don't," out of her.

"Hush," he'd said, borrowing the word he'd heard her use with Nick. And tried not to think about the fact that the jacket had already spent the night in her room, as he had in his dreams.

While she was no doubt thankful he hadn't claimed the payment she'd thought he was after.

Yes, they were going to have that discussion on the way back.

Now, when she reached for the side of his jacket, he thought she was going to pull it off and hand it back since they were inside. He was distracted for a moment by the down button lighting up on the elevator panel, indicating somebody else would be riding it down. When he turned back, to his surprise, he saw her reach into the pocket of his jacket and pull out his sketchpad.

"I know you're furious with me, and rightfully so," she said, in an almost timid tone that irritated the hell out of him. "But Nick's done nothing wrong. So may I show him your drawing?" He stared at her. She'd seen it? "I didn't snoop, not really," she said hastily, that same apologetic note in her voice. "It fell out when I accidentally knocked your jacket off the chair. I'm sorry if—"

"Stop apologizing." He'd wanted to snap it at her, but with what he'd realized last night, thanks to his mother's knack for understanding, he couldn't find it in him. So he added quietly, "Please."

"I…" She stopped as if she couldn't think of anything to say other than that apology. Or that she didn't want the worried-looking couple that had just exited the elevator to hear her.

"Going to apologize for existing?" he asked as they stepped into the waiting car.

"Sometimes I want to."

It was barely a whisper, but he heard it. Heard it and it stabbed deep, causing an ache he was sure was minor compared to the one that had made her admit it. This was going to stop. Whatever it took, this was going to stop. And he added one more topic to the list for the long ride home.

"Show him the damned thing," he said as he hit the button for Nick's floor and the doors slid shut, leaving them alone in the moving space. "Hell, give it to him if you want. I don't—"

He stopped abruptly, suddenly remembering. Had she seen that, too? Had she seen the next page in the sketchbook? When he'd done the one of the two of them, it had seemed only natural—a loving reunion in a hospital after a medical issue. And he was, as always, the observer, that half step back, taking it in, processing, and then letting it out again in physical form. Focused on capturing the emotion between two other people, the love and caring. Much like she had in that series of photographs.

That had been safe, distant.

The second drawing was neither.

He hadn't even meant to do it. He'd only been barely aware of flipping to a fresh page and starting, almost as if he were still mentally in the previous image. It had poured out in a rush, that second image, his hand moving more swiftly on this one. And he'd done it almost without looking at her, as if every detail was already present in his mind.

If she hadn't seen it, he'd just practically guaranteed she would, by telling her to give the first one to Nick. But then, looking at her, seeing the way her eyes darted away, he knew.

"You saw the other one."

He knew he hadn't imagined the way she stiffened her spine before she turned to look at him. "Yes." She took a quick breath. "I didn't think you did that."

He drew back just as the elevator stopped at their floor. Was she angry, that he'd sketched her without…what, asking permission? "Did what?"

"Flattery."

He blinked. She stepped out of the elevator, not even looking at him as she went. Which was just as well, because he couldn't think of a thing to say.

He left her alone with Nick the rest of the morning, wandering back to the cafeteria and grabbing more coffee, something he'd been doing a bit much of lately. Maybe that was his problem, he was just too wired, too much caffeine. He sat by a window for a long time, searching for answers that seemed elusive.

When a pretty young woman in hospital scrubs asked if she could share his table, his earlier thoughts made him tell her it was all hers, he was just leaving anyway. She looked disappointed, and he wanted to tell her not to, she wouldn't have been getting any bargain in his company today.

The doctor came in a little after noon. Nick was checked out and inspected—like a steer ready for market, he groused, making Ry smile despite his touchy mood—and the paperwork started. An hour later, with the barest of assists, he was in the passenger seat of the truck. Kaitlyn climbed into the smaller crew seat behind, and Ry wondered if she was relieved that she didn't have to sit next to him.

They got Nick back to the assisted living place where he had a one-bedroom apartment that could have been anywhere, except for the emergency call buttons and pulls strategically placed throughout. It was small but not cramped, and spotlessly clean. And judging by the group of staff that met them at the door, Nick was a favorite. There were many worse places he could be.

And might be, if not for Kaitlyn.

Once reassured that he was home and safe, Kaitlyn seemed to relax a little, and he got to observe more of the relationship between them. And even he couldn't miss that she was never this relaxed around him. And that bothered him, although it shouldn't; the man had been in her life a long time. Certainly a lot longer than the week he had known her.

And it still boggled him that it had been such a short time, considering how much of his energy and attention she consumed.

Finally Kaitlyn realized how much time had passed, and that Nick, despite his protests to the contrary, was tired after a long, eventful weekend. Ry shook hands with the man who meant so much to her, then excused himself to leave them alone for goodbyes.

"Take your time," he said to her, the first words he'd addressed directly to her since she'd made that crack about flattery.

Yes, the ride home was going to be…interesting.

"HE DID THIS?" Nick asked, staring at the pencil drawing she held out to him.

"Yes. He said I could give it to you, if you want it."

"I'd love it. I will frame it and put it where I can see it every day." He gave her a sideways look. "This is the man who insists he's not an artist?"

She nodded. "And won't even discuss it."

"I'd like to see him do a portrait of you."

Her breath caught. Nick was uncannily sharp, but there was no way he could know. "That would be boring." She tried for a laugh. "There's a reason I prefer to be behind the camera."

"Yes, there is. Because you don't see yourself as others do. And that, my sweet girl, is a pity."

She didn't want anyone's pity. But Nick's words stuck in her mind all the way out to Ry's truck. He was leaning against the driver's door, legs and arms crossed, his head leaning back against the top of the cab, his face turned toward the sun that had broken through the clouds while she was inside.

She stopped in her tracks, staring, her fingers itching for a shutter in that familiar way. But she didn't have a camera with her, so she simply looked at him. Soaked in the beauty of him, memorizing every detail for the time after, when she would go back to her life and he would go back to his, no doubt glad to be rid of the annoyance of all this.

She didn't think she'd made a sound—although she could have sighed overly loudly—but his head came up and he looked toward her. She still didn't move, but simply stood there savoring the way his lean, muscular body moved, that savage grace as he straightened and started toward her. When he stopped in front of her, she would have sworn she could feel his heat even from a foot away. As if he had some kind of burning aura around him that warmed anyone who got close.

Anyone lucky enough to stay close would be warm forever.

"You get him all settled?"

"Yes." It was all she felt safe saying.

"He seems good."

"Yes."

"Ready to head back?"

"Yes."

She saw his gaze narrow at the third monosyllable. But he only nodded and turned around, holding his arm out as if to escort her back to the truck.

She had a few minutes of peace as he got them out of the parking lot, onto the side road that led to the boulevard that would take them back to the interstate. She thought she'd worked out what to say, but somehow seeing him like that, like some beautiful creature the sun had decided to break through the clouds to bless, had stolen all the words from her head. Finally, once they were on I35 she decided to just come out with the easier part.

"Nick said to thank you for the drawing."

He glanced at her, then went back to the road ahead. "Did he recognize the woman with him?"

She blinked. "What?"

"In the drawing."

"Of course, why—" She broke off suddenly as she got his point.

"Not *too* flattering then."

Apparently that had really gotten to him. She hadn't meant it as a jab, to her it was just simple fact. Uncomfortable, she tossed off the first explanation she could think of.

"Who else could it be, there with him like that?"

"And the drawing of just you?"

She thought of that image, a woman as lovely as…perhaps her mother, at a younger age, before the booze had done its damage to her looks. Yet gentler, kinder than her mother could ever be. Lovely on the inside, too, so much that it shone through.

A woman she would never be.

"I didn't show it to him. That's no more me than some portrait of a royal by an artist currying favor."

"So that's what I am now? A sycophant?"

"I didn't say that."

"Didn't you?"

She was breathing again. This, she could do. Much easier than delving into that portrait he'd done. "You keep saying you're not an artist at all. Why?" Steadier now, she added firmly, "And 'I'm a craftsman' is not an acceptable answer."

He gave her an irritated glance. "But it is the answer."

"Why?" she said again. "Why would you deny what's so obvious? Anybody who looked at those drawings would call you an artist."

"I don't care what anybody else calls me."

She was getting to him, she could tell; that had come out rather clipped. But to get what she wanted out of him, she was going to have to push harder, because this was buried deep. "So no one knows what an artist is except you?"

"No one knows what I am except me." That came out even sharper.

"Let's ask the expert on it, then. Obviously you have a criteria in mind. So who do you think of first, when you think of an artist?"

"My father was an artist."

And there it was, the opening she'd been after. "Yes. Yes he was. And of a rare caliber."

"Yes." His tone had softened then, with that touch of pain she heard in all their voices when they spoke of the man.

"Then tell me, Rylan," she said, very softly, "isn't denying you are also an artist in essence denying you inherited your talent from him? And in a way, denying him?"

He didn't look at her, not even a quick glance. He stared down the interstate as if it was a runway and he was at the controls of a fighter jet. Only the jump of the muscle in his jaw and the tightness of his grip on the wheel betrayed that her words had stabbed home.

He was silent for so long she thought she might have accomplished two things. She'd learned she was right on target with her observation. But she'd also made him so mad that it was entirely possible he'd never speak to her again. Which might let her escape from the apology she knew came next. And unlike the casual ones she had gotten into the habit of tossing out too frequently—as he had repeatedly pointed out—this one she needed to make.

The apology for thinking even for a moment that a man like him would want a woman like her in the way she'd accused him of.

She'd probably been more wrong in her life, but she couldn't think of when.

Chapter Twenty-Six

B Y THE TIME they hit Georgetown heading south, he'd had enough of over-civilization. He bailed off the interstate onto State Route 29 and headed west. It would take longer, but he needed to think. And besides, he felt much better on the smaller, lesser traveled road. He didn't want to have the rest of this discussion and try and focus on freeway traffic at the same time, even on Sunday.

Especially after she'd already blown him to bits with that little observation of hers.

He'd known, deep down, for a long time, that his father was the reason he turned his back on being called an artist. Some part of him simply and firmly insisted he was not and could not be what his father had so clearly been. A genius-level artist. And so he'd clung to the word *craftsman* as if it were a shield. He was good at what he did, but what he did was not of the same caliber as the man who'd done the paintings they held so dear.

He just hadn't expected anyone else—especially someone he'd just met—to get it. He suspected Mom knew, on some level, but she'd never broached the subject. And she certainly hadn't fired a broadside at him the way Kaitlyn had.

Isn't denying you are also an artist in essence denying you inherited your talent from him? And in a way, denying him?

He'd never thought of it quite like that before. She seemed to have a knack for that, putting things in a different light, much as she did with her photography. And this light made him feel…he wasn't sure what. Denying the man he'd practically worshipped? Denying the man who had encouraged him to explore what talent he had? He could never do that.

But had he been?

You've got a gift, son. It can enrich your life or make it hell. What it can't be is ignored. Trust me, I tried.

He'd never forgotten what Dad had told him that day when he'd found the drawing Ry had done of Buckshot, his prized stallion. He'd carried it in his mind and chewed on it, as Dad said, and had come up with a raft of questions he wanted to ask.

But the very next day had been the last day, the final time he'd had with the man who had shaped all of their lives.

He had burned the drawing the day they got the news. And had never done another until he'd had to, once the leatherwork had taken off. He'd justified that by telling himself it wasn't really art, it was simply a design, like a blueprint for the belt or saddle or whatever the project was.

And he'd never touched actual paints in his life. Just the thought hurt too much.

He felt more than saw her looking at him. She hadn't

questioned the obvious change in route. He fought the natural instinct to explain. He was so tangled up right now he was afraid of what might come out if he spoke. So he did what he usually did under those circumstances, stayed quiet. As Chance said, silent running.

He focused on driving as if he hadn't done this route a dozen times. And he stayed quiet.

They went through Bertram and Burnet, where he thought about cutting south to Marble Falls and Johnson City, but kept going past the Buchanan dam and lake. She turned her head and looked out over the lake as they passed. He stayed quiet.

He took the turn onto SR16, dropping down to Llano, then continuing south. They passed the gates to many ranches, some he knew of and some he didn't. He stayed quiet.

He was a little surprised she also stayed quiet. Most women he knew would have felt the need to at least break the silence. His mother always wanted to know what he was thinking. Sydney was such a dynamo, he didn't think an hour went by without some phone call to some distant place. Ariel, maybe. Yes, she could do this. Chance had told him once that some of the best times were when he and Ariel just sat quietly at night, reading. That when she looked up and simply smiled at him, he felt...healed. Ry knew what a tremendous breakthrough that was for his brother, and he would be forever grateful to the woman who had caused it.

Kaitlyn, on the other hand… Her silence was different. And he suspected it was born of uncertainty. No, maybe certainty. Certainty that he didn't want to hear anything she had to say. And yet again he had an extremely uncharitable thought about the woman who had done so much damage to her daughter.

When they hit the outskirts of Fredericksburg, he realized with a little jolt that he'd gone two hours without saying a word. So much for that discussion he'd been determined to have with her. And she hadn't said a word either. He didn't think he knew another woman who could manage that. Maybe it was just a sign of how tangled up things had gotten.

When they pulled up at the inn, she jumped out the moment the truck was at a full stop. Anxious to get away from him? *Not so fast, Ms. Kaitlyn.* His resolve returned, albeit a bit late in the game, after the long, silent drive. But that discussion still needed to happen, and while it was nearly dark, it wasn't really that late.

"You don't have to walk me in," she said hastily when he got out and came around the front of the truck.

"I'm a Texan, ma'am," he said, exaggerating the drawl. "Of course I do."

She kept giving him quick, sideways looks, nervously, like a rabbit who knew a coyote was in the area. When he started up the wide staircase with her, toward her second-floor room, she opened her mouth as if to say it again, then stopped and looked away.

At the door to her room, she unlocked it then stopped. He heard her take in a deep breath, then she turned to face him. And when she spoke, her voice was smooth and even, as if she'd practiced what she was going to say. Maybe she had.

"I know you've said to stop apologizing, but this one is necessary." He started to speak, but she didn't stop. "I'm sorry for what I thought last night. I should have known better."

"Yes, you should have," he said, his own voice a little tight. The memory still rankled.

She gave him a sad smile then. "I apologize for the insult, for thinking even for a minute that you would want or expect that. From any woman, but especially me."

His annoyance vanished at her last three words. That qualifier that put her words in an entirely different light. And he didn't like it any better than he had liked her assumption last night.

"So are you saying thinking I expected sex as a payment was the insult, or thinking I might want it with you was the insult?"

"Either. Both."

It took every bit of what patience he had left to ask evenly, "Why?"

"Why?" She looked genuinely bewildered. "Why would you want…me?"

She put special emphasis on the "you." As if he were on

some other plane than her. And he knew that was what she thought. He couldn't decide if it was the most pitiful or the most heartbreaking thing he'd ever heard. Both, maybe. And he couldn't think of a damned thing to say in answer.

But he could think of something to do.

"Maybe this is why," he said, moving even as he spoke. He cupped her face in his hands and tilted her head back. And kissed her.

It was everything he'd suspected it would be. And more, because it happened faster than he'd thought possible. At the first touch of her mouth beneath his, fire leapt to life and raced along every nerve.

She'd stiffened for an instant. The still-functioning part of his brain ordered that if she stayed that way, he had to stop. But the moment the thought fully formed she went soft and pliant. He heard her make a tiny sound that echoed what he was feeling, stunned and at the same time hungry for more.

He deepened the kiss, probing, tasting. How could something be so hot and so sweet at the same time? It was like the spicy sweet potato dish they sometimes had when Mom was in the mood, neither flavor overwhelming the other, and together an impossible taste unlike any other.

Just as Kaitlyn Miller was unlike any other.

And when he felt her tongue move tentatively forward, the first sign of his own fierce wanting returned, it almost put him on his knees. He ran his own tongue along the even ridge of her teeth then past, swiping over hers, relishing the tiny sound she made again.

As an experiment, the kiss was conclusive. As a measurement of desire, it was off the charts. It was all he could do, took all his willpower not to push harder, harder than he knew she was ready for. He wanted her, more than he'd wanted anyone. But no matter how little time he'd known her, he knew enough to know if he pushed he would lose.

And he didn't want to lose. Not this, not her.

He broke the kiss. Stepped back. Spent a silent moment savoring the almost dazed look in her eyes, because he knew it meant she'd felt what he'd felt. This was different. Special. Together, they were incendiary.

"That's why," he said with emphasis. Then, with the best casual tone he could manage, he added, "See you tomorrow, Kaitlyn."

He walked away. Walked away knowing that this woman, who had looked so broken when she'd thought he'd wanted sex as payment yet so strong when she apologized for thinking it, was unlike any other he'd ever met. And he wanted more than anything to unravel the puzzle that she was.

And he couldn't stop himself from, at the end of the hall, looking back to be sure she was safely inside.

He was a Texan, after all.

Chapter Twenty-Seven

"H E'S A GOOD man, Kaitlyn. A true Texas gentleman."

She sat on the edge of the bed in her room at the inn, her grip tight around her phone as Nick spoke.

"Yes," she agreed, her thoughts fixated on the way he'd proven that last night, kissing her until her toes tingled and then walking away. Walking away, when she knew if he had pushed even a little harder, she would have given him everything.

And almost wishing he had. Or, more shockingly, that she had.

All the hard lessons of her life piled up to try and out-weigh those precious, amazing few moments, trying to tell her she was a fool for believing, even for a moment, that what her senses, what her body told her was true.

Some men would, perhaps had to, take sex wherever they could get it.

Rylan Rafferty wasn't one of them.

A wave of sadness swept over her. As painful as it would be to have him once and never again, she wasn't sure never having him at all might not be worse. And for the first time she had the thought that perhaps this was how her mother felt when she went on one of her sprees with a new man.

The moment the thought formed she recoiled from it. Because there was absolutely nothing similar about those men and Ry. Nothing.

"—you all right?"

She snapped back to reality at Nick's question. "I think I'm supposed to be asking you that."

"I'm fine. Good, in fact. Incision's sore, but I expected that. But honestly, honey, I think I feel better already."

That news lightened her mood considerably. "I'm so glad, Nick."

They talked on for a while, mostly about the work she'd been doing. Then a nurse arrived to check on him, and he had to go. But he took time to say one last thing.

"I think Rylan is an honest man, Katie. He might hide from his feelings, but he would never fake them."

And then he was gone, leaving her staring at her phone, wondering what on earth that was supposed to mean. Because Nick couldn't know how she'd let herself get so scrambled when it came to Ry. He was perceptive, and smart, just as Ry was, but... Had she somehow betrayed to him how she felt? He did know her better than anyone. But had she really somehow given away that Ry got to her in ways no man ever had?

She gave herself an inward shake, irritated at how easily

she lost herself in useless pondering when it came to Ry. She didn't know why he'd kissed her, but she'd be a fool to read into it.

Rylan is an honest man, Katie. He might hide from his feelings, but he would never fake them.

She trusted Nick's judgment. She always had, even when she'd doubted she had the talent he insisted she had.

He was right about that. Why not this?

Maybe he just didn't see Ry as a woman would. Beautiful, stunning, unattainable. Unless the woman was equally beautiful, stunning, and unattainable.

She had a sudden image of Ry and Jillian together, attending some gala function, dressed to the nines and with camera flashes going off all around them as the media reacted to the simple gorgeousness of them as a couple.

And as if her thought had summoned her up—like calling up a demon? she wondered wryly—the phone still in her hand signaled an incoming call. Signaled it with the rather bitchy ringtone she'd assigned to the woman she'd just been thinking of.

She automatically lifted the phone to answer, then stopped. Did she really want to have to talk to Jillian just now, when her mind was so…distracted? Her thoughts were so messed up who knows what the woman might trick her into saying. Or admitting. Because if nothing else, Jillian Jacobs was famous for getting what she wanted out of people sooner or later.

She let it go to voice mail, noting the time so she could plead being in the shower or something. And then she put off listening to it for a while longer, but when she started worrying about the woman showing up here momentarily and wanting her ready to go, she decided she had to. Not that Jillian was much for advance notice—she simply expected everyone to be prepared to move on her whim. And that put pressure on everyone she dealt with.

She listened to the message. After the first ten seconds or so, Kaitlyn felt that pressure ease. *I'm still in Austin. I have a lead on something big. I'll be back there to hicksville in a couple of days. Just do your thing.*

But then the message went on, and her stomach plummeted. *I need a juicy hook. Find something for me, something sensational or scandalous about your boy. Sleep with him if you have to.*

Sleep with him if you have to.

Kaitlyn sat there for a long time, wondering if she'd gotten this message yesterday it would have changed last night. If she somehow would have found the courage to urge Ry on, if she'd been under orders to do so.

And you know how well it turned out the last time.

She'd convinced herself the professor's interest was genuine, and Jillian had just been teasingly egging her on. She wasn't going to make that mistake again. No matter how much she wanted to follow that order.

No matter how much she wanted Rylan Rafferty.

"Where are you off to?"

Ry straightened from greeting the ever-amiable Quinta and looked at his mother over the rim of his coffee mug.

"Over to the inn."

"Kaitlyn?"

He nodded. "The exalted Ms. Jacobs is delayed, so she doesn't have the car."

His mother looked at him consideringly. "You don't sound disappointed."

"I am," he said. "In a way anyway. I want her gone. I've had enough of this media thing."

"Including Kaitlyn?"

"No," he admitted. "She's…different. She doesn't ask questions that feel like she's looking for dirt." *No, she just comes out with things that make me think, about things I've avoided most of my life.*

"So you're glad she's coming back."

He wasn't sure what she wanted him to say. Or rather, he was sure that he wasn't about to say it. Because it would have to be something like, "I kissed her last night, and it about blew my boots off." And he could imagine quite clearly her reaction to that.

So he said simply and with a negligent shrug, "Sure."

And his mother gave him a smile, one of those too know-ing, motherly smiles, as if she saw right through his façade of nonchalance. "So am I. I like her."

"Mmm." He didn't dare say anything, not the way he'd been thinking lately. If Mom ever got it into her head he was hot for the photographer, he'd never hear the end of it.

"You know," she said, and he braced himself as her voice took on that tone that warned him she'd been using that Mom intuition again, "I think you two are a lot alike." He blinked at that. She went on. "You've just been doubtful about different things. Seems like she's sure of her talent with a camera, but nothing else. You grew up knowing you turned heads, but you've never been sure of the genius you were born with."

"It's just a knack," he said. He tried to shrug, but Kaitlyn's words echoing in his head made it impossible.

... denying him.

He knew sloughing it off had been a mistake when his mother set down her own coffee mug rather sharply. "You can belittle my opinion, because I'm here to defend it. But your father isn't."

He drew back. What was that supposed to mean? "What are you—"

"Your father knew what talent you had. I remember the night, after you'd gone to bed, that he sat right where you're sitting and went through that old sketchbook of yours. And he looked up and said, 'He'll outshine me someday.'"

Ry stared at her. "You never told me that. Neither did he."

The old, too familiar pain glowed in her blue eyes for a moment. He was sorry about that, but he was too stunned by what she'd said to want to divert this.

"Because," she said, that pain in her voice as well, "he assumed there would be a next time. But that night was his last in this house." She stopped, and Ry swallowed hard as he watched his mother, this petite woman who had held the Raffertys together, steady herself. As she had done so many times. "And after that, I couldn't bear to. But I should have told you. When you first started denying you were an artist, I should have told you."

He couldn't stop himself; he crossed the few feet between them and pulled her into a fierce hug. She so rarely let the old pain show, so he knew how close to the surface it must be now for her to let it out.

"He said it with such pride, Rylan," she said, her voice muffled against his shirt. "Such fierce, fatherly pride. Only a loving father could be so very glad that his son would one day outshine him."

For a moment longer she lingered, but then the strong, steel-spined Maggie Rafferty was back, and she straightened.

"You get going. I have to go check on Two. He's still a little mopey about being weaned."

"He loves his mother. I get that," Ry said, holding her gaze. "I love mine too. More than she'll ever know."

The smile she gave him then was almost blinding. And when she headed for the barn, Quinta dancing at her heels, he thought yet again that despite tragedy, the Rafferty family was pretty darn lucky.

He glanced at the painting on the wall. "You built well, Dad," he said softly.

Then he finished his coffee, grabbed his mother's abandoned mug, rinsed them both and put them in the dishwasher. And headed out to his truck to go get Kaitlyn, who had had much more tragedy, and was long overdue on some luck.

Chapter Twenty-Eight

"**Y**OU'RE AS BEAUTIFUL as your rider, aren't you, m'boy?"

Kaitlyn crooned at the big black horse who nudged her with his nose. He whickered softly, and she smiled as she patted him. She'd come ahead into the barn while Ry paused to take a phone call, wanting to see how Two, the colt being weaned, was doing. But Flyer had stuck his head out and snorted at her as she went, as if offended she'd passed by without saying hello.

"And about as easy to ignore, too," she said, stroking the silken smooth nose.

"I'm glad to hear that."

The light, amused voice came from so close behind her Kaitlyn almost jumped. She turned to see the irrepressible Sydney Brock.

"Hi," she said, feeling a bit awkward that the woman might have overheard her incautious comments to the horse.

"He is beautiful, isn't he?" When Kaitlyn hesitated, the blonde chuckled. "That applies to both of them."

Kaitlyn felt her cheeks heat, but it was impossible to be

too embarrassed when it was clear Sydney was laughing with her, not at her. Still, she was glad when Sydney continued, relieving her of the burden of coming up with a response.

"I've often wondered which combination would be more striking, the matching duo with Ry aboard this guy and Cody aboard Chance's palomino, or if they switched."

Kaitlyn smiled, remembering her own musings on the topic. "I had the same thought. I decided that if they were together, the opposites. Individually, the match."

Sydney looked thoughtful, then smiled and nodded. "Good call. But then, you do have that artist's eye. Speaking of which, where is the resident non-artist?"

"On the phone," she said, nodding back toward the tack room. "Slater, the man from the saloon, I think?"

"Ah. Slater Highwater. Yes, he runs the Last Stand Saloon. Must be about the party Wednesday."

"Highwater?" She hadn't heard his last name before. "Any relation—"

"Yes. His brother." Sydney grinned. "And yes, it's an interesting family. You'll meet them there, at the party."

She'd been wishing she'd never agreed to go to this thing. "I...don't know. I don't have any party-type clothes. Here, I mean," she added hastily, not wanting to admit she didn't have any, period. She had one dress suit she kept for interviews, a simple black thing she'd bought for its permanent style, but that was the extent of her up-dressing wardrobe. She had nothing at all party worthy.

Sydney took a step back, looking her up and down. "You're too tall for my things, but Ariel might be a good fit. We'll find you something. Meet us here at five or so, and we'll get you set up before we head out at seven. And don't forget, as soon as you're done with this assignment, I want to talk to you about that work for me."

"I won't forget." She wasn't likely to forget the chance to do some work for something the size of *The World in a Gift*.

"And here's the other half of this gorgeous pair, so I'll leave you to it."

Sydney was gone practically before Kaitlyn could take a breath. And she knew she must look a bit besieged, because Ry was grinning at her as Sydney walked away. "Feel like a tornado just went by?" he asked.

"Is she always like that?"

"Pretty much. Although Keller's calmed her down a bit."

"Then she must have been overwhelming before."

"She's just what my brother needed," he said, and there was no mistaking the complete satisfaction in his voice.

They walked down to the stall where Two was now housed. His mom, Ry told her, was out in the big corral, far enough away and with some other mares for company. The colt would be turned out later today in the smaller corral on the other side of the barn, for some playtime.

"We're all working with him," Ry said. "The more people he gets used to messing with him now, the better later."

The youngster seemed to be adjusting, and appeared

both interested and playful with them. He'd made her laugh with his antics, suddenly taking off to run full tilt around the small enclosure, looking all legs and elbows to her. Then Ry patiently showed her how to saddle up the equally if not more patient Latte, and they got ready to ride.

It turned out to be one of the best days she'd ever had in her life. They'd headed out with no particular destination in mind. But when they reached a place that looked familiar, and she realized it was a vista she'd seen replicated on the governor's saddle—he'd been born here in the Hill Country—she'd simply had to take a photo of it.

"Side by side with an image of the saddle," she'd murmured, framing the shot in her mind before she even had the camera out of the saddlebag.

It had taken her a few moments to get in just the right position, and several shots before she was satisfied. Only then did she realize Ry had never said a word, had simply waited. And when she'd started to apologize for the delay and for getting lost in the idea of showing the reality next to his vision, she suddenly stopped herself. Because he was looking at her with total understanding.

"Good," he said softly. And she didn't know if he meant the idea, or that she hadn't apologized.

They'd ridden on, to some places they'd been before, and some new ones. Past peacefully grazing cattle, over the stream swollen from a storm up country last night then out to Chance's place, where Tri greeted them with calm alertness and Chance was working with another, clearly edgier dog on leash.

"The peace here must be good for them," she said as she stayed in place, watching Chance calm the animal. The other man nodded approval at her words, or perhaps her care at making no quick moves. She was introduced to the dog now known as Bowie, and the animal eventually tolerated a stroke from her hand.

Then, at Ry's nod, she broached again the subject of some photographs, with the idea of broadening the reach of the fundraising for *They Also Serve*. Chance gave her a steady, assessing look, and crazily all she could think was that this man should be the one who flustered her, with that warrior's gaze. But no, contrary as she was, it had to be his brother who rattled her cage.

And suddenly the cage simile she often used seemed a little too appropriate. Because here, in this fabled area, on this ranch, with this family, she felt as if she truly had been living in a cage until now.

"You, I think I could stand," Chance said.

As they were riding away from the cabin a few minutes later, Ry gave her a sideways look. "You have no idea what a tribute that was."

"I think maybe I do," she said, "because I felt…honored."

The smile he gave her then, instead of flustering her, made her feel a burst of warmth somewhere deep inside.

She paused several more times when something intriguing, from a rock formation to the hawk circling overhead, caught her eye and demanded her lens. Each time Ry waited, patiently, although he'd looked at her rather intently when she wanted the perfect shot of a view between two hills that seemed to frame a big oak whose shape reminded her of the hanging tree over east in Kyle. Backlit by the lowering sun, the contorted tree was an amazing image.

And each time, she consciously made the choice to simply thank him instead of apologizing for taking up his time.

"I get it," was all he said, and she knew he did. And that was another pleasure she'd never experienced before.

She even loved the time when, back at the barn, they untacked and groomed Flyer and Latte. It gave her a different kind of pleasure to take care of the big sweetheart of a horse, even if her still-unconditioned riding muscles protested. And when Maggie Rafferty called out to both of them to come inside and have dinner, and Ry smiled, she didn't hesitate to go with him into the big house.

Cody was there along with Keller and Sydney, and it turned into a cheerful, talkative meal that made her feel welcome even as it made her impossibly nostalgic for something she'd never had. After the meal and the cleanup, she wandered over to look once more at the painting on the wall. Now that she'd been to the place depicted a couple of times, it seemed even more vivid to her.

"Do you know," she asked Ry when he came over to

stand beside her, "did he do this there, at the location?"

He shook his head. "He never did that. He always worked from memory."

She nodded slowly. "He wanted the heart of it, not just the details."

Ry went very still beside her. Had she said something wrong? Maybe she shouldn't have voiced such an assumption about his dead father.

"Come with me," he said, an edge of tension in his voice. But she could no more not follow him than she could have stopped herself today from taking image after image of this amazing place. She grabbed up her backpack and followed him.

He led her across the ground between the main house and his studio. They hadn't been back in there since the round of photographs he'd allowed her to take. Inside she saw that it didn't look much different, except that the floor around the easel with the big drawing pad was a bit more littered with discarded pages. He didn't even pause but kept going, and after a moment she realized he was headed for the stairs at the back of the space. The stairs that must lead to the loft, where he'd said he lived most of the time.

A million chaotic thoughts crashed into her mind. She had to focus on each step one at a time to try and keep any kind of control over them.

He lived up here.

He slept up here.

He was in essence, leading her to his bedroom. And she was following, without questioning. She—

She almost collided with him as he stopped dead at the top of the stairs. Her pack shifted, almost slipping from her shoulder. She caught a glimpse of the big space beyond, which covered at least half of the barn's area. A couch, a table, a pile of books, a flat-screen TV, and...a huge-looking bed on the far wall. Her gaze darted away from that just as he stepped to one side, and she saw why she was really here. Saw the painting on the wall at the top of the stairs, so obviously by the same brilliant hand as the one in the house.

A painting of nearly the exact view she'd photographed today, of the twisted oak tree framed by the hills to either side, backlit by the lowering sun.

Chapter Twenty-Nine

"HE SAID EXACTLY what you said. That he wanted the heart of it, not just the details."

Ry knew his voice was a little raw, but he couldn't seem to help it. It had dug at him when she'd stopped to take those photos of this scene, but he'd pushed it aside, thinking that he already knew she had an artist's eye. But when she'd said that in the main house, using almost the identical words his father had used, it had pushed him over the edge. He stared at the painting he saw every day as if he'd never seen it before, but really it was to keep from looking at her.

He knew his family loved him, despite all his eccentricities. He knew his place in the tight fit they all were. Keller had gotten their father's love for this place that had been his family's for generations. Chance had taken up their father's sword to defend the country he'd loved. Cody had had the least time with the man who had shaped them all, but even he had dedicated his life to trying to save others who served, by eliminating the hazard that had caused his death.

But he had gotten something else from that man, something he'd never really wanted, and it was something that put him into the difficult place of either denying it and going stark-raving crazy, or channeling it down a path he could accept. There was a reason he'd never tried painting. It quite simply hurt too much to even think about. His leatherwork had eased the itch without triggering the pain, and he was satisfied with that. Even happy with it.

Kaitlyn got it. She understood, in a way few did. She understood that you did what you could to live with the pain, once you realized that while it changed, it never went away. And she understood the passion of it, the need to let out what your mind saw, to express it in some visual way. She did it herself, with the same unerring eye his father had had. That he hoped he had. She knew what it was like to be so lost in the image you were trying to capture that all else faded away; he knew that from the way she hadn't even heard him speaking a couple of times on that ride today.

No woman he'd ever met had understood the way she did.

His jaw sent out a signal warning him he'd been clenching it too tightly. He had to consciously relax the muscles. Then, finally, he looked at her.

She was still staring at the painting. And he saw, to his shock, tiny droplets trickling down her cheeks.

"Why?" It broke from him almost against his will. "Why does this make you cry?"

He saw her swallow, knew she was fighting the tears. And failing. She kept her gaze on the painting. "Because he saw what he saw. Because I know how brilliant he was, and that I saw the same thing makes me feel…" She swallowed again and then went on. "Because I wish I'd known him. Because—" she turned her head finally, and met his gaze "—you showed this to me."

"I…" This time it was he who could not find the words.

"I get why it's…up here. I don't think you share it with everyone."

"I share it with no one." He hesitated, then thought to hell with it and plunged ahead. "And to answer what you didn't ask, no woman has ever set foot up here."

Her eyes widened. She started to back away, toward the stairs. As if he'd told her she shouldn't be setting foot up here either. He reached out and took her hand, holding her there.

"That wasn't a cue to leave, it was pointing out you're an exception."

She froze, staring at him almost as intently as she'd stared at the painting. "Why? Why would you make an exception for me?" She sounded genuinely puzzled.

"Why not?" he demanded.

"You…your work is dazzling. You are dazzling. Even your horse is dazzling. I'm…not. I'm just plain me."

He ignored the compliments. They didn't matter, not right now. "Someday, I want to meet your mother," he said, his voice tinged with the anger he was feeling; now that he'd given in to roiling emotion, he couldn't seem to control which one he let loose. "I want to tell her how much I loathe her for what she's done to you."

She looked away from him then. "You'd understand, if you did. She's beautiful. Do you remember that ad campaign for that new perfume, ten years ago? The one with every ad near a swimming pool, where every guy who saw it drooled over the woman? That was her. She was the model."

He did remember. For a while it seemed like the images of the admittedly gorgeous, sexy brunette had been everywhere. He also remembered she'd never been seen again.

"Why wasn't she everywhere, after that?"

Kaitlyn didn't answer, but he suspected he knew why. If she'd already been drinking, as Kaitlyn had said, she'd probably hit the tipping point where all her beauty wasn't worth the problems that came with it.

But then something finally clicked in his mind.

"That's it, isn't it? It isn't just that you don't drink, you don't want to be anything like her in any way, so you actually try to be the plain you keep calling yourself." He could tell by the way she wouldn't meet his gaze that he was right.

"I am plain. I don't have her looks, or her charm."

"I'd argue that, but more importantly, you have none of her weaknesses either." Her head came up sharply. And as he looked into those eyes the next logical step hit him. "And that's why you're always behind the camera, so you never have to be in front of it."

She sucked in an audible breath, and still avoided his gaze.

If you're going to do it, do it right. Mom's oft-given advice echoed in his head. And he took the next plunge.

"And I assume she managed to blow all the money she must have made from that? And didn't make any provisions for her daughter?"

Kaitlyn shrugged, but still didn't look at him. "I was eighteen then. An adult."

"So is she, but you're paying for her rehab."

"That's different."

"She convince you of that?"

"No."

"Then who? Your father?"

She winced, and he almost regretted saying it. Almost. "Yes," she finally said, barely above a whisper and she never took her eyes off the painting. "He said she was…different. Fragile. Special. And needed to be looked after."

"Is that why he stayed with her? Because he thought she needed looking after?"

"Probably."

"And look what it cost him."

That struck hard, because she finally turned on him. "You think I don't know that?"

He found himself welcoming the snap in her voice. "He made the decision to stay with her, Kaitlyn. Just like you've made the decision to let her keep deciding who you are."

She stared at him. He couldn't tell what she was thinking. Mom had always said he was perceptive—You have an artist's perception of people and things, she'd told him, and he'd countered with his usual protest that he wasn't an artist—and right now he hoped she was right. Because he thought he might have found the key.

"She doesn't deserve that," he said softly. "She doesn't deserve to control what you think you are, not when you've proven yourself worth so much more than she ever has."

"But she—"

"Stood in front of a camera? Cashed in on something she had nothing to do with? While you use your heart and your mind and your soul to produce images that stir all those things in others?"

She was still staring up at him, but he saw something change in her gaze, in her eyes. And her voice matched that new softness when she asked quietly, "Like you do?"

He opened his mouth to say there was no comparison. But something in the way she was looking at him stopped him. Stopped his words because it fired something else in him, that sudden, fierce heat that shot through him like wildfire. He was staring at her now, at the warmth and softness in her eyes, at the spray of tiny freckles that danced across her pert nose, at the way her lips were parted, as if her breathing had kicked up just as his had.

"I love your freckles," he said, inanely.

She blinked. Looked startled. More than startled. "You

do? I've always…hated them."

"Don't you dare. They're real. They're you."

And then, because he didn't seem to have any choice, he kissed her.

This time, it seemed as if she'd been waiting for it, maybe even hoping for it, because her response was instant, and eager. He tasted her hungrily, driven to prove to himself that it was as he'd remembered, hot and impossibly sweet. He deepened the kiss, much more quickly than he had before, because he felt driven. More than he had ever felt before. He knew on some level this was about what he'd just said about her heart, her mind, her soul, that he wanted, needed, had to connect with all three, because with her nothing less would do.

But then he could barely think at all, because every nerve in his body had snapped to life with only one end in mind, slaking this ferocious need that only she had ever roused in him. Nothing else mattered, not who she was, not who he was, not even the people who had made them what they were, for good or ill. The one thing that mattered was that triumphant cry he heard in his mind, his only coherent thought.

At last.

Chapter Thirty

HER HEAD WAS spinning. Maybe because this time she wasn't caught off guard. She wasn't stunned.

She wasn't resisting. Wasn't resisting how this made her feel. Wasn't dwelling on how she didn't deserve this, or him.

You've proven yourself worth so much more...

He'd meant it. All of it. What he'd said about her had come from what he believed about her.

With the last bit of her mind that was still functioning amid the sudden flood of heat and sensation, she shoved away all her thoughts that no man like this would ever want a woman like her. Because it was so obviously not true; he was here, kissing her, tasting her, driving deeper with every moment, with a hunger even she couldn't deny. And even if she could, there was no way she could deny the readiness of his body, his erection was close and hard, prodding her. If it had been anyone else she would have assumed he just wanted sex and she was handy. But this was Ry, and he wasn't one of those. Which left her with only one answer.

He wanted her.

He truly wanted *her*.

And no matter what happened after, no matter if this was the one and only time, she had to have this, had to have him. If she had to, she would live on the memory of this for the rest of her life.

He broke the kiss, but pulled back only far enough to softly speak. "Kaitlyn?"

"Yes."

She heard him suck in a breath. "What are you saying yes to?"

"Who."

"What?"

"You mean who am I saying yes to."

"Me, I hope?"

"Back to answer one. Yes."

And she couldn't help it, the silliness of the exchange made her smile. And the smile she got back from him made her feel crazily giddy.

And then he was kissing her again and her world was spinning in a new, different way. Joy was building inside her. Joy, and a hunger she'd never known. She wanted him, wanted that lean, muscled body next to hers, preferably naked. But she couldn't find the words, so she used her hands to stroke him, savoring the feel of him as she urged him on. And when he began to tug at her clothes she took it as the signal she'd wanted and began to do the same. She was vaguely aware of the tangle of fabric and the clunk of boots as they hit the floor, but then they were skin to skin and she could think of nothing else.

She ran her hands down his back, to that taut backside she'd so often admired in his jeans. He made a low, harsh sound, and then his hands slid up to cup her breasts, her nipples rubbing against his chest as he lifted them. She moaned at the arrow of heat and sensation that shot through her, awakening part of her that had been yearning for him forever. And then his mouth was on her, teasing those nipples to a tightness she'd never experienced, and she moaned again, nearly gasping this time.

His hand slid around to her back, as if to pull her even closer. And suddenly he went still. Her heart missed a beat. She'd forgotten. She'd actually forgotten.

His fingers moved, over the puckered, hardened flesh of the three-inch almost round scar on her left shoulder blade. She felt as if a bucket of ice water had doused the heat as he stepped around her to look. She didn't fight him. Didn't try to hide it. He might as well know.

When she knew he could see she held her breath, waiting for him to recoil, to pull away. But instead his fingers slid over the burn scar once more, gently, as if he was afraid it still hurt.

"Kaitlyn?"

"I know it's ugly," she said, trembling and unable to stop it. "Even though it's old."

"Almost twenty years old?" he asked softly.

She wasn't surprised he'd figured that out. "Yes."

He was silent. And then he moved, to her shock pressing his lips against the thickened flesh and skin. When he came back to stand in front of her, he seemed to be studying her, as if he had a question he could find the answer to just by looking at her.

And then he said, in such a tone of pained wonder it made something ache deep inside her, "You went back in yourself. To try and save him, just like he tried to save you."

He wasn't asking, so she didn't answer. And then he leaned down and seized her mouth again, kissing her long and hard and deep. As if he'd never seen the ugly scar.

Or as if it didn't matter.

When he broke the kiss at last it took her a moment to remember how to breathe.

"Tell me we don't need a condom, because I don't have any," he said, sounding as if the words were coming through gritted teeth.

Somehow the idea that he wasn't prepared only sent her higher. "I get the shots," she said breathlessly. "My work doesn't always take me to the nicest places."

"No more alone," he grated out.

She could think of a couple of ways that could be interpreted, but then he was kissing her again and thinking wasn't an option.

"I wanted to go slow," he muttered, now against the shell of her ear.

"Don't you dare," she said, not even recognizing the

woman she'd become with him.

"Later," he said in apparent agreement.

He picked her up as if she were some tiny, delicate thing. And then they were on his bed, and she gave in to what she'd wanted from the moment she'd felt the heavy prod of his erection against her. She slipped her hand down his body, savoring the solid sleekness of him as she went, until her fingers curled around him. He groaned, low and deep, and she felt his every muscle go taut against her.

She'd never felt anything like him, so strong, hard, yet so silken smooth. She stroked, exploring, and when she felt a drop of moisture at the tip she ran her thumb over it. There was no word she could think of for the sound he made then. But she was barely thinking at all now.

And then he was sliding into her, his way eased by a body that had been ready for him, wanting him, since the first time she'd seen him. She cried out at the exquisite fullness as he drove home and thought it might end for her right then. But then he moved and she lost track of everything except the growing, expanding need.

Then he shifted, just slightly. One more long stroke and her body exploded with fierce, drowning sensation. It rippled through her and she cried out, aware of nothing except the sheer, overwhelming pleasure until the moment when she heard him say her name in a voice that sounded exactly like she felt.

SHE WASN'T SURE at first what had awakened her. It wasn't morning, not judging by the level of darkness. For a moment she was afraid to open her eyes, afraid she'd dreamed it all. But then the very atmosphere of where she was proved that wrong; she could feel how different this place was, as if even the air pressure was different in a place as big as this barn loft.

Ry's loft.

Her eyes snapped open. What had awakened her was him, getting out of the bed where she'd spent the most amazing night of her life. And she had a feeling it would keep that ranking maybe until the end of her life.

But Ry was leaving. He was pulling on the jeans she'd so eagerly helped him shed last night. For a moment she lay frozen, unable to breathe. Her fingers curled at the sight of him, of the shape of that tautly muscled backside as he tugged the jeans up.

So quietly she knew she wouldn't have heard it had she still been asleep, he covered the distance to the railing where it looked down over his studio in four long, barefoot strides. She watched, entranced now by his sleek, sculpted back and shoulders. Then it struck her he hadn't even looked back.

Could he be in a hurry to get away, maybe regretting last night? She knew all the jokes about morning-after regret, and if she'd had to say which of them would feel it in the morning, she of course would have guessed him. But he was still barefoot, so he couldn't be really leaving, could he? He—

He grabbed the railing and went over the side.

She stifled a gasp of shock. He'd simply…jumped. It had to be a twelve-foot drop, and he'd simply jumped. Her stunned mind tried to tell her he was that desperate to get away. From her. But to believe that, she had to believe that Rylan Rafferty was the worst kind of liar.

I share it with no one…you're an exception.

Belatedly she realized she hadn't heard any crash or anything beyond a slight thump as he hit the floor. He'd landed with no more noise than if he'd been that big cat she always thought of when he moved. And it occurred to her that perhaps this was his usual method of getting downstairs.

Driven by a need to see what he was doing, to see him, as if now that he wasn't beside her she couldn't quite believe any of this had really happened, she rolled out of the bed herself. Forgoing underwear and shoes as he had, she pulled on her own jeans, but added a T-shirt. His shirt, telling herself it was because she wasn't exactly sure where hers had ended up. It smelled like him, that combination of wild sage and Ry that made her breathe deep.

She crept downstairs. Saw him standing before the easel, jeans low on his narrow hips because they were only half-zipped. He half-turned to pick something up from the workbench, and that downward arrow of dark hair she'd traced last night drew her gaze and kicked up her pulse. Then he was drawing, moving in quick, sure motions that told her this was what had driven him. He hadn't been leaving her, he'd been going there. Because he had no choice.

Her fingers were itching, and she walked as quietly as she could back to the spot near the top of the stairs where he'd set her backpack when he'd slid it off her shoulder last night. She had the camera in her hands in seconds, and was back at the rail. She snapped off several shots, framing, focusing, trying to capture the pure energy of the man, that fluid grace.

And then she stopped. She set the camera down and stared at her hands. Because they were still itching, fingers curling with the need that had always meant she needed to do what she'd just done. But this time, it wasn't enough. It wasn't her camera, that device she used to both capture the world around her and to insulate her from it, that she wanted.

That's why you're always behind the camera, so you never have to be in front of it.

No one except Nick had ever understood that before. But Ry did. He understood that—and her—better than anyone ever had.

And it was Ry she wanted her hands on.

But she couldn't interrupt him, not now, not if he'd been driven by a vision strongly enough to take that literal leap. So she tiptoed down the stairs into the studio, but stopped several feet away. For now, she would content herself with watching. Watching, and marveling that this amazing creature, this beautiful, powerful man, wanted her.

Chapter Thirty-One

"GOOD MORNING."

Ry nearly jumped. His mother had always had that knack of being able to sneak up on you. It was merely unsettling now; when he'd been a kid it had been a definite hazard of doing anything he wasn't supposed to be doing. But this morning he'd only come in for coffee, because he'd been out at his place.

"Hi," he said, finishing pouring the coffee.

"Up late last night?" she asked, her motherly tone just a shade too light and airy as Quinta politely sat at their feet.

He froze. There was no way she could know, was there? "Uh…"

She laughed. "It's about time, Rylan. It's about time."

"What is?" he asked cautiously.

She rolled her eyes at him, then looked pointedly down at the kitchen counter. Where he'd just filled two mugs. "Oh," he said lamely.

"Not to mention that cat that got the canary look in your eye."

"Oh." Just as lamely.

She smiled then. "Why do you think I kept leaving you two alone together?"

"Oh." It suddenly seemed to be the only word in his vocabulary. But she had done that, now that he thought about it.

"She'll take some special care, Ry. She's had a rough life."

There was no point in denial, not in the face of the mom mind-reading. He pulled himself together. "I know. She's hiding in plain sight. What's that you used to say? Hiding her light under a bushel?" He told her as much of what Kaitlyn had said as he thought he could without betraying a trust. Because he knew his mother's heart. Then he held the gaze of the woman who'd been the rock of all their lives since he'd been thirteen. "She could use some mothering. Your kind. The right kind. The best kind."

He saw the sudden sheen of her eyes. "I think I can manage that. Because she's perfect, for you. Tell her welcome for me, until I can do it myself."

She stretched up and kissed his cheek, patted his arm. And then she was gone, the ever-loyal Quinta at her heels.

When he got back to the loft Kaitlyn was awake, but still in bed. He handed her the coffee mug, and after she'd taken a long drink, said casually, "Mom says welcome to the Raffertys."

He knew she tensed because he saw the ripple in the surface of the coffee. "Welcome to...she knows I..."

"Did I forget to warn you she's a mind-reader?" he said

lightly. Then, almost wryly, he added, "Or in my case, apparently my smugly satisfied expression was enough."

He saw her swallow. Then, hesitantly, she asked, "Are you?"

He stared at her for a moment. Satisfied? Is that what she meant? How could she doubt it, after the night they'd spent? She'd driven him crazy, then sent him flying so many times. How could she—

Kaitlyn. This was Kaitlyn. With her past, her history, her casually cruel, in his book murderer mother.

He leaned down and took the mug from her. Set it and his down on the upended crate that served as a nightstand. Shed his clothes as fast as he could and rejoined her.

And proceeded to show her what he couldn't find the words for.

THE NEXT DAY was the happiest Ry had had in longer than he could remember. They went back to the inn so Kaitlyn could pick up some things, then he took her to his favorite places in Last Stand. First stop was Kolaches, which she confessed she'd succumbed to that first day. Which got them talking about that encounter and had them both laughing at what she'd naturally thought and how he'd felt when he'd realized it.

And he nearly backed out of the parking space into a

passing delivery truck when it occurred to him that someday being in that obstetrician's office for real might not be so bad if he was waiting on Kaitlyn.

He clamped down hard on that thought. A kid, with Kaitlyn? He was already thinking…like that? That was crazy. He was crazy.

He shoved the thought back into a mental cave, but he had the feeling it wouldn't stay there. He made himself focus on driving. They went by the police station, and he gave her more Highwater history, then took her by the Outlaw Tequila building, and told her about the contentious history between the Highwaters and the once literal outlaw Delaneys. They stopped at Java Time for more coffee—they hadn't, delightfully, gotten much sleep at all—and then at Yippee Ki Yay because Kaitlyn wanted to look at the belts again. And as he watched her looking at them, touching them with her delicate fingers, he got to thinking what else those fingers had done, and he had to take a walk around the store. Which seemed insane after the night they'd spent, but his body wasn't listening to logic today.

He didn't know how long he'd been standing there, staring unseeingly at the display of boots on the wall, when her soft voice beside him startled him out of a reverie.

"Need new boots?"

"I…no. I was just thinking."

And the answer had come to him—what was needed to finish the design that had burst into his mind last night. The design he planned to put on the belt that would be her official welcome to the Rafferty clan. And that he was thinking this about a woman he'd first laid eyes on nine days ago didn't seem at all odd to him. When you'd been looking for something all your life, wasn't it logical that you'd know it when you finally saw it?

He thought of the burn scar he'd seen, and it underlined the answer in his mind.

Especially when it was someone who, even as a child, risked her life trying to save the one person she loved?

It was after that that all the doubts, the uncertainty had been layered on by that pitiful excuse for a mother. But underneath all that he knew the core was still there, the brave, determined person she'd been even at nine years old. She just need to shed all the crap that had been dumped on her. And he was filled with a determination of his own, to help her do just that.

Because when Kaitlyn Miller finally broke free, it was going to be an utterly amazing thing. And he wanted to be the one who reaped that harvest.

That determination held even after Kaitlyn told him the next day, after another spectacular night where they'd learned even more about each other, and he'd discovered the particular pleasure of expanding her riding lessons in a much more personal way, that Jillian had texted she was on her way back from Austin, and wanted a final, long deep-digging session with him.

"Is that what she calls it?" he said with a grimace.

"Among other things. She said she'll be here in half an hour. She—" She broke off with a small gasp. And suddenly she was looking at him wide-eyed.

"What? What's wrong?"

"She can't know," Kaitlyn said, a trace of something a little too akin to horror in her eyes.

"Can't know what?"

She looked up toward the loft, as if she could see the bed they'd turned into a tangled mass of sheets and blankets. "Us. This."

He felt a sudden chill. The nosy reporter couldn't know that they were sleeping together? "Why," he said carefully, "would she even care?" Kaitlyn didn't answer. Or look up. Something occurred to him, a memory from when Ms. Jacobs had first appeared. "If she thought I'd ever sleep with her, she was extremely wrong."

Her gaze snapped back to his face at that, and he didn't think he was wrong thinking there'd been some pleasure in that look.

"I…she knew that, early on." She looked down again, this time fiddling with a flap on her ever-present backpack. "She said you might have a thing for…the needy ones."

His brows lowered. "She said what?" Then it hit him. "Wait. That's what she calls you? Needy?" Her only answer was a shrug. "Is that why she can't know?"

She sucked in a deep, audible breath. And then, as if it

was the most difficult thing she'd ever done, she lifted her head and met his gaze.

"No. She can't know because she told me to sleep with you. To try and find out some juicy secret she could use."

He stared at her. Was vaguely aware of his stomach knotting up, his muscles tensing as they did when he spotted a rattlesnake out on the ranch. It made his voice cold when he said, "Is that what this was?"

The horror in her eyes was definite this time. "You can't believe—"

"Hey, you two!"

The buoyant call came just as the door swung open. Sydney stepped in, followed by Ariel. If they were aware of the tension they'd just walked in on, it didn't show.

"Knock?" he said, barely managing not to say it through gritted teeth.

"Not when we came to kidnap your lady," Ariel said. "We need to prep for the party."

Well, that was a distraction. "The party that's not for two hours yet?"

"Spoken just like a man," Sydney said with an exaggerated sigh.

Sydney was a cheerfully relentless force, and Ariel a quiet but inexorable one, and together they were unstoppable. Before he could really get his chaotic thoughts together, the three women were gone. And it seemed significant that Kaitlyn grabbed up her backpack as she was ushered out the door.

And he was left to ponder the fact that Jillian had told Kaitlyn to sleep with him.

And why.

Far too soon after that, while all he could think about was Kaitlyn and what was going on in the house, he was again face-to-face with the beautiful, confident, ice-cold woman who'd done it. He didn't let her inside his studio. In fact, he told her he had work to do in the barn, knowing she'd probably turn up her nose at the idea. Which she did.

"It's fitting," he said flatly. "We can both shovel shit."

She looked startled at the crudity, then just slightly worried. He savored that as he walked into the barn and indeed grabbed a shovel. It was all he could do not to confront her, and only that fact that he had no doubt she would take it out on Kaitlyn if he did stopped him.

He gave her nothing. One-word answers when possible. If it wasn't directly about the work itself, he didn't answer at all. He stymied her until her frustration was obvious. She clearly never expected him to stonewall her, had assumed she was doing him a favor by even deigning to do this story. Or maybe she just assumed no one would ever buck the media in general.

"This story can make or break you!" she finally exclaimed. "Why are you being so contentious?"

"I'm a Texan."

"So?"

"Haven't you heard?" he said, his voice way too bland. "A Texan'll start a fight at the drop of a hat. And he'll drop the hat."

She stared at him, clearly dumbfounded. She'd come here expecting him to tread carefully around her, maybe cater to her or at least flatter her. Expecting it because she really thought she could make or break him.

Which only proved she didn't know jack about Texans.

Chapter Thirty-Two

"NO, NOT YET," Sydney said. "One last thing before you look."

The blonde reached out and swiped the soft brush she was holding over Kaitlyn's cheeks.

"That's it," Ariel said approvingly.

Kaitlyn didn't know what to say, and even less what to expect. She felt as if she'd been caught up in a tornado as the two women worked on her as if she were some project they were taking great delight in. They'd led her into what had to be the master bedroom, which made her feel even more uncomfortable; this was Ry's mother's space, after all. But she had said welcome. At least, Ry had said she had.

But that was before he'd found out about Jillian's order. Which she had stupidly told him.

What were you supposed to do, lie to him?

True, not telling him about Jillian's instructions in the first place wasn't the same as lying in words, but lies of omission were sometimes worse. Like when her mother let her go on thinking she was staying sober only for her to get that tearful phone call that revealed she'd been drinking again for months.

They had sat her down on a chair facing the bed, and she had immediately spotted the painting on the wall above it. As with all the others, there was no mistaking the hand that had produced it. But where the others she'd seen poured out love for this place, this Hill Country, this one exploded with love, adoration and devotion to one thing. One person. The beautiful woman in the portrait, unmistakable even now, two decades later.

"Beautiful, isn't it?" Ariel had said softly.

Kaitlyn was speechless.

"When I first saw it," Sydney said, "I thought I could die happy knowing a man with that kind of talent had seen me that way."

"Yes," Kaitlyn had whispered before her throat knotted up altogether.

And I almost had that.

It had taken everything she had to keep herself even slightly steady while the two other women went to work.

They'd worked on her hair, her face—especially her eyes—with makeup she didn't even know the name of, and then put her in a dress, a flippy little gold number she would have laughed at the very idea of wearing if she'd seen it in a store. Not to mention the heels they apparently expected her to wear, something she hadn't done in years. But Ariel, who was loaning them since they were the same size, promised they were more comfortable than they looked, because she insisted on it.

And through it all they wouldn't let her look in the mirror above the dresser.

"Now," Sydney pronounced, "one more thing."

"What else could there be?" she asked, almost plaintively. She couldn't help the undertone; she'd already lied by omission by not telling them there was every likelihood Ry would want her disinvited to this whole thing now.

"Something you have to understand," Ariel said quietly. "That this has nothing to do with how you look every day. This does not mean you're unattractive or as I hear you think, plain and ordinary. You're neither."

Sydney picked it up there. "All what we've done here means is that a woman can be anything she wants, whenever she wants. And for whoever she wants."

"Helps if he's a drop-dead hunk, though," Ariel said, with a quiet smile.

Ry. They were doing this for Ry. Or rather, to make her attractive for him. She would have gone along with this eagerly had they only shown up five minutes earlier. Before she'd blurted out what Jillian had told her. Ordered her.

But she knew she wasn't wrong about how angry he'd been. Angry enough that she'd been glad of the escape.

"Done yet?" Maggie Rafferty's voice came from the doorway. Kaitlyn couldn't help herself, she jumped to her feet.

"Yep," Sydney said cheerfully.

Maggie stepped into the room. And stopped. She looked Kaitlyn up and down, as if she were a horse she was looking to buy. And given how she'd spent the last two days with the woman's son, she could have done without that being the simile that popped into her head.

"Ah," the woman said, a wide smile spreading across her face. "Now that's the woman I knew was in there."

Kaitlyn blinked. And to her shock Maggie Rafferty crossed over to her and enveloped her in a hug. A warm, welcoming, almost loving hug. The kind she'd known so rarely in her life.

"You need to know this is for *you*," Maggie said firmly. "Rylan doesn't want or need you to do this, or to be anyone other than who you are. That's who he fell for. This, he would tell you, is just window dressing. Now. Come look."

As if her words were the final approval on this project they'd embarked on, Sydney and Ariel finally walked her over to where a full-length mirror hung on the back of a door. With every step all she could think of were Maggie's words.

That's who he fell for...

A stranger looked back at her from the mirror. A woman in a sexy gold dress and shoes, with huge, warm brown eyes flecked with gold the dress seemed to make pop, fringed with impossible lashes, cheekbones that wouldn't quit, and a riot of waves in thick, shiny, sun-kissed hair that looked anything but like her plain brown.

She had the inane thought that she was lucky they'd had sex before this transformation, because at least she knew it had been, in that moment, real. If this had come first, she would have always assumed that was why.

Because this was a woman worthy of Rylan Rafferty.

This was the woman he'd drawn in that sketch.

But underneath all the artwork was a woman he'd never want to see again.

THE SALOON WAS exactly the kind of place she'd imagined it would be from the outside, down to the jukebox and the drawing of the building over the bar, showing how it had once been the only building that had any chance of standing up to a Mexican barrage. Maggie had personally driven her here, teasing her easily about lugging her backpack along. In general acting as if she'd truly meant that "Welcome to the Raffertys."

Once inside Kaitlyn met the Highwaters, including the police chief who looked just as imposing as he had at the library, and the brother who ran the place and was married, improbably, to the librarian she'd also met, and several others, including a couple of familiar faces—the Buckleys who ran the Hickory Creek Inn. She tried to focus on all that instead of the grim fact that Ry wasn't even here.

"He'll be along," Maggie had assured her, and Kaitlyn

couldn't find it in herself to explain why he likely wouldn't. His mother seemed to sense her doubt—that mind-reading thing he'd mentioned?—and added, "I can't wait for him to see you. He's already crazy about you, but tonight you're going to blow him away."

Crazy about you.

It was stupid to believe it for even a second. All the makeup and curling irons and sexy dresses in the world couldn't fix this. Why would he believe her even if she ever got the chance to tell him what Jillian had said had nothing to do with what had happened between them?

She was listening with interest to Sydney telling Lucas— he'd been allowed to come since there was food being served and, Maggie had said with a grin, Chief Highwater would be there and the boy wouldn't dare even try to sneak a drink under his nose—about some kind of crazy cross-country horse race she'd participated in in Mongolia. It seemed he'd already heard the story, but wanted to hear it again, with more details.

When the tale was told, Lucas looked at Kaitlyn and smiled shyly. Sounding a bit worried, he asked, "She won't come here tonight, will she? The woman you're working with?"

Kaitlyn felt a ridiculous burst of pleasure at the very idea. Jillian Jacobs would be furious to be considered to be working even with her, instead of Kaitlyn working for her.

"If she does," Kaitlyn said seriously, "we'll drive her out

with the twangiest country music we can find on that jukebox."

Lucas grinned, and everyone around them, which included Maggie, Sydney and Ariel and their Rafferty men, Joey the librarian, an elegant Hispanic woman who was married to another Highwater brother, burst out laughing.

It was barely a moment later when the entire atmosphere of the place shifted. At least it did for her, and she knew why without even looking, knew from the sudden tension along her spine.

Ry was here.

She couldn't stop herself from turning to look, toward the back of the saloon. And there he was, standing next to a woman with long, flowing hair that looked like autumn, as if all the colors of all the leaves, from burnished red to polished gold had gathered there. They were clearly having a serious conversation, leaning in toward each other in a familiar sort of way that made Kaitlyn's stomach knot. Because this was the kind of woman she would expect him to be with, beautiful, stylish, confident...

"Ah, there he is," Maggie said in her ear. "He'll be looking for you."

Only to avoid me. "Looks like he's...busy right now."

Maggie studied her for a moment, and Kaitlyn suddenly remembered Ry's joke about her mind-reading. It had been a joke, hadn't it? "That boy of mine is many things, but fickle isn't one of them." Then she smiled, widely. "Or stupid.

That's Lily Highwater, Shane's wife."

"Oh."

"Go to him," Maggie urged. "I want to see his face when he gets his first look at you."

Only because you don't know what he thinks of me right now. But Kaitlyn started walking, because she didn't seem to have any choice. Maybe she'd just keep going, right out the back door Ry had come in through. She was certain Ry wouldn't stop her.

He saw her. His eyes widened. But the woman next to him was speaking, and he wasn't rude enough to cut her off. And then he shifted his gaze to the redhead, his expression changing completely.

Then she got close enough to hear his next words. Angry words. "That tears it. Who the hell does she think she is?"

She stopped in her tracks, then dodged into the hallway that led to the restrooms, out of sight. The other woman said something to him, but her voice was too low and quiet for Kaitlyn to hear anything except her last words: "…could have warned you, if I'd known it was her."

Her brow furrowed. She tried to think if she'd ever encountered Lily Highwater before. She didn't think so.

"I'm going to—" Ry, still sounding furious, broke off when his phone rang. He looked at it. "There's the callback from the magazine. This ends right now."

Lily patted his arm in a commiserating sort of way, then left him there, striding confidently into the saloon's main room, probably looking for her massively impressive husband. Frozen in place, Kaitlyn heard it all in Ry's taut, heated voice.

"I don't care that it's after hours, Jackie." Jackie. The editor at *Texas Artworks*. And at the moment, essentially Kaitlyn's true boss. "I'm not dealing with her. Get her out of here."

The chill that overtook her then was the most awful thing she'd ever felt. She'd felt horrible, crushing things in her life, but she'd also never had much to lose. Now, she'd thought she had everything, or at least a shot at it. And it was crumbling right in front of her. He was done with her, what they'd found together mattering nothing in the face of what she'd foolishly admitted to him. He would never believe that Jillian's order wasn't why she'd slept with him. As if any woman would have to be ordered with a man like him.

You should have known. You should have known it was too good to be true. Ugly ducklings like you don't land the handsome prince. Didn't you learn that yet?

"She makes a slug seem cuddly," he was saying, his voice practically ringing with disgust. "I don't know why you hired her in the first place. She's just a fancied-up troublemaker."

Fancied up.

What Sydney and Ariel had done, good as it was, hadn't fooled him one bit. She still wasn't enough for the likes of Rylan Rafferty. She never would be.

"Look, you're the ones who wanted this piece done. I couldn't care less. So get rid of her, now, or forget the whole thing. I'm good either way." He ended the call, and she heard him mutter, "Damn that bitch."

Fitting words, she thought numbly. Because that's how she felt. Utterly and truly damned.

The moment he was out of sight she ran.

Chapter Thirty-Three

R Y SCANNED THE saloon again, searching for that vision in gold he'd spotted in the moment before Lily Highwater had dropped that little bomb on him. He'd thought she'd been headed for him, but apparently she'd been aiming for the ladies' room. He'd been anxious to talk to her, since they hadn't exactly parted on the easiest of terms.

It had taken him a while to process what she'd told him. For everything he'd learned about her to outweigh his gut reaction to the fact that the woman she apparently accepted as her boss had ordered her to sleep with him. And she'd done it.

But everything he knew about her told him that wasn't why. She wouldn't. She just wouldn't. Not Kaitlyn. If he had to believe that, then he might as well give up right now because he was too stupid to live. That leveled him off, which in turn let him focus all his anger on the proper target: Jillian Jacobs.

So when Lily had cornered him in the back of the saloon, what she told him didn't surprise him. But that didn't make him any less angry.

"I recognized her the minute I saw her coming out of Yippee Ki Yay the other day," Lily had told him. "I'd seen her before, at a media conference we were both at a couple of years ago. And I remembered the scuttlebutt I'd heard then, that she's ruthless, lies with ease, and is always looking for the big scandal that will make her famous." Lily's nose had twitched as if in disgust. "And she's been poking around town, looking for gossip."

"Gossip?"

"About you. She was asking everyone about you. Hoping to find some dirt, I imagine. Obviously that was fruitless."

Some juicy secret she can use. Kaitlyn's words, uttered in that stricken voice, echoed in his head.

Lily had hesitated then, and he'd said, "What?"

"I talked to some people I know in Austin. Rumor is, your friend the former governor is going to make a presidential run."

He'd been disconcerted by the seeming change of subject. "Not surprised. I know he's been playing with the idea. But what's that got to do with—"

"According to what I know of the way Ms. Jacobs works, and my friends agree, she's quite capable of trying to find dirt on you to manipulate him into giving her his first interview when he announces. As in give her the interview, or she'll go public and destroy you."

He'd blinked. "But there's nothing to go public with. Unless she thinks me getting hauled in by Shane's dad for drinking with my buddies down by the creek when I was fifteen is life-destroying."

"Ry," Lily said gently, with a touch of pity in her voice, "do you really think she wouldn't just make something up if she had to?"

The anger he'd been feeling, prodded by not being able to get to Kaitlyn, who had been turned into some kind of picture-perfect vision in gold, burst free. "That tears it. Who the hell does she think she is?"

"Queen of the muckrakers? The kind who gives all of us a bad name?" Lily suggested under her breath. Then she gave a sad shake of her head. "I could have warned you, if I'd known it was her."

He'd been about to blurt out some choice words when his phone had rung, with a callback from the chief of staff at the magazine, where he'd already left an irate message after Kaitlyn had told him what Jacobs—she was reduced to a last name in his mind now—had told her to do. Lily had patted his arm and left him to it.

The conversation hadn't been pleasant. He wasn't one to normally badmouth anyone, but it wasn't badmouthing if it was the truth, was it? Jackie had been soothing, saying she'd handle it, but he was mad enough calm didn't come easily. That woman had used Kaitlyn, tried to manipulate her, and somehow that infuriated him more than anything. Kaitlyn had gone through more hell in her life than any person should have to. And damned if he'd stand by and let the woman he was half in love with be treated like that.

After some choice observations about Jacobs, he ended the conversation with an ultimatum, because at this point he truly didn't care.

"Look, you're the ones who wanted this piece done. I couldn't care less. So get rid of her, now, or forget the whole thing. I'm good either way." He ended the call muttering, "Damn that bitch."

An image of Jillian Jacobs poking around Last Stand, looking for someone, anyone, to say something shocking about him was bad enough, but to then use that to try and blackmail the governor into an exclusive…and suddenly he'd almost laughed; if she thought she could manipulate that man, she had a surprise coming.

But the amusement faded when he'd put his phone away and looked around for Kaitlyn. It truly had taken him a moment to be sure it was her when he'd spotted her. He didn't know what all Sydney and Ariel had done, but it had produced an amazing transformation. Kaitlyn had looked as if she could easily swim with Chelsea's crowd.

Oddly—or perhaps not—while the look had been breathtaking, he now found himself wanting the real Kaitlyn back, that sweet, genuine, woman underneath the flash they'd added. He'd had enough experience with the flash to know that it was what was underneath it that mattered. Chelsea hadn't had much.

Kaitlyn had…everything.

And he realized that he'd been wrong. He wasn't half in love with her.

He was headfirst, all the way, completely in love with her.

"THAT GIRL NEEDS some confidence-building," his mother said. "Do you know when she saw you with Lily she thought you were *with* Lily?"

"So she thinks I'm suicidal?" Ry said dryly, glancing over to where Shane and his wife were slow dancing to the beautiful ballad playing on the jukebox.

His mother laughed. "No, I explained who Lily was. Where is she, by the way?"

"That's what I'm trying to find out. I saw her heading for the ladies' room when I got here about fifteen minutes ago, but then Lily hit me with…some information and I lost track of her."

"Information?"

"I'll tell you later, right now I need to find Kaitlyn. And she's nowhere in sight."

"You said you did see her, though?"

"Yes." He smiled. "In all her Sydney and Ariel glory. She's beautiful." He met his mother's gaze, held it. "But she always has been, to me. And I want the old Kaitlyn back when this is over."

He was a little surprised when she reached up and cupped his face in that way she had. And she was smiling in warm approval as she said, "Right answer, Rylan. Right answer. Now, I'll go make sure she's not still in the ladies' room."

Then she was off, briskly heading for the hallway that led to the restrooms. But in a moment she was back, a look of slight concern on her face.

"She's not in there?"

"No." She looked thoughtful, then worried. "The last time I saw her was soon after we sent her off to waylay you. She said she needed to get something out of my car. I just unlocked it from here with the fob, and told her how to lock it back up from there."

"What did she have in the car?"

"Her backpack. She's almost never without it, isn't she? I teased her, but I assume she wanted her camera, to take some pictures here." She frowned. "But now that you mention it, I haven't seen her since."

A chill was starting to creep over him "Which pack? The big one or the smaller one?"

His mother frowned. "The one she was carrying that first day I saw her. Seems pretty big to me."

The big one. Which held more than just her gear. "When you women duded her up...what did she do with her other clothes?"

"She just stuffed them into that pack. What are you saying, Rylan? Did something happen—"

With uncharacteristic rudeness he left his mother without explanation and headed for the parking lot out back at a near run. He found her compact SUV parked three slots from the back door. In the light from the fixture above that door, he could see into the front seats. And on the passenger seat was a swath of silky gold fabric he'd last seen sleekly caressing curves he thought he could already recognize in the dark. Gold that was the same color as those flecks in her eyes.

His mother arrived and stopped beside him. "What on earth?"

He heard the beep, realized she'd unlocked the door. He yanked it open. There was a square of paper or cardboard on top of the carefully folded dress. He grabbed it. Realized vaguely it was one of the coasters from inside. But all that really mattered was what was written on the back, cramped in order to fit.

Dear Maggie,

I'm sorry. I'm sure Rylan will explain what I did. Please tell him it was never, ever in my mind until Jillian texted she was almost here. He won't believe it, but it's true. I'm sorry I'm too much of a coward to face him.

Thank you for all you did. And thank Sydney and Ariel for me. You all made me look at myself a little differently. On the outside, anyway.

Kaitlyn

Ry stared at the small piece of cardboard. Inanely, all he could do was wonder how and where she'd changed clothes. In the ladies' room inside? Possibly. Things were just getting started and it wouldn't have been a busy place yet. Or maybe she'd gone into Java Time across the street, then come back. It didn't matter. All that mattered was the pain that fairly radiated from the written words.

On the outside, anyway.

Somehow that line above all the rest jabbed at him.

His mother's voice came from close beside him; she'd clearly been reading over his elbow. "What on earth does that girl think she did?"

Interesting that she put it that way. Not what did she do, but what did she think she'd done. He only vaguely registered this.

"Rylan?" his mother said, more insistently when he didn't speak. "What was it that wasn't in her mind?"

She told me to sleep with you. To try and find out some juicy secret she could use.

He had no doubt that was what she meant. That Jacobs's order hadn't been in her mind. The horror in her eyes when, prodded by his gut reaction, he'd asked if that's what it had been proved that to him beyond a doubt.

Doubt.

Hadn't that driven Kaitlyn for most of her life? At least since her father had died trying to save that life?

So now she was doubting…what? Him?

He won't believe it, but it's true.

Him. She was doubting him. Or at least, that he would believe her. As if he could believe she would do something like that, on the order of a woman she loathed. No matter what was at stake.

I'm too much of a coward to face him.

The woman who as a child had run into a burning building for the father she loved.

"Oh, yeah?" he murmured. No one who'd done what she'd done both in and with her life could possibly be any kind of a coward.

No, Kaitlyn Miller was Texas born and bred. Only the circumstances had made her so uncertain. He knew that as surely as he knew that the revelation he'd had when he'd hung up from telling *Texas Artworks* they either got rid of that Gila monster Jacobs or they could write off the article altogether was the bone-deep truth.

He loved her.

He loved her, and he wasn't about to let her ride off into the sunset and leave what they'd found together behind out of some crazy idea she didn't deserve it.

He shoved the coaster into his back pocket.

"Rylan Rafferty, what is going on?" his mother demanded, in that voice that usually brooked no denial. But for maybe the first time in his life there was something more important to do.

"I'll explain later."

"You'd better fix this, whatever it is," his mother said.

"That girl's right for you."

"I know."

He turned on his heel. He was three long strides away before he heard his mother again. "Where are you going?"

"I'm going," he said fiercely, "to bring her home."

Chapter Thirty-Four

NICK VEGA EYED Ry warily. The man actually looked considerably better, not just in looks but in the way he was moving, acting. That pacemaker seemed to have resolved a few of his physical issues.

"You look better," he said.

"I feel better," Nick admitted. "No more dizziness, more energy. Thinking about maybe leaving here."

"The staff would miss you," Ry said. Trying to lighten the mood he added teasingly, "Especially the ladies."

The wariness slammed abruptly into suspicion. "There's only one lady I want to talk to you about. What the hell did you do to my girl?"

He blinked. Felt a rush of heat as the memories of what they'd done in his bed slammed through him. *Damn near everything is your answer. And she did the same to me.* But he didn't speak it, because he knew that wasn't what Nick had meant.

"Where is she?"

"Why should I tell you?"

"You know, then. Where? She's not at the most recent

address I found."

She hadn't been answering her cell, so he'd had Cody run a check. He'd been relieved when he'd found an apartment address. But the relief had vanished when he'd gotten there and found she'd moved just under a month ago, and they had no forwarding address.

"Maybe she's off on a world cruise," Nick said, and Ry knew the snark was intentional.

"She's not. She wouldn't spend money on herself." The snark faded. That had obviously been the right answer. "So where is she? What's the new address?" A sudden panic seized him. "Tell me she's not living in her car somewhere."

"You think I'd let her do that?" Nick demanded, drawing himself up as if to face down an enemy.

"Then tell me where she is."

"I repeat, why should I?" Nick said, sounding almost belligerent now. In defense of "his girl." *My woman.*

"I don't know what she told you—"

"She told me she'd been unforgivably stupid and she never should have taken that job because now she'd probably never get another one."

Ry stared at the man now, brow furrowed. He pushed aside the rest and focused on the last thing he'd said. "Never get another? Why?"

Nick glared at him. "Because you made sure of it."

He pulled back sharply. "I what?" he snapped out.

"Look, whatever she did, she would never intentionally

hurt another human being. It's just not in her to—"

"I know that!" He was starting to feel utterly confused. "She didn't do anything, except put up with that bitch she was stuck working with."

That seemed to surprise Nick in turn. "Then why did you have her fired?"

Ry knew he was gaping now, but he couldn't help it. "Fired? What the hell are you talking about?"

Nick stared at him. "You…didn't?"

"She thinks I did?"

How the hell could she possibly think that? The only person he'd wanted rid of was Jacobs, and he'd…he'd done that in the saloon. The call had come in right after he'd spotted Kaitlyn, that vision in the gold dress, walking toward him.

The probability of what happened slammed him in the gut. She'd heard. She'd heard and thought, somehow thought, impossibly thought, it was her he was talking about. It wasn't that Jacobs had told her to sleep with him, it was that she thought he believed that was why she had.

He ran that call back through his mind, his side of it, what she'd heard. The call that had ended with: *So get rid of her, now, or forget the whole thing. I'm good either way.* And his final imprecation after he'd hung up. *Damn that bitch.*

No wonder she'd run. Because that was exactly what Kaitlyn Miller would expect out of life, another body blow.

"Nick," he said hurriedly, "you're going to have to trust

me. I need to know where she is."

"Why?"

He drew himself up and faced the man she considered a father head-on. And chose the plainest, clearest words he could think of.

"So I can tell her I love her."

It took a moment, but a slow smile gradually spread across Nick's face. As if he were looking at someone who had finally seen what was obvious to him. "I was afraid you hadn't realized that yet."

"I love her," he repeated. "And I need to tell her. In person."

Within the hour he was on the road back to Austin, his GPS screen showing an address glowing as the target.

KAITLYN STARED AT her phone screen, beyond puzzled. It wasn't that Nick didn't text her now and then, although he preferred calling because, he said, he liked to hear her voice. But he also liked sayings and quips and aphorisms, especially what he called "Texas-isms," and he would text those. Things like his opinion on Jillian. *She was raised on concrete, and it was softer than her heart.* Or her favorite: *She's got horns holding up her halo.*

None of which explained why he'd now texted her the words: *You may be deceived if you trust too much, but you will live in torment if you don't trust enough. ~Frank Crane*

She had just typed in a string of three question marks when a knock came on her door. She'd seen Mr. Palaski, her landlord, out puttering about earlier, maybe it was him. If so, she hoped it wasn't to raise the rent.

She nearly laughed pitifully out loud at that; she had enough to pay one more month, and then she'd be completely broke. And then what would she do when Nick's expenses came due again? She'd been counting on the payment from the *Texas Artworks* job to hold her for a while, but now…

With a heavy sigh she headed for the door, still wondering what Nick had meant. He knew perfectly well she wasn't one to trust too much. They'd talked about it enough, so it had to be the other part…*but you will live in torment if you don't trust enough.* What did he mean by that? It was too pointed to just be something he'd tossed out there, that had been aimed at her. She—

She stopped dead, her hand still clutching the knob of the door she'd just opened, forgetting the peephole entirely in her distraught state.

Ry.

Standing right there on her cracked concrete doorstep. His hair was tangled, his jaw unshaven. He looked tired. He looked worried.

He was beautiful.

Because he always was.

The pain she'd been fighting since she'd left the Last Stand Saloon swept over her in a wave. She was half convinced she was hallucinating, that she'd imagined him here because she wanted it so badly.

When she'd first gotten back, she'd gone through her routine by rote, unpacking her gear, hooking her camera up to the computer to download the last batch of images. And then she'd seen the shots she'd taken when he'd gone over the railing in his loft, only half-dressed.

Her heart had started to slam in her chest as she stared at him, at how perfect he was. She thought she must have idealized him a bit, that no man could be that beautiful. She'd had the camera between them at the time, giving her that tiny bit of distance, but with the image full screen, stealing what little breath she had left, there was no denying what she was seeing. And she knew he was everything she'd remembered.

Now the real thing was here, standing on that cracked doorstep.

She pulled back, her hand tightening on the doorknob she'd never let go of.

"Don't, Kaitlyn." His voice was a rough, tight whisper that sent a shiver of fire and ice down her spine. "Don't shut me out."

Why was he here? She could feel her fingers protesting the prolonged tight grip on the brass of the knob, but it was only a vague sort of awareness, on some other level. Some level beneath the pain and need and wanting that just the sight of him brought on in her. She couldn't move, couldn't speak, especially couldn't say his name.

"We need to talk."

Why on earth would he want to talk to the person he hated enough to call her boss and demand she get her away from him? And how had he found her in the first place? She'd not given her new physical address to anyone except—

Nick.

"Trust me, Kaitlyn. Please."

Her breath caught. *You will live in torment if you don't trust enough.*

Was that what that text had been, a message, advice from Nick to trust Ry? It would be just like him to hide it in some quotation from someone she'd never heard of.

"It wasn't what you think, Kate. Let me in."

That voice. That low, rumbly, man's voice.

You will live in torment if you don't trust enough.

Almost without consciously deciding, she stepped back a half step. Ry took it the rest of the way, coming through the doorway in a single stride. In almost the same motion he pushed at the door. He was so close, so nerve-shatteringly close, she was barely aware of letting go of the knob, barely heard the sound of the door closing and catching. The four hundred square feet of her apartment had never seemed smaller.

She'd thought it little when she'd arrived home, told herself it was only natural after days spent looking out over land where the glorious hills met the horizon so far away, the hills portrayed so beautifully in an incredible painting. But now it seemed absolutely tiny. Ry's presence dwarfed it until she thought if she turned, if she tried to back away, she'd hit a wall. She groaned inwardly at the double meaning of the phrase. She'd already hit the wall, on so many fronts it was dizzying.

He was so close she felt more than saw him move. His arms came up and wrapped around her. The common sense that told her to back away warred with her heart's urge to hug him back, resulting in a stalemate that had her simply staying there, not moving either way.

"You heard me on that call, there at the saloon, didn't you."

It wasn't really a question, but she felt compelled to respond as the probable answer came to her. No matter how he felt about her, Ry wasn't a cruel person, and he wouldn't have wanted her to hear him say what he'd said that night.

"It's all right," she said, hating the shaky sound of the words even as she was surprised she managed to say them at all. "I understand."

"Kaitlyn—"

"I said I understand. You didn't have to come here to say it in person. I overheard something I shouldn't have. I know you would have been…kinder if you knew I could hear."

He went very still. And then, as she'd been expecting all

along, he pulled away from her.

"Kaitlyn Miller, look at me." It was one of the hardest things she'd ever done, but she did it. And looking into those stormy-gray eyes made her feel as if she were back in the Hill Country, where that horizon was the only limit. "That call," he said firmly, "was not about you. How could you even think that, after that night we had? And after what she told you to do?"

"I thought…that's why, because you thought that's why I…"

"You thought I believed you slept with me because she told you to? You really thought that?" He looked so aghast it blasted any lingering remnant of that idea out of her head. And her heart. "It was Jacobs I was telling the magazine to get rid of. To get her the hell out of my life because she's nothing but a…a…"

He broke off like a man who'd been about to descend into profanity.

"Fancied-up troublemaker?" Kaitlyn said, staring up at him as she quoted his words back to him.

"I said that, yes. I was thinking self-serving, arrogant, manipulative and a few less kind things."

"I thought…you meant me. The dress, the makeup."

Something changed in his eyes then. His entire expression changed. "You," he said, sounding almost breathless, "were incredible. When I saw you walking across that room I nearly lost it. But then the phone rang, and knew I had to get rid of that…witch, get her out of our lives."

Our lives.

She was now feeling breathless herself.

"You looked incredible, sweetheart. But this Kaitlyn," he said, reaching up to grip her shoulders as his words started coming in a rush, like someone who'd feared he'd never get the chance to say them, "the one who gets up and faces every day despite the odds, who sacrifices endlessly to help others, who is loyal beyond belief, the Kaitlyn who has that eye, that knack of seeing and framing the world in such incredible ways, the one who would understand when I get crazy and obsessed with capturing something a certain way, the one who made me finally face why I was denying the core of who I am—an artist—that's the Kaitlyn I love."

That's the Kaitlyn I love.

The words rang in her head, and that inner voice, that thing that had been with her since childhood told her that was the only place she was hearing them, that a man like this would never truly say something to her. Not her, plain, ugly duckling Kaitlyn who had none of her mother's looks or charm.

I'd argue that, but more importantly, you have none of her weaknesses either.

She stared up at him, this man who had seen her as no one ever had.

That's the Kaitlyn I love.

"Ry?" It was all she could get out, and her voice trembled even on the single syllable.

"I know it's happened fast, and we'll have to give it time to be sure but give us a chance. Please, Kaitlyn, give us a chance." He swallowed visibly. "Give me a chance."

She wondered, surely inanely, if Rylan Rafferty had ever had to beg a woman before. Even the idea was laughable. Yet here he was.

He hadn't been talking about her that night. Jillian. It was Jillian he had called…well, everything Kaitlyn had ever thought about her. And he'd told Jackie Hyland that he'd cancel a project any artist would covet because he wouldn't deal with her.

Any artist.

…the one who made me finally face why I was denying the core of who I am—an artist—that's the Kaitlyn I love.

Had she really given him that? Was she the reason he embraced the fact now, that he was an artist? A fulfillment like she'd never felt before swept through her. That alone was something to live on for a very long time.

Time spent with Ry?

Give us a chance.

Us. A couple. A unit.

The images that brought on were nearly overwhelming. To have a chance at that, it was worth any risk, wasn't it? She suddenly wished she had a recording of everything he'd said, to play back whenever she was flooded with those self-doubts. And then it hit her—if she did as he asked, gave them a chance…maybe she could hear those things any time she needed them. Because Ry was the kind of man who, once decided, wouldn't stint. He'd give it his all, just as he gave his all to his work, because that's who he was.

That's the Kaitlyn I love.

And in that moment, stupidly, all she could say, and in a tiny voice, was "You…love me?"

He pulled her back into his arms. "I think," he said against her hair, "the question is…do you love me? At least, enough to give us that shot?"

She was utterly lost. Lost in the feel of his arms around her, the warmth of his embrace, the words, all the wonderful words he'd said. This was too big for words, almost too big for her heart, a heart that seemed to be expanding in her chest as if it were only now reaching its full potential.

So she answered him in the only way she could.

She kissed him.

Chapter Thirty-Five

THERE WAS, RY decided, a lot to be said for a smaller bed. What it might lack in area for more strenuous activities, it made up for in forced proximity.

Not that he would ever have to be forced to stay close to this woman.

He let out a long, relaxed sigh of satisfaction that was not simply physical, although they'd certainly managed that this afternoon. He hoped he'd also managed to prove to Kaitlyn that everything he'd said to her was true, down to the bone. Despite his own hunger, he'd turned it all over to her. Whatever she wanted, the only proviso was she had to ask for it. He knew it was difficult for her. The constant color that rose to her cheeks told him that. But anything she wanted, he did. Even when it took every bit of restraint he had not to just drive himself into her and ease the screaming ache she caused in him. And when she'd finally broken and flat-out demanded he take her, and now, it was worth it. And when she practically screamed his name as her body clenched around him, he felt more triumphant than he had about anything in his life.

He edged himself a little closer to her, savoring the feel of that sweet backside against him as they spooned together.

"I'm sorry it's so small."

Ry blinked at the sleepy words. "And here I was just thinking there were great advantages to a smaller bed."

He thought he heard a faint chuckle. "I meant my apartment."

He raised up on one elbow. "It's not that much smaller than my loft."

"But that seems so much bigger, with all the other room."

He hesitated, thinking it might be too soon. Decided to not phrase it as a question, but to just plant the idea. "Maybe even big enough for two. You'll have to decide if two artists could survive."

She went very still. "I have to decide?"

"I've already made my decision." He heard her let out a small breath. He didn't want her to feel pressured so he said quickly, "By the way, I invited Nick out to visit the ranch."

She rolled over then, to look at him. "You did?"

"Yep. He's already doing so much better, and I checked with the staff and they said they thought he'd be fine."

She smiled. Soft, loving. The kind she'd given him after the first time they'd made love today. Because it had been that. They'd done the rip-roaring sex later.

"He is doing better."

"Much. And I'm glad."

"I believe you."

"All I ask." He said it lightly, but inside elation was building. "Oh, and if you're agreeable, Lily Highwater is going to actually write the profile for *Texas Artworks*."

Her eyes widened. "What?"

"She's been writing them for the local paper, *The Defender*, for almost a couple of years now. I sent Jackie some samples, Lily said she could make the deadline, and they went for it. "Lily had one condition, of course. That you stay on the project."

She blinked at that. "The chief's wife said that?"

He nodded. "She felt bad about what happened. That you heard us. When she called to say she'd accepted the project, she told me I'd better find you, and fast."

Kaitlyn gave a slow shake of her head. "You did all this in one day?"

He leaned over and gently kissed her. "I wanted it all fixed. Because it doesn't seem like anything's ever been fixed for you."

"Oh, Ry…"

He thought he'd never heard anything as sweet as that note of wonder in her voice. And decided to go for it. "Do you know any art supply stores here in the city?"

She drew back at the non sequitur. "I…yes, there are several. Why?"

"I'm thinking I need to buy some paints."

He heard her breath catch. "You're…going to paint?"

"I'm going to try. Somebody—" he leaned down and kissed her again "—gave me the nerve."

He couldn't even describe the look that came into those wide brown eyes of hers then. The golden flecks fairly glowed. He wondered if he could capture her subtle beauty in color, in paint. As his father had captured the beauty of the land he loved. And of the woman he loved, as he had in the portrait of Ry's mother that hung in her bedroom, so full of love that it practically poured out of it into the heart of the viewer.

Was he good enough? Could he do that?

He'll outshine me someday.

His father's words sang in his mind. He didn't know about that, but for the first time in his life, thanks to the woman in his arms, he had the nerve to try.

IN A MATTER of a few weeks the ranch felt more like home to Kaitlyn than anyplace ever had. The happiness was bubbling up so strongly inside her that sometimes she found herself smiling for no reason at all. She had bonded nicely with Lucas and Cody, she and Ariel and Sydney were already friends, she adored Maggie, and while Keller and Chance still intimidated her a bit, she admired and respected them both. She was utterly joyful over the turn her life had taken, but she never forgot how lucky she was. So many pressures had been removed, and for the first time since her father had died, she felt safe, secure, and wanted.

Having the Raffertys at your back was no small thing.

She was even humming as she went about cleaning her gear. She was upstairs at the desk, while Ry was down messing with the paints they'd picked up in Austin before they'd left. It was a learned skill, he'd said, but he was learning. And he was, fast. He already had progressed past many supposed successful artists, at least in her admittedly biased view. He—

Her cell phone—the new one Ry had insisted on, because she needed better reception out here—rang. Still humming, she picked it up without even looking and gave a cheerful hello.

Moments later she was sitting in the desk chair, her stomach churning. She should have known she hadn't left the past behind completely. No one ever could.

Slowly she got to her feet. She went down the stairs, concentrating on each step far more than necessary, just to keep her rocketing thoughts in check. When she stepped into the studio area Ry, who had been bent over a sketch on his workbench, turned to look at her, smiling.

His smile faded the instant he saw her face. He tossed down the pencil he'd been using and strode across the room to her. Putting his hands gently on her shoulders he said urgently, "What? What is it? I heard your phone."

She drew in a deep breath. Met his stormy gaze. "It's my

mother."

He stiffened. "What about her?"

"She walked out of rehab. She was arrested last night in San Marcos for drunk driving. She wants me to come bail her out."

She saw anger flash in his eyes. But when he spoke his voice was neutral. "What do you want to do?"

She drew herself up. Took in a breath. Somehow knowing he would support whatever decision she made, made the right one easier. "I'm not going to do it."

The smile he gave her then warmed her to the core. But then he surprised her. "I think we need to go there."

"What? Why?"

"I think we need to formalize the new...policy."

And so she found herself once more standing in a jail waiting room, to see the woman who'd borne her. After getting to know Maggie Rafferty, she couldn't bring herself to call the woman mother any longer. To Kaitlyn she was barely recognizable as the woman of that decade-old ad campaign.

"Well, well," the woman said when they brought her out and she spotted Ry. "Your taste has certainly improved." She shifted her bloodshot gaze to Ry. "Or did she just luck out with a ride-share driver?"

"Shut up," Kaitlyn said, with utter calm.

Her mother blinked. "What did you say to me?"

"You heard me." She nodded at Ry. "I'm only here because he wanted to meet you."

"Well of course he did," she said, the insult apparently forgotten.

"She reminds me of someone," Ry said, looking only at Kaitlyn. "Same sort of self-centered, undeserved high opinion of herself."

Kaitlyn couldn't help it, she laughed out loud. She looked back at the woman who had made her life so miserable. "I'm not bailing you out. And I'm never helping you again. You're a lost cause, and this is me, washing my hands of you."

"How dare you! You'll be sorry for this—"

"She will not," Ry said, and his voice was so icy cold even her mother stopped to stare at him. "And I'm here to warn you, you pitiful excuse for a human, that if you ever, *ever* hurt Kaitlyn again, physically or emotionally, you'll answer to me."

Kaitlyn had never seen her mother so stunned. Ry was looking at her as a person looked at a cockroach. And then, utter disgust on his face, he shook his head.

"How on earth did you ever have a beautiful daughter like her? You've got to be the ugliest person I've ever met."

Kaitlyn smothered a gasp. She was certain she'd never told him her mother's usual lament, about how a beautiful woman such as herself had ever had such an ugly child. But somehow Ry had known exactly what to say. And Kaitlyn knew she would treasure the memory of her mother's shocked expression for a very, very long time.

KAITLYN LOOKED UP from the laptop screen at the woman who'd written the lengthy profile she'd just read. One that captured the essence of a man, his talent, his love of his home, his history, his family, and how deep his roots went in this demanding but rewarding corner of the country. More than once she'd teared up reading it; Lily Highwater definitely had a way with words.

"It's wonderful," she said, her throat tight. "I hope they don't change a word."

"They didn't. It's been accepted as it stands," the other woman said with a wide smile. "And I'm sure a big part of that was your amazing photos."

"Thank you," she said, instead of shrugging as she might have before the last few weeks spent savoring Ry's unstinting and constant support.

"And—now don't get mad at me—I pitched them another piece, and they're enthused about it."

Kaitlyn's brow furrowed. "Why would I get mad about that?"

"Because I sort of promised we'd both do it."

Kaitlyn couldn't stop the smile that spread across her face. "I'd like that. A lot."

Lily grinned at her. "You don't even know what it is

yet."

"Don't care," Kaitlyn said, meaning it. She'd learned quickly that working on something with Lily Highwater was far different than that woman she refused to name even in her mind any longer. "But what was the pitch?"

"That Texas itself, in all its diversity, is a natural work of art worthy of their magazine. And that you were the perfect photographer who could show that. And don't worry, I know you'll have to fit it in with your work for Sydney and The World in a Gift. We'd have to do some traveling, but I think Ry could spare you for this, don't you?"

"I think," Ry said from above, where he was just coming downstairs from the loft, "that he'd love to go along and schlep bags or whatever."

Kaitlyn laughed, not at the idea of the man who was about to blast into the Texas consciousness with the article she'd just read lugging baggage, but at the fact that she knew he meant it.

Lily said her goodbyes then, because she had an appointment to get to. Kaitlyn watched Ry watch rather intently as she left. She remembered the night in the saloon, when she had seen them together and had wondered if there was something between them. Now she just smiled, contentedly.

She was still adjusting to this odd, unexpected, unaccustomed state of near-constant happiness. She'd given up her tiny apartment almost with regret because of that long, loving week they'd spent there, with Ry not caring a whit how small it was. But here on the ranch she felt as if she'd truly come home. Her riding was progressing until she dared to take the sweet Latte out on her own now and then, although she preferred riding with Ry, or Lucas, who seemed to enjoy showing her around the place he, too, had come to call home. They were going to pick up Nick next weekend, and the two men she loved more than anything in the world would be together in one place, getting to know each other better.

And in a family gathering last week, she'd not only been informed that from here on her opinion would be required on any family action, she had also been presented with the belt she now wore, a Rylan Rafferty original, replete with images that brought tears to her eyes. An amazing replication of her father's image from the photograph that had mysteriously gone missing a week before, the Llano River slab, for her hometown, her camera, and another amazing image of Nick. And anchoring it all an image of the small converted barn that was now her home, the place where she'd never been happier. As a welcome to the family, it had been overwhelming.

"She tell you what that appointment was?" Ry asked as Lily drove off.

"No, why?"

He turned to look at her then. "I saw her coming out of a doctor's office yesterday."

Kaitlyn frowned. "You think she's sick?"

A smile quirked one corner of his mouth. "No. I think Shane's in for it."

She blinked. "What?"

"Remember where we first met?"

"When you almost knocked me over with—" She broke off, remembering exactly what door he'd almost hit her with. Her brows shot upward. "You think she's pregnant?" Then, before he could even answer she nodded. "Yes. Yes, I believe it. There was something different about her, but I didn't know what it was."

For a long moment he just looked at her. Then he said softly, "Maybe someday it will be us."

The idea didn't even scare her anymore.

"I want a boy with your talent," she said, gesturing at the painting on the stairway wall, beside the one his father had done. It had an entirely different feel, that image of a woman, almost undeniably her, astride a paint horse riding not into but out of the sunset. But it was no less skilled, no less powerful.

"And I want a girl you can teach what really matters," he said.

She took a deep breath. "I suppose you can learn even from a bad example."

"You sure learned what not to do," he said with a grin. And then he pulled her into a fierce hug. "You'll be the best kind of mom, Katie," he said, using the nickname that pleased her because he was the only one who did, and because her mother had never allowed it. Her mother, who this man had put in her place fiercely and forever.

"I love you, Rylan."

"I know," he said, pulling back a little and still grinning. "I'm thinking we'd better give Mom time to recover from Keller's wedding, and then Chance's before we spring another one on her."

She looked up at him. Her life had changed so much, she had so much she'd never dared hope for, let alone expected, that she had to remind herself that it was all real. Except he'd never actually proposed to her.

"Was there a question in there?" she asked.

The grin widened. "Didn't they tell you?" His hands slid down to her hips, and the belt he'd done with such care. For her. "Accepting this is like saying yes."

"To a proposal I've never gotten?" she asked, with no small amount of wonder at herself, and her newfound spunk, as Nick called it.

Instantly Ry dropped to one knee. He reached up and took her left hand. "Will you marry me, Kaitlyn Miller? Will you take on all this crazy?"

The joy almost bubbled over. "It's the best kind of crazy. Yes. Yes, yes, yes."

To her surprise he took something out of his pocket and slipped it onto her ring finger. "That's just until we pick out a real ring," he said. "One you want."

She looked down. Saw it was a band of leather carved with their initials entwined.

"This," she said, her throat almost unbearably tight, "is as real as it gets. I want this one."

He stood then and held her so close and strong she thought she could almost feel the last of the pain and doubt flitter away.

"Welcome to the Raffertys, Katie."

And Kaitlyn knew she had somehow truly landed in clover.

THE END

Want more? Check out Chance and Ariel's story in
A Texas Christmas Miracle!

Join Tule Publishing's newsletter for more great reads and weekly deals!

If you enjoyed *Once a Cowboy,*
you'll love the next book in…

The Raffertys of Last Stand series

Book 1: *Nothing But Cowboy*

Book 2: *A Texas Christmas Miracle*

Book 3: *Once a Cowboy*

Book 4: *Cowgirl Tough*
Coming in April 2022!

Available now at your favorite online retailer!

More books by Justine Davis

The Texas Justice series

Book 1: *The Lone Star Lawman*

Book 2: *Lone Star Nights*

Book 3: *A Lone Star Christmas*

Book 4: *Lone Star Reunion*

Book 5: *Lone Star Homecoming*

The Whiskey River series

Book 1: *Whiskey River Rescue*

Book 2: *Whiskey River Runaway*

Book 3: *Whiskey River Rockstar*

Available now at your favorite online retailer!

About the Author

USA Today bestselling author of more than 70 books, (she sold her first ten in less than two years) Justine Davis is a five time winner of the coveted RWA RITA Award, including for being inducted into the RWA Hall of Fame. A fifteen time nominee for RT Book Review awards, she has won four times, received three of their lifetime achievement awards, and had four titles on the magazine's 200 Best of all Time list. Her books have appeared on national best seller lists, including USA Today. She has been featured on CNN, taught at several national and international conferences, and at the UCLA writer's program.

After years of working in law enforcement, and more years doing both, Justine now writes full time. She lives near beautiful Puget Sound in Washington State, peacefully coexisting with deer, bears, a pair of bald eagles, a tailless raccoon, and her beloved '67 Corvette roadster. When she's not writing, taking photographs, or driving said roadster (and yes, it goes very fast) she tends to her knitting. Literally.

Thank you for reading

Once a Cowboy

If you enjoyed this book, you can find more from all our great authors at TulePublishing.com, or from your favorite online retailer.

Made in the USA
Las Vegas, NV
02 February 2022

42884109R00189